db wolfe

db wolfe

2011

DEAD MONEY

Betty: Viva Las Vegas

Books by db wolfe:
available at db_wolfe@yahoo.com for personalized copies
TRYING NOT TO DIE IN THE TROPICS
DROP DEAD ON RUE DAUPHINE
YELLOWTAIL

Book by db martin
SOUTH OF CANCER, NORTH OF CAPRICORN

Google db wolfe for tv interview

ISBN: 1453895876
ISBN-13: 9781453895870

BEFORE THE GLITTER
AND THE GRIEF

The first gamblers to enter the valley were indigenes peoples ten thousand years ago in search of the usual elements of survival; food, water, and shelter. Their stakes were the original all-in. Losing meant death and winning promised only the barest existence. Some succeeded well enough to leave petroglyphs behind as a record of how they did against the first house game; man versus nature. The rock carvings are perhaps the cave version of modern t-shirts proclaiming the wearers' time spent in Vegas as a CSI or as a parrot head on the strip.

Europeans entered the valley known for abundant grasses and water in force early in the 1800's and so the name *The Meadows* or Las Vegas in the Spanish tongue of the new settlers became how it would be known. John C. Fremont found two fresh water springs and wrote about it in papers for the burgeoning population back East. This rare commodity, only miles from Death Valley is situated perfectly for the railroad line between Salt Lake City and Los Angeles. Water to make steam qualified as one of the few factors limiting the ever growing railway expansion out West. Nevada soon became the 36th state.

Prostitution, long a mainstay of cowboy towns where the ratio of men to women often approached twenty to one, is legalized in the period before statehood but not regulated. Contrary to how visitors may think, its existence to this day is a point of contention, the newcomers being against it and the native Nevadans in favor. As a statewide compromise, counties with a population over 400k may not legalize prostitution which is a poorly disguised nod to the newbies since Clark County-Las Vegas contains seventy-five percent of the state's population.

Only eight counties in the state contain twenty-eight brothels. Paying drivers thirty percent of one's take to bring customers to outlying counties, health and drug exams, room and board to the house, and a requirement that legal prostitutes must register with the local sheriff, creates no shortage of illegal hookers in Sin City.

The Comstock Lode hit around the 20th century making Nevada the silver state. Mining and the railroad the main sources of economic growth, suffered greatly during the Depression until the building of the Hoover Dam began in 1931. Since 1910 gambling had been illegal in Nevada, one of the last states to prohibit it, but a budget crisis from the economy and a need to somehow tax the influx of workers from the dam to pay for education, set the slot machines ringing again.

The outlying areas of the desert were perfect for the military and Nellis AFB became a major employer during WWII. When the war ended Bugsy came to town and the Flamingo became one of the places to be on the highway between LA and Vegas, The Strip.

With Siegal leading the way, the Mob back East found Vegas the perfect place to skim the take and avoid the IRS. After the state lost an estimated one trillion in revenue and gamblers complained of shady games, the Nevada Gaming Commission came into existence in 1959. After years of corruption, the commission became one of the bright spots in Vegas. One most likely will lose when in Vegas but one won't be cheated. It's not worth it to the casinos and not necessary. The odds are in favor of the house. That's not to suggest the house won't change dealers or decks if you're hot or not burn a card on a shift change if the opposite is true. As they like to say, it's just business.

The 1950's were boom times when tourists watched above-ground nuclear blasts from The Strip like unexpected fireworks shows and Betty Willis designed the iconic *Welcome to Las Vegas* sign. When the commission under the pointed suggestion of the federal government finally got its act together making scenes like those from the movie *Casino* as rare as a winner, corporations bought into the game.

The Vietnam War like all wars poured billions into the economy and Vegas got its share of the action. Elvis began his meltdown in full view of packed audiences as his success slowly strangled his talent. Even his voice, unable to save the career, couldn't salvage the man either.

Post Vietnam War everything got tight but Vegas came roaring back with cartoonish looking megaresorts and attractions for families. New arrivals poured into the valley and the county population screamed from 478K in 2000 to 1.4 million in 2008.

Like the boxers that come to town for championships and riches, only to find broken dreams and noses to match, the housing collapse gutted Vegas worse than any blackjack team from MIT or a random number processor scam.

Foreclosures were cheaper than making the mortgage note, thousands choosing to rent and take the hit on the credit score, others packing up in the night and leaving. Why pay $2500 on an ARM when owners were desperate to rent the same house for $1000. Squatters and meth heads moved into $500,000 houses with no one to notice for months, the banks so completely inundated with losses. Particularly entrepreneurial spirits leased homes to others for which they had no ownership, only being found out when the out of state owners stopped by for a visit.

But lest one cries for Vegas, the worry may be premature. It's been down before but never for the count. Poker rooms throughout the city have action 24/7 with no risk and little expense to the house. Month long poker tournament series are found in multiple locations throughout the year. The rules for blackjack now so favor the house with eight deck shoes, 6-5 blackjack payouts, machine shufflers, and hitting soft 17, the only players at the table have no clue. The real gamblers are at the poker tables and that's fine with the house.

In a reflection of the land grab during the Great Depression, investors with money are buying houses for pennies on the dollar. On the Strip, three corporations own ninety percent of the properties, one large construction site saved in mid-completion by one of the mega corporations and an established casino just off the strip had its debt purchased by the largest casino corporation in town. Giant cranes still tower over the landscape, construction-destruction-construction a way of life on The Strip.

The *new* Miami financed its rebirth in the seventies and eighties with South American drug cartels and money laundering. Regardless of the fact that we all study history, most of us are surprised when it repeats itself.

Vegas will be back. It holds all the cards. It's like arguing with the referee; it never changes the call.

*Criminal: a person with predatory instincts who has
not sufficient capital to form a corporation.*

– Howard Scott

5757 Wayne Newton Boulevard

Las Vegas, Nevada

Wolfe hated the flight to Vegas and he hated the flight
home more. Stepping off one of the multitude of flights that
stop at the glitter in the desert, Wolfe always chuckled when
he remembered the address of McCarran Airport. One may
think that Vegas is about gambling which it certainly is but it
is more about marketing and the airport address was only one
example. If Wolfe heard "whatever happens in Vegas stays in
Vegas" one more time while in town he might barf up his $15
sixteen ounce prime rib he always managed to eat at an old
eatery on the Strip. If they wanted something to stay in Vegas they could have his red meat overdose. Lately, it had been
his money. Yet he returned often enough to know the town as
well as Hilton Head. The dance with the dangerous lady had
intrigued Wolfe ever since he ran a casino in his basement as
a teenager. Pennies and nickels had transformed to hundreds
and then thousands of dollars as he aged. Funny how one's
gambling stakes grow into one's income over time.

Wolfe had arrived for his annual pilgrimage to the World
Series of Poker. The quintessential six weeks of lying, deceit,
fear, blustering, and acidosis, known as high stakes tournament
poker culminating in the main event.

Poker, the only game when one didn't play against the house. One played against other gamblers. Make no mistake the house made plenty of money without any risk but the gambler operated with the same odds as his opponent which could not be said about all other forms of gambling. Think of the house rake more like interest on stock margins. Shuffle up and deal.

"Daga. You have your carryon? "

"Si, Wolfie. What's the temperature outside?"

"It's June. Probably somewhere over one hundred."

"But you told me to bring sweatshirts and long sleeved tops?"

"The casinos keep the A/C in the sixties. A few hours of poker and you get cold."

"Maybe *un poco*, but I'll be at the pool most of the time."

"Yeh. Try not to cause too many heart attacks among the hung over conventioneers. It might affect the economy. Come on. Let's get our checked baggage."

"You mean it's not right here?"

"Nope. We have to take a train to get to the baggage claim. This is a major airport for being a destination and not a hub. Most passengers that land here stay here. Forty-seven million sheep last year. Projected to be at capacity fifty-three million by 2017."

"Sheep? Why do you call them sheep?"

"Because the majority loses. They fly great distances to walk into the slaughter house. Vegas operates on the law of large numbers. Ninety-eight percent lose a small amount. Maybe two percent win a few dollars and a miniscule number actually win a life-changing amount. Everybody believes they'll be in the two percent. In the end, Vegas wins. But the winners always go home and brag about winning which is the best PR in the world. Vegas is the actual capital of the United States. Regardless of what we learn in school. Vegas can move politics in any direction it wishes. The best mathematicians in the world do not work for NASA. They work in Vegas. Trust me."

A few minutes at the baggage carousel always started the Vegas trip badly for Wolfe. Actually, a few minutes would be bearable but it seemed always to be closer to an hour in order to make the transition from gate to taxi. It didn't matter if it were Monday mid-morning or Friday night after work hours for the Angelinos. Either way, thousands of taxis take their turn picking up passengers and taking them to the butcher shop. The victims are often in high spirits.

"Harrah's, please. That's with an H." Wolfe and Daga scrambled in the passenger compartment while the driver threw the bags in the trunk.

"With an H? I see you're not a Vegas virgin."

"Somehow those two words make an oxymoron."

"Well, yeh. Sexually, you'd be looking at pretty stiff odds. Pardon the pun. It's our term for first time visitors. Harrah's sounds like Paris over the phone and in person. Newbies don't always make it clear,"

"I understand. I learned the hard way after I got a ride from Convention Center Boulevard to the entrance of Bally's before I realized where the cabby was headed. My eyes were closed at the time and that's my story and I'm sticking to it."

"What're you in town for?"

"WSOP."

"Ever cashed?"

"Not big. Satellites for bracelet events. Looking to turn it around this year."

"You and everybody else."

"Do you play?" The driver nearly injured his neck trying to see all of Daga and drive simultaneously.

"Me, chico? No. Not at poker."

"Other games?"

"Yes. Dangerous ones."

"Like what?"

"The ones you only lose once."

While the driver digested Daga's last response Wolfe made crazy eyes at his girl. He mouthed the word *relax* and gave her a soft kiss on the mouth. She tried to respond in kind and he blocked her with a single finger. "Later", he whispered.

The short drive onto Paradise Road and then to Harrah's finished quickly and they headed into the lobby. Wolfe liked Harrah's for its location. Mid-strip, plenty of choices for food, and away from the autograph hounds and spectators at the event, made his time away from the tables relaxing. He didn't have to worry about them being bothersome, he wasn't famous, but the wandering throngs at the Rio made doing daily routines like exercise at the gym a hassle. Wolfe thought only of poker. This time of year he concentrated much differently then hanging out in a basement or garage drinking beer and playing every hand. Time to be serious would be his watchwords.

In spite of a detailed game plan, Wolfe knew in Vegas luck isn't always a lady.

Check-in, cleanup, count your stake, head to the Rio. Scheduling one's day during the WSOP didn't require a personal secretary. Had Wolfe known the evil that would come to be omnipresent he may well have turned and boarded a flight out of town *or* maybe not.

WASHINGTON, DC

Sam Sauria boarded a thrift airline itching for a drink. He hadn't flown commercial for awhile. Back in the day, landing thirsty in Vegas didn't seem very likely. Not having correct change did not occur to him. He didn't know it but happy wouldn't happen today.

Nothing could be worse than the grilling he had just taken at the hands of Democratic Senators concerning Dick Cheney's JSOC transgression. Only in the mind of the Great Poohbah himself could it seem inconsequential. Cheney had spent his entire public life sending young men to war and yet had never served in the military. Apparently, he had been too busy defending himself from DUI charges and multiple attempts to graduate from college.

JSOC, one of Cheney's marionettes during the Bush administration, stood for Joint Special Operations Command. They reported only to Cheney and were essentially hit squads for high value targets during his eight years in office. Cheney found international law cumbersome. Sam did not but found himself violating the statutes more and more during his stay at Gitmo. Now Cheney enjoyed retirement and Sam got skewered by congressional counsel.

Working on this new assignment would only be slightly less illegal. The CIA charter forbade operating on US soil but that line had been blurred by the Patriot Act following 9-11 when it had been discovered that information held by the intelligence community had been mistakenly withheld from the FBI. The information might have saved many lives.

In the expected knee jerk response after the attack, Congress approved guidelines which allowed the CIA to operate within US borders in matters of national security. Those guidelines had been stretched to the point of breaking like an overused bungee cord. Sauria's superiors at the CIA, acting on the Bush Administration's interpretation of that law by the now tainted Justice Department responded accordingly. Sam found himself headed to Sin City.

The new president would be informed after the operation had begun. A well-worn tactic employed as early as 1961 when Dulles, then CIA Director, pulled the young JFK into Eisenhower's planning for the Bay of Pigs. Dulles had hoped JFK could be roped into invading Cuba. When JFK chose to not intervene with American soldiers, the CIA-trained invaders, all ex-pat Cubanos recruited by the Miami field office, were stranded on the beaches to be killed and captured by Castro's troops, Dulles got fired and the CIA old-school began to plot against the President. Sam hoped he hadn't been selected for a new version of an old failure.

Three hours later the aircraft wheels screeched to a landing in the toasted desert landscape. McCarran Airport frames the South end of Las Vegas Boulevard. The Strip is the home to modern versions of exotic cityscapes and pyramids meant to give the visitors a since of escape although the tarmac inhabits a patch of sand only forty-five minutes by air from LAX.

Sam gathered his bag and disembarked to find his old friends. He couldn't imagine this unexpected rendezvous doing anything but evoking incredulity in Wolfe and murderous rage in Daga. Aruba involved amateurs. His new targets were trained professionals with cold hearts, cold cash, and hot lead.

"Harrah's with an H." Sam directed the driver.

BARRIO TEPITO, MEXICO CITY

Nestled in the North Central portion of the city inside the 150-190D beltway, Tepito is quaint and dangerous when one begins to describe it. For purposes of government, its location is the Delegación de Cuautémoc but laws and police are both looked upon in disdain while illegal activity of any kind imaginable goes on in plain sight of either the helpless or bribed cops.

Bounded by federal districts on the East and West, it is an endless series of rat holes, alleys, warrens, street stalls and vendors. Some have colorful blue or yellow ceilings while others, *los ambulantes*, push their wares down alleys so unforgiving to newcomers, one feels as if one were a mouse in a human-sized maze.

All things can be purchased. Illegal but relatively harmless CD's, DVD's, designer clothes and perfume some of which are pirated and others are stolen push the foot traffic into a narrow space between the curbs. It's the flea market of choice for those who dare to come. Even the locals call it *El barrio bravo de Tepito*, the tough neighborhood.

But farther along, not a great distance from Callé Jesús Carranza, where police chase illegal vendors daily, half-heartedly, only to have them return after siesta, one finds other merchandise for sale. Drugs of one's choice ranging from over the counter to marijuana are easily attainable in distribution size amounts. Weapons are flashed plainly for sale. Most are made in the US or purchased there. Handguns are common and not lonely for company. With the correct amount of money, one can purchase military radios and the frequencies used by the Federales. Body armor including Kevlar helmets hangs on display like suits in the NY garment district. Shoulder-launched M72 rockets, grenades, and TNT are available for the serious criminal.

This little section of Tepito is under the control of the drug cartels that see it as their fiefdom. In fact, those that come from here consider it an honor most likely the result of daily chanting of the neighborhood cheer. "ser Mexicano es un privilegio pero ser de Tepito es un don de los Dios." *To be a Mexican is a privilege but to be from Tepito is a gift from God.*

The cartels run a pretty tight ship. Many of the people one sees lounging in the barrios are actually at work. If only the government were as organized in its endeavors efficiency would not be such a strange word for bureaucrats everywhere. *Los Halcones,* The Hawks, keep an eye on the distribution end of the business using two meter radio band. No product or contraband moves without them knowing about it. *Las Ventanas,* The Windows, are juveniles on skateboards, bicycles, rollerblades, or just walking along that signal when law enforcement or strangers enter the barrio. *Los Mañosos,* The Picky Ones, buy and sell arms and only the best.

Two of the more dangerous subordinate groups are *El Dirección,* Command, which is the techies, the NSA of drug cartels and *Los Leopardos,* The Leopards, the prostitutes. The Command has over twenty members who intercept phone calls, trail possible enemies, and coordinate kidnappings and executions for payment or retribution.

Notice the prostitutes are Los Leopardos not Las Leopardos indicating that the group is of mixed gender. Their job besides the obvious is to make money and gather information from drunken johns who have powerful connections or positions.

At the pinnacle of this RICO operation is *Los Zetas,* The Z's. Ironic of course is that the acronym for Racketeer Influenced Criminal Organizations spells rich in Spanish. The Z's were formerly members of the Grupo Aeromóvil de Fuerzas Especiales, GAFE, air mobile special forces.

Trained at the School of the Americas at Fort Benning, GA and exposed to additional tactical training by the Israelis and French, the Z's were the elite officer corps of the Mexican Army. Their on-hands experience included rapid deployment, aerial assaults, marksmanship, ambushes, small group ops, intelligence collection, counter-surveillance, and prisoner rescues.

All of this information concerning drug cartels and their new paramilitary security forces could be gathered from open source material like *Jane's Intelligence Review* or Congressional subcommittees. Apparently, US authorities had more pressing agenda items to read.

These aforementioned Tepito streets spawned José Jesús Dominguez. His alias *Zarilla*, the skunk, referenced his over use of cologne common among the newly wealthy. People fresh from a death scene overused as well hoping to extinguish any lingering sensory reminders. On any given day Zarilla might be both. One couldn't be sure why the heavy cologne but it announced his arrival as surely as if his presence were made known by a court crier.

Zarilla had been a GAFE. Now he occupied the position of Padrino and Patrón. He had plans for the great land north that his forefathers once owned and had conquered by killing or converting the indigenous people. The recent inhabitants who had stolen the Southwest under their policy of *Manifest Destiny* would never see it coming until their children were Mexican citizens.

However, today the patron headed to the Iglesía de Piedad, The Church of Compassion, deep in his familiar barrio. Every Wednesday when he was in town he stopped to make an offering to Santa Muerte, Saint Death. Santa Muerte is not officially recognized by The Vatican but to many people of Mexican heritage it is as important a religious icon as any other and easily distinguished.

Characterized by a human skeleton and adorned with white lace in the manner of a virgin bride, Santa Muerte is a form of facing one's fears. People who swim that are afraid of water or who parachute from airplanes because they are afraid of heights exhibit similar behavior. In the case of this icon, the belief follows the logic that if one worships death then one is protected from death. Offerings left daily at her feet consist of cigars, cigarettes, rum, tequila, and money.

This particular Wednesday Zarilla left a special gift to his patron saint. A nine millimeter live round wrapped in a US hundred dollar bill. He knelt before her and whispered prayers for his family and friends. Similar to the Cosa Nostra in the US, Mexican criminals often exhibited extremely religious behavior before going to commit murder. They cried like babies at the funerals of friends and family and then committed homicide without hesitation. Zarilla was no different. They had the unique ability to compartmentalize extreme compassion for others close to them from the ice cold blood that ran in their veins when torturing and killing enemies. Zarilla had work to do today.

HARRAH'S LAS VEGAS

Daga lounged in the chair while the crisp desert rays warmed her brown skin. The misters sprayed clouds of cool water and combined with the low humidity made it seem almost brisk outside although the thermometer hovered at 105F. Wolfe sat upright reading newspapers and books depending on his mood. These early afternoon sessions at the pool energized him for the laborious hours of stressful poker play ahead. Nothing occupied his mind. Just get a tan, smoke a cigar, enjoy the view for now.....

"Hi everybody. Viva Las Vegas!"

Wolfe's eyes flashed at Daga's. She mirrored his facial expression, one of total surprise and curiosity. In perfect simultaneous motion, both their necks rotated towards the source of the sound.

"What's a matter with you? You can't see me?" The voice seemed to be coming from the mist like a bad horror movie.

"It can't be!" yelled Daga.

"It's impossible!" Wolfe agreed.

"Sure it's possible." The creature from the Black lagoon soon made its presence known as its shadow and then body separated the vapor.

"Sam! What are you doing here! Are you retired?" Daga hugged their old friend warmly while Wolfe glanced over her shoulder to see several young men noticing the clinch; their faces belying puzzlement as to why the old guy got all the skin from the hot chica.

Sam shook his body like a dog leaving a river. His entire shirt dripped water from Daga. "Nope. Can't say that I am. But I'm not working at Gitmo. That's an improvement."

"Sa—m. What do you mean? I'm here to play poker. That's it." Wolfe shook Sam's hand but not overly warmly.

"Well now, Wolfe. Some of my friends back at the office thought you two might be of help. Seems they liked the work in New Orleans and some scuttlebutt reached them about Aruba as well."

"So what. I'm playing poker. That's all I'm doing."

"Sam you can't do this. Aruba still bothers us, New Orleans too for that matter." Daga slumped back in her chair.

"What ya say we go have dinner tonight after poker. Let me explain my position. I think we can work it around your schedule. Give it a chance?"

"Fine, Sam. But if I bite on this one you should be selling used cars not doing what you're doing."

"Good. It's a date. 2330h at Battista's Hole in the Wall."

"How do you know we like Battista's?" Daga asked.

"Daga, Daga, Daga. All this time we've spent together and you think I don't know where you stay, where you eat, where you tan? What hour you go to the gym and when you go to sleep whenever you're in Vegas? I'm old but not that old."

"OK, Sam. Don't rub it in. We'll be there. You're buying and no lying. Anything interferes with the tournament we're both out." Wolfe shook his head. He knew how this would turn out.

"You drive a tough bargain, Wolfe. See ya there."

Sam shuffled down toward the pool bar in his usual tasteless tropical shirt, wrinkled khakis, and sandals with white socks. Wolfe chuckled softly. If anyone ever made Sam for an intelligence operative they had to be thinking out of the box. Way out of the box. Off the chain. Funny but somehow that gave Wolfe a warm feeling all over just before his stomach turned two flips and Daga gave her bugged eye look as well.

II

MATAMOROS

Zarilla made a call on his disposable cell phone. It had been a quick Gulfstream GS-II flight from Mexico City to the border town across from Brownsville, Texas. He made the trip because he wanted to do this one in person. Insubordination could not be tolerated and he planned on making a statement written in screams and body parts.

"Is the package ready?"

"Sí, padrino. At the ranchero."

"Make sure all the equipment is prepared. We will be there shortly."

The black Cadillac Escalade, carrying Zarilla in back, with a heavily armed driver and another guard in the shotgun seat pulled away from the parked plane and headed out of the gates to the secluded ranch house in the desert south of town.

Zarilla did not find disciplining his men distasteful. He felt more like a father teaching his children obedience. The child to be taught a lesson would never make another mistake. José Jesús Dominguez entered the ranchero and kicked the dirt off his cowboy boots of crocodilian leather. The object of his visit sat up wide-eyed and trembled.

The cloud of cologne accompanying Zarilla reached the nose of the captive. Instead of being comforting it announced the arrival of his demise. The lowly underling had no misconceptions about what to expect. He hoped against all reason it would be quick. Consciously, he knew otherwise.

The indiscretion had been a common one. Motivated by greed yet making more money than most Mexicans, the drug runner had been cutting the drugs and keeping the difference.

Zarilla's heels clicked across the wooden floor towards where the subject sat naked duct taped to a wooden chair. His arms, legs, ankles and neck were restrained. Silver tape replaced his smile. A bright light from above shone in the face of the subordinate placing him in a cone of brightness and leaving the remainder of the space in blackness except for a small table covered in white linen.

Placed on the table top were the instruments of pain. In another setting, the tools could be mistaken for everyday objects or medical devices. Today they had a different role.

Standing in the shadows out of sight of the victim were two members of the Hermanos Pistoleros Latinos. A street gang operating in the Nuevo Laredo area, Las Zetas used them for muscle and minor hits. Sitting in a far corner, a medical doctor in white lab coat sat reading a newspaper. To the uninitiated, the presence of medical personnel seemed counter-intuitive but the function of the doctor would soon become apparent.

Dominguez had been at the torture and killing of DEA agent Enrique "Kiki" Camerena. The agent had been kidnapped in front of the US consulate in Guadalajara by Mexican cops working for the cartel. He had been sacrificed by the CIA and DOJ in order for Oliver North to continue to supply the Contras in Nicaragua. Strangely, the CIA even had a recording of the torture.

Zarilla removed his jacket and rolled up his sleeves.

"Good evening, my friend."

A grunt served as the answer. The eyes told more than any conversation might have done.

"Do you remember Kiki Camerena?"

He shook his head in the negative.

"Well, I do. He suffered terribly. I consider myself a student of that session. You are going to die. The question before us is the manner of your death. This, of course, is your choice. It will depend on the information you give us. Comprende?

Yes was the answer by way of moving his head.

"Bueno. How many others have you told about stealing from the cartel?"

Zarilla glanced at his guards. One of the pistoleros stepped forward and tore the tape from the mouth of the prisoner. Half of the moustache came off with the tape.

"Nobody! Nadie! It was for my abuela. She is dying. I needed the money."

"If she is dying, you don't need the money. She is old. You are young. Yet you are in the grave before her. Not a good decision. Were you ever arrested by the Americanos?"

Zarilla , of course, already knew the answer. It satisfied his desire to kill.

"Yes, just once. They caught me crossing the border. I had cocaine stashed in fresh oranges."

"And you told them nothing? Nada?"

"Nada."

"Were you followed?"

"Nunca! Never!"

"I don't believe you. That is of no matter, however."

Zarilla approached the table. On the linen lie an object that resembled a threaded top like the children's toy made of clear plastic. Its proper use was to pry open jaws when one suffered seizures. Clenched teeth were nearly impossible to open. The oral screw, its medical name, provided leverage for EMT's to open mouths. The attending personnel placed the tip beneath the overbite of the upper teeth and turned the handle until the mouth had opened enough to make airways breathable or clear physical obstructions like regurgitated food. It prevented the victim from biting off the end of a finger as well.

Zarilla juggled the screw in the air near the face of man. "Do you know what this is?"

"A butt plug?" The answer came out high-pitched and wobbly.

"A butt plug? Are you loco? What clubs do you go to in Matamoros? Are you a marícon? You like men? I should shoot you now but that is what you want.

No, this will open your mouth so we can talk in case you choose otherwise. I guess you don't have any problem keeping it open." Again Zarilla motioned and tape soon covered the eyes of the captive.

Unknowing, the man left his jaws apart like a willing dental patient. Zarilla grabbed a pair of pliers from the table and quickly grasped a lower cuspid. The shrieking stopped much before the blood ceased flowing.

The doctor appeared at the chair and checked vitals. Slightly elevated heart rate and breathing were indicated. Traumatic shock had not yet manifested. He returned to his reading material.

"Now, let us continue. You want me to believe that you stole a relatively small amount, that you were arrested by the gringos and told them nothing and you will never do anything like this again. Correct?"

The sí muffled by streams of blood stumbled from the man's mouth.

"I see. Well, unfortunately for you I don't believe you. Perhaps your memory will improve with help?"

At the far end of the main room, a fireplace burned mesquite wood. The flames burned a mature bright red.

Zarilla stripped the tape from the eyes of the moaning lump of flesh before him. He sobbed and begged continuously to please kill him. Zarilla would have none of it.

"Do you know what this is?" Zarilla held it down to the face which now dipped low on the chest.

"It is re-bar. The metal used to reinforce concrete. Now it is only a plain brown. Soon it will be a glowing red. The fire waits. Are you sure you didn't tell them anything?"

Red spittle mixed with unintelligible words rolled down the man's torso.

Minutes later, the pistoleros tipped the chair with the victim still attached on its side. They placed a garrote on his neck and warned him it would only tighten if he moved. They removed the constraints on his arms and legs in order to take away the chair and then replaced the bindings so he lie naked on his side with his hands behind his back and feet bound together. Zarilla approached. He waved the glowing hot metal in the face of the condemned man close enough for the skin to blister on the face.

"Are you sure you told them nothing? Maybe our methods and contacts? Our schedules? Our preferred routes?"

A form of no repeatedly could be distinguished among the pleas for a merciful death.

Using the same method that had been used on "Kiki" Camarena, Zarilla reached for a fresh re-bar and inserted the glowing tip in the rectum of the man. The shrieking continued until exhausted or dead, the smuggler fell silent.

The doctor appeared soon after. "He is dead. Either from shock or internal bleeding or a combination."

Zarilla spoke. "Why do I have you here? We were only getting started."

"I can't help he is of little constitution." The doctor shrugged his shoulders.

"Make sure the video gets seen by others. It is of no use if they don't know how he died. Remove the skin from the fingertips and burn. Cut off the hands, head, and feet and feed them to the desert. Pull out the rest of the teeth and throw them out as you drive. Leave the body for the birds."

Zarilla washed his hands, sprayed too much cologne on his neck, and lit a cigar as he entered the SUV and the guards drove him away.

III

BATTISTA'S

Located behind a convenience store one block east of the strip on Flamingo, Battista's is unassuming but perfect for business and seclusion. Separated into multiple cubby holes, privacy is easily achieved. The fact Sam had requested 2330h made it more so. The walls were plastered with Rat Pack and other celebrity photos. Faces flush with wine were pictured shaking hands and bussing the owner and his wife.

"What ya think? Pomodoro gravy?"

"Come on Sam. Is there anything else in a joint like this?" Wolfe chided.

"Sam, we love you but get to the meat." Daga sipped her full-bodied chianti made by the owner and his adult children.

"As you might have guessed, we've got a problem. Basically, the Mexican drug cartels have taken over the government of Mexico and where there is resistance there is all out war. Last month there were over two hundred murders along the border mostly in broad daylight.

The police chief of Nuevo Laredo resigned or faced annihilation of his men. Eight police officers had been murdered in broad daylight before the chief succumbed to their demands. The clear threat received stated that he would leave walking or his men would leave feet first. The ol' plata o plomo deal. Silver or lead. The bribe or the gun. There were major shootouts in business districts. Civilians and cops alike. President Calderon actually has some cojones. He called in the federales but even they're outgunned."

"What are you doing in the middle of it? You're prohibited from operating within the US except for Patriot Act stuff. This sounds more like DEA and Border Patrol/ICE. I mean New Orleans involved Al Qaeda but this is different."

Sam chuckled. "Wolfe, have you ever read the Patriot Act? It basically dissolves the constitution when it comes to protection of individual rights and frees up the charters of the FBI, NSA, and CIA to pretty much do as they see fit as long as it has to do with national security. All bets are off. Practically, no judicial oversight. The Ivy League boys are in charge."

"OK, what do you need from us?" Wolfe glanced at Daga and happy didn't come to mind when describing her countenance.

"Wolfe, the CIA has been involved in the Mexican drug trade since the eighties and the Iran-Contra deal. We no longer have an interest in Nicaragua and finally there is a Mexican president who actually can't be bought. It's spilling over the border. American girls are going missing, held for ransom, Phoenix is now the kidnap capital of the US. There are home invasions this side of the Rio Grande weekly; I have orders to stop it."

"That brings you to Vegas?"

"They're making so much money that it is ending up here. Along with all the problems associated with such. Besides everything else, it's a laundering operation. The worst part is we are dealing with well-trained ex-military types with good intelligence and equipment. They don't mind killing cops. They sure won't mind killing you."

"Are you trying to recruit me or chase me away?"

"I thought you'd like the truth."

"What's that have to do with the World Series of Poker and us?"

"With fifteen hundred dollar buy-ins minimum and some as high as fifty thousand, besides laundering money, they're destroying the integrity of the game through collusion."

"Okay, Sam. We get it. Finish your cappuccino. Give us the details."

"We're treating this like a national security risk. We' have carte blanche. Judge, jury.....

Think of it like the Somalian pirates. Eliminate when possible. We have to be somewhat more discreet. We can't have Delta forces operating in Vegas. That's where we come in. It's a basic search and destroy mission in an urban setting and completely off the books.

You continue to play in the WSOP and the two of you identify targets. Then we move against them. The problem is the Zeta's are well-prepared. If they get a sniff of the op, they'll move on us without a second thought. They have resources better than most militaries and police forces and they don't hesitate because of uniform or nationality. If they even get suspicious, we'll have communication techs and street people on us pronto.

We don't want to go head to head. We have to stay below the horizon. What do you think? You in?"

"We're in."

"Yeh, thanks Sam. It is how we wanted to spend our summer." chimed in Daga. She leaned over and gave Sam a peck on the cheek. "Dinner's on Sam."

"Of course, it is. Don't worry, you'll earn it."

Sam reached under the table and handed Daga a Gucci shopping bag. She smiled too quickly before Sauria could wipe the grin from her face.

"Sorry Daga. It's not what you think. Just a little operational security. Inside beneath the gift paper one will find the briefing papers on our targets. Los Zetas and all of their henchmen. It's rather extensive. Read and flush in very small pieces. Questions?"

"No. Pass the garlic bread and the chianti, please." Wolfe didn't let listening interfere with a delicious meal.

"We'll meet tomorrow at Venus' pool around noon. We should be up and running by evening. Got to collect intel before we take any action."

"Hey, isn't that the topless pool at Caesar's?" Wolfe smiled and Daga glanced up from pasta and pomodoro sauce.

"It sure is. I figured there'll be fewer people and more security. Why? Is that not good?"

"It's OK with me. I'm already a little tired of how uptight you Americans can be." Daga returned to her plate with a playful wink at Wolfe.

"Well, I know it will be OK with Wolfe. See ya then"

Sauria slapped Wolfe on the shoulder. He left the restaurant happy with his day. Wolfe and Daga finished their meal silently. They knew that this would not be their usual visit to Sin City. They hoped that their bodies wouldn't be *what stayed in Vegas.*

IV

VENUS' POOL

SOMETIMES Daga struggled with her obvious natural gifts. In an area sprinkled nicely with young beautiful women in various degrees of nudity, Daga had managed to stop all other human activity except the rubbernecking by most of the males and all of the females. The reason she didn't affect all of the males pertained to the fact those men were attempting not to be punched in the arm by their girlfriends.

It seemed normal to her. She walked the length of the pool deck to the shower wearing only an oversized white t-shirt. Drenching herself as she would at home, she arched her back and allowed the water to run endlessly down her front and back. Soon her cover up became transparent, a fact that had no bearing on the length of the show. Wolfe and Sam sat chuckling at the cabana.

"Does she do it to upset the women or tantalize the men?" Sam reached for his champagne and Chambord cocktail.

"She does it naturally although she is quite aware of the affects on others. She refuses to change because others have problems. Problems that she does not recognize as being hers."

"How's that work for you?"

"Oh, when we first met it bothered me but when I realized she is completely her own being it actually made me proud. Besides, there's always the idiot that wants to know why she is with me."

"What do you tell them? Bugger off?"

"Noo-o. I tell them something which plays on their insecurities and repressed psychological self-hate."

Sam raised his eyebrow, the one that stretched above both eyes. "Are you going to make me ask?"

"I tell them that '*I can't show you here*.'"

Sam spit out half his drink laughing. "What does *that* mean?"

"Nothing really. Whatever they imagine. They usually start mumbling to themselves and go back and crawl under their favorite rock."

"You should have been in psychological warfare, my friend."

"We're in it every day."

Daga walked up and sat down. "That shower felt good."

"I'm sure many people would agree." Sam smiled at his minor humor.

"Now then, it's time to talk turkey. Wolfe, you and Daga are going to work. The main purpose of which is to find out who exactly we are chasing."

"Don't you know?" Daga asked while combing out her long tresses.

"Seems like a reasonable question, Sam."

"Oh, it is Wolfe. We know the organizations, the hierarchy, and the so called capos in Mafia-speak. But similar to the mob the top bananas aren't anywhere around the action. We want to weaken the Vegas end of things and see if we can coerce the padrinos to come check things out."

"Start a little fire?"

"Exactly. When people and money start disappearing the boss has questions. He'll send a couple upper management types and then if that doesn't do it he'll show up himself. That's the basics."

"Gee Sam; you make it sound so simple. It's the details about money and people missing that I'm sure are a little more complicated."

"I'll make sure it's worth your time. I know you've wanted to play in more bracelet events."

"Always watching out for us." Daga rolled over on her belly, removed her cover up and stretched out in the desert sun. Even Wolfe had a difficult time listening to Sam's pitch.

"Wolfe you're going to play poker. Keep your ears and eyes open. Human intel. Daga, you'll work as a stripper which based on your tanning habits shouldn't be that big a stretch and actually a bonus. A full body tan does wonders for the tips."

"Looking for what? Shaved coochies?"

"That would take about thirty seconds. We're looking for evidence of laundering. Strip clubs are a cash business which makes them perfect for washing large amounts of cash. There should be plenty of drug use but maybe more than the usual one might expect. Easy availability close to the source. Questions?"

"Yeh, where is this place?"

"Over on Industrial between the railroad tracks and the boulevard. There are quite a few over there but you're looking for *The Chocho Rosado*. It means....."

"Don't bother Sam. I can figure it out. Remember I'm Dominican."

"Right. Sorry." Sam glanced back to Rebelle. "Wolfe same for you."

"What? I got to go dance? I don' think.."

"Easy cowboy. You're the boyfriend. When you're not playing poker you're hanging at the club. The easygoing caballero that's not jealous and is cool with his girlfriend stripping. Go there often enough and you become part of the décor.

After you get squared away I'll find you. Don't get sunburned." Sam got up and strolled through the statuary of Roman goddesses on his way out. The earthly ones ignored the frumpy man in the bad tropical shirt. The heavenly ones smiled upon him.

V

CHOCHO ROSADO

It didn't take long for Daga to find it. Shaped like half an apple if one were being generous. It nearly blocked out the view of the not far away Trump Tower. Outlined in pink neon lights, the bulbs throbbed to some unknown beat like swollen vulva in ecstasy. She glanced at her watch. The numerals flashed back two in the afternoon. She had the right place.

Rehearsals were in full swing. With the economy completely in the dumps, secretaries, house-wives, and teachers scrambled to make ends meet. The joke circulating in Vegas was that men were starting to have sex with their wives.

Still, there were customers. Salesmen and realtors who had no action of their own, could pass away the afternoon watching aspiring entertainment without the guilt of not tipping or the chore of telling their wives that the business luncheon went nowhere again. After all, the women were dancer interns.

Interns, the catch all phrase for free or cheap labor common during the Bush years. When did the word *interns* stop meaning doctors in training? Daga shook her head and walked over to the bouncer.

"Hi. I'm looking for work."

"Pahrump is a thirty miles west of here?"

"What does that mean?"

"Are you a hooker? I guess not. Well, what kind of work do you want to do here?"

db wolfe

"Entertain?"

"Entertain. You mean strip? OK, fine. Did you bring any costumes?"

Daga's silence answered the question.

"You *are* new. Happens all of the time. Go in the dressing room and see the house mother.

There's always some clean hand me downs to use temporarily. When you're ready come on out and we'll get you up on stage. Just relax. By the way, I'm Bobby. Everybody calls me Bobo. Don't know why. They just do. If this works out, I'll introduce you to the boss and you can talk details. Good luck."

Daga learned fast. She watched the others. When it came her turn, she imitated what she could and free-styled everything else. The natural rhythms of her birthplace served her well. The meringue music of her childhood still beat in her heart. One elderly gentleman even gave her a dollar.

Daga left the stage to a smattering of applause and drunken hoots. A man in a well-tailored suit met her at the bar.

"Hello. I'm Carlos. Mucho gusto."

"I'm Dagmar. Nice to meet you." Daga hadn't used her Christian name in years.

"Is that your real name or professional name? It's very sexy."

"Professional."

"You look Latina? Habla español¿

"Not so much anymore." Why tell them useful information thought Daga.

"Well, you looked very interesting on stage. Come on back in my office and I'll break everything down for you."

Daga bit her lip and followed Carlos into his office. If he did one stupid thing, Sam would have to do without her.

Inside of Carlos' office resembled a designer's worst idea of a Hollywood casting couch from the 1930's. Framed nudes of the female form were displayed on every wall. Not even real paintings, they were the step-children of the velvet Elvis sold on every street corner in Vegas. Shadows cast themselves across the desk with only a few limited sources of light to contest them. The requisite leather sofa stretched out languidly nearby in silent invitation for the next needy woman with few skills and plenty of expensive habits.

"Make yourself comfortable, please. This won't take long. Would you like a drink?" Carlos gestured at the couch which represented the only other seating available besides the single chair at his desk.

Carlos José Jueza - the judge — reached beneath his desk for a bottle of Patrón. He removed his jacket and rolled up his monogrammed French cuffs with the stylized letters of HPL, exposing tattoos covering his arms. Daga tried not to look but he had noticed her glance as he had hoped she would. He poured two glasses of liquor equal to a glass of wine each. He presented one for Daga as she had not yet taken a seat.

"Please, please. Sit. Don't worry about these. Childhood fancies." he acknowledged with a nod his exposed ink.

Daga took a seat. Sitting rigid on the very front edge of the sofa with her legs tightly crossed, she rubbed the back of her neck. Her ever present friend comforted her with a steel kiss. She forced a smile while thinking of what sounds Carlos would make with a blade between his ribs. These self-assured practiced come-ons of a rapist instantly silenced as the knife severed his liver.

The tattoos told a story to those who could read the modern skin hieroglyphics. The left forearm flashed the letters HPL encased in a spider web while the other arm displayed Santa Muerte. Had he lifted his shirt, which he hoped he would soon, Daga would have seen a tattoo of a .45 caliber handgun at his waistline as if it were tucked in his belt.

Carlos represented Los Zetas in this particular scheme. A lifelong member of the Hermanos Pistoleros Latinos, HPL, his duty involved washing all of the cash that came through the club. Most HPL members were hired killers for Los Zetas in the Nuevo Laredo area but Carlos showed a little more ambition and brains and received a position requiring both. The fact that he benefitted otherwise from the enterprise concerned no one as long as the numbers made sense.

Laundering money through a dance club involved very little imagination. If the Chocho Rosado did 100K on a particular night, he deposited 200K. The difference came from the boxes of dirty cash in the storage facility listed in his dead mother's name. The Feds, both FBI and IRS, had given up on chasing cash businesses even in Las Vegas. Terrorist plots, false driver's licenses, and Islamic charities kept them occupied. The state of Nevada paid some attention but comp nights at Caesar's and free VIP lap dances in the seclusion of the Platinum rooms took care of any difficulty. The Las Vegas bankers filled out the requisite forms but asked no questions that weren't required. If the Feds didn't have any problems, why should they?

"And now, a toast to your new job. Salut!" Carlos downed the tequila, Daga took a sip.

"What you don't like it? That's good shit." Not another hard nut to crack thought Carlos.

"I'm not big on tequila or shots for that matter. I'm here for a job. Can I take it that I've been hired?"

"Sure. Sure. You got a boyfriend?"

"Yeh, he's playing poker at the Rio."

"I don't want any drunk boyfriends causing trouble with patrons. Does he have a name?"

"His name is Wolfe. He won't cause any trouble. He has a few drinks, talks to the other girls. We actually like each other's company."

"Lobo, huh?"

"Yeh, lobo not loco. He's cool."

"You know how this works? Your pay and all?"

"Yeh, pretty much. I need the exact numbers though. Early girls pay less to come to work 'cause it's slow and bad tippers.

Late girls pay more. They might make more per hour. Depends how their luck runs. How am I doing?"

"Fifty at 6:00pm. One hundred at 10:00pm. No charge for nooners. Ready for another drink?"

"Nope. On my way out. I'll call for my required days. I might work some doubles."

"Fine with me. Next time relax a little around me."

"I don't relax until I learn the tune."

"See ya tonight."

AMAZON ROOM, WSOP, THE RIO

Wolfe settled in to his seat number five at table 229. The event represented the most common type held at the WSOP; No Limit Texas Hold'em, $1500 buy-in. As usual he got there on time, a few players already in their seats, and the majority standing around trying not to look too anxious or eager for the game to start. Twenty – eight hundred players meant two hundred eighty got at least the buy-in back with the final table getting seventy percent of the prize money and the winner getting thirty percent of the final table money. With a prize pool of 3.8 million after the house take, the motivation to do well permeated conversations, metabolisms, last minute self-encouragements, and all consciousness.

If all of the usual factors didn't stoke one's competitive spirits, then the giant room with 280 plus tables with ten players each might be enough. Larger than life photos of former main event champions stared down upon the masses silently daring the crowd to first win a bracelet and then come for the daddy of them all, the 10K buy-in WSOP Championship. The championship changes one's life, fame and fortune continuing to flow well after the win itself, the ultimate checkmark on every poker player's bucket list.

Wolfe surveyed his opponents as the table filled. These would only be the first of many. A few rounds would give him an idea about each player's style and with that information he could begin to make moves rather than play *mom and pop poker* where one either got cards or didn't and played them when one had them.

Today's poker didn't resemble any game the baby boomers played in the kitchen. The young gunslingers dominated the action and even professionals adjusted to the new and successful style or went out trying. Wolfe studied this phenomenon and tried to utilize it. Guys in their twenties some barely old enough to play legally in the USA were capable of going all in at anytime with any range of hands. Many had played more poker hands on the internet by age eighteen than seasoned pros in the game for years. When one re-raised an internet young turk one should reasonably expect his opponent to push the pot regardless of his hole cards.

Wolfe liked to use the only play that he had found that threw the fly boys off their game; the check raise. The usual response arrived in one of two forms. The unexpected fold or the all-in could be expected ninety percent of the time. Some East coasters might just call. These thoughts and many others raced around the corners of his mind.

His job, as Sam had described it, involved scouting. However, he still wanted to win and with the pressure off thanks to Sam providing the buy-in, he could enter more tournaments. The majority of players could be divided in to basically two groups; the internet group and the pros. Small sub-groups encompassed the older males who have made a small income on the side playing poker for years, successful people of both genders playing for the adrenaline, and true dead money. Dead money consisted of the people who had nothing but a dream; the mom and pop people.

White American males, all though numerous, were under-represented. The majority of true Caucasians playing actually were descended from the steppes with large contingents from Russia and the Nordic countries. Thirty percent of the gamers were west coast Asians. Asians at any age played aggressively. Under-represented were Latinos. If that changed, Sam wanted to know.

The tournament director entered the room. "Shuffle up and deal." The rectangles potentially worth millions flew across the table at Wolfe. The watches and cell phones around the room were on 1200h.

Six hours and three fifteen minute breaks later the tables broke up for dinner. Upon the players' return, floor men directed players to new tables and chairs re-mixing the remaining field. That's when the picture changed.

Seated at Wolfe's table were three men with Latino gang tattoos. Although not impossible, they seemed to know one another. The men displayed ink from HPL, Texas Syndicate, and MS-13. Three men affiliated with three different gang loyalties seated at the table and getting along amicably set off Wolfe's radar.

Then it got worse. The Latinos played nearly every hand regardless of position, wagered heavily, and often were in hands with one another. Other players got wedged between the Latinos and were chased from the pot or put all-in to decide if seeing the river met pot odds. Often, it did not. Wolfe watched from his seat at number 8 waiting patiently for a premium hand. One hour in to the fourth session Wolfe found the hand he needed.

Sitting on the button, Wolfe had hit A-K suited. He had position, a premium starting hand, and enough chips to play. However, A-K didn't make a hand unless something came on the flop. He settled into his seat. The attack came as suspected.

All three Latinos called Wolfe's raise of 3X the big blind. The remainder of the players folded and eagerly began to watch the action. The flop came 2-3-A rainbow. The Latino under the gun raised the pot, the second one called as well as the third. Wolfe's play; he only called. Fourth street popped as a five that made two spades on the board and four for Wolfe to hit the nut flush.

The Latino in first position went all-in. The other two gangsters called. They had Wolfe covered. Rebelle called as well.

The dealer flopped a non-spade 8. The other two Latinos stuck in a side pot went in with what chips were left. Unbeknownst to them, it represented a major strategy flaw. Previous to going all-in the two had other options. Now all four hands had to be exposed.

The Latino in first position had 4-6 in the hole; a straight. Wolfe had the pair of Aces. The other two Latinos had total trash and seemed to care less. One of them won the side pot with a ten high. The first Latino now had about eighty percent of the chips on the table. Wolfe stood up. He had something to tell Sam. But he had something to say before he left.

"Wow, you guys are good. One guy calls out of position with a 4-6, one guy has 10-2 and another has 7-9. For all the money. He hits a straight which gives him a monster chip lead and one of you is still alive. I feel silly for playing A-K and hitting an ace on the flop. Good luck with the tournament."

Wolfe walked out of the convention space and up the hall to the main casino. He scratched his head and smiled. These guys weren't even trying to hide it.

CHOCHO ROSADO

Daga made her way past Bobo at the door. Happy hour had recently ended and the place might be full of leftover salesmen and cheese balls warming up for a night on the town. The three twenty-somethings at the door waiting to get past big boy glanced at Daga and one made an audible gasp. She started to turn and respond but caught herself. Oh good, she thought. I'm not even inside yet.

The title of dressing room described some other space than the one she entered. The actual area resembled more of a locker room for a minor league hockey team. The main difference centered on the fact hockey players don't need or use mirrors. Double stacked khaki-colored lockers covered wall space not used for makeup. The floor, littered with the detritus of stripping for a living, made walking in CFM pumps a risky endeavor. CFM's, come fuck me pumps, were capable of making nuns look like working girls. The house mom met her at the door.

'Hi. I'm the house mom. Everybody calls me Mom. Find an empty locker. If you have anything valuable make sure you lock it up. If you don't have a lock I'll keep it till you get one. Any questions?"

"When do I go on?"

"Go down and work the crowd. Try to get some lap dances. When you hear your name announced by the DJ, you got about fifteen minutes to report back to here. Good luck."

Daga changed into a white thong covered by a matching wrap around skirt that she tied in a knot at her waist. A simple white polyester top clung to her bare breasts and seemed to be as much a part of her as her own skin. Simple sandals completed the ensemble.

"Where you going dressed like that?" A tall, model thin girl met Daga as she exited the dressing room.

"Are you talking to me? I don't know you." Daga's defenses were up.

"Oh, I'm Kathy. Everybody calls me Kat. I use that on stage as well. It's just that none of the other girls dress like that to work."

"Well, I don't want to look like the other girls. You know; something a little different."

"Suit yourself. As long as it's cool with Carlos. Oh, hey. Do yourself a favor and stay away from the chick in the green sequin gown. Ludmilya Laparova. A real bitch. Too much powder if you know what I mean."

"Thanks for the tip. See ya." Daga headed for the bar. As she turned to leave, Carlos appeared and dragged Kat by the arm into his office. She went without protest.

Daga ordered a Cruzan rum on the rocks and sat down at the bar waiting for the inevitable drunk to sit next to her to start a conversation. She felt the presence of a body squeeze into the seat behind her and turned to face the customer.

"Hey, honey. You're in my seat."

"I didn't see anyone's drink around. I kind of like it here."
Daga stared into the face of Laparova.

"Look. I know you're new but this is my favorite spot."

"Might want to get here earlier. There's plenty of space.
I'm Daga." She extended her hand. Laparova ignored it.

"You can have it. Today. But if you try this with some of my
regulars there's going to be hell to pay."

"What's your name?"

"LOL. Lots of Love."

"Well, LOL. This intimidation routine might work on
Mary Lou from Waterloo. But with me it's a waste of time. I
paid money to come to work. Keep your distance and we'll do
OK. Pendejo." With that final insult, Daga swung around to
face the bar.

"You won't last long." Ludmilya stormed off in the direction of the customer tables.

HARRAH'S
Sam walked in off the street. Wolfe and Daga waited at
Bill's Bar just inside the door. They had a two drink lead on
Sam when he arrived.

"So how'd your first day go?"

Daga didn't wait for Wolfe to speak. "Well, the manager
is covered in gang tattoos and uses the girls as his personal
harem. He tried his creepy come on to me but I cut it short. I
met two of the dancers. One I feel sorry for. The other is Russian and high on something. Probably cocaine. Thinks she's the
boss. I set her straight."

"That's good. Stir things up and see what floats. How'd the
poker go Wolfe?" Sam turned his attention to Rebellle.

"Higher number of Latinos than other years. They were
playing high stakes cash and bracelet events. Covered in Texas
Syndicate, HPL, and MS-13 tats. Strangely, they all seemed to
get along. Basic bully strategy. Push all the money in all of the
time. Didn't seem to care if they won. But of course they did."

"Yeh, they're the washers. If they make a payout, the money is all of sudden clean. Daga, what about the cash at your end?"

"You'll have to check the deposits but from where I stood during my cashout he had about 400K on his desk. Not bad for an afternoon."

"Did that make sense? Did you do that much business?"

"No way to know. They have the usual private rooms. Anything could and probably does go on in there. Who knows how much legit business goes down and how much prostitution and laundering. I can tell you that they're not going broke."

'OK. That's a good start. We're going to take some of their money and see if we can get them to up the ante. Keep doing what you're doing. I'll be in touch." Sam threw a hundred on the bar and it disappeared in bartender Big Ernie's paw. Sauria wanted to be remembered.

VI

BARRIO TEPITO

Zarilla settled into his mansion fortress. Leather furnishings and ebony tables dotted the tiled floor. Vaulted ceilings interrupted only by great arched windows provided openness and uninterrupted views of the tropical flora beyond. He would spend the evening reading financial reports from the well-paid accountants of Los Zetas and then finish the night going over intelligence reports from Los Halcones. Always, he searched for new enemies or sources of income. From the street, La Forteleza looked like a plain stucco wall void of color. Four meters high and one block square, it jogged the interest of some only by it size. The locals of course were less than eager to know what lie behind it. In this part of the world, curiosity really did kill the cat.

Planted across the top, cacti of every shape and variety grew lush in the bright sun. Hidden amongst the succulents, razor wire crossed low and high, strung so densely rodents often could not escape its cutting tentacles. Laser motion sensors picked up miniscule movement initiating live feed digital images by fiber optic cable to the four man security force provided by La Dirección. The obvious cameras at the gate provided solely as a distraction to those who would wish to enter unannounced.

Like many in his line of work, he loved his children and wife dearly. This, however, could not be gauged by the time spent with them. They lived in a separate part of the compound from his offices, his children tutored on site. Any sexual drive remaining after the workday he satisfied with young new prostitutes recruited into Los Leopardos. None could work if he had not *sexed them in,* using the lingo of the gangs for the passage of initiation.

Only rare events of pleasure or danger could ever entice Zarilla from his velvet cage.

LAS VEGAS

Carlos rolled up to the storage facility in his black Escalade. He had gotten new orders from his *jefes* to launder even more money. Apparently the drug and kidnapping business in northern Mexico didn't reflect economic downturns and recessions. He backed his SUV up to the garage door, removed the combination lock, and swung up the portal. What he saw he could not believe. Worse yet, his bosses would not believe. They would not believe it even after he had been tortured to death. Five million US dollars in unmarked moving boxes no longer existed in this unremarkable storage with a little old lady's name attached to the lease. Security cameras surrounded the place both those of the owner's and the others he had added. He swallowed hard, his heart racing to break through his chest. Once the money doesn't add up the bodies start to stack up.

The videos told it all. Five individuals wearing night camo, their faces masked and carrying M4 assault rifles descended through the chain link fence to the garage door. One stepped up and worked the lock. It delayed entry by thirty seconds. They took care to replace the lock for re-use making any explanation by Carlos suspect. One held up a hand printed message, 'thanks for the tip, Carlos' turning slowly to make sure it could be seen by all cameras.

Three men took perimeter while the other two loaded the money into the van. Ten minutes after it had all began the scene on the camera returned to normal.

Questions bombarded Carlos' brain, who were they? Why his stash? Why frame him? How could he explain it? Should he run? Where? Carlos collapsed in his tracks. He had no answers. Perhaps he had one.

LA FORTELEZA

Carlos called the emergency number. He spoke two words of code, removed the SIM card and left the phone on the bus. He got off and walked around the corner. Standing upright, his sunglasses off, he presented himself to the front gate of the fortress. Cameras whirred though not the large obvious ones and moments later the gates opened and the guards escorted him within.

Carlos' knees shook uncontrollably. His eyes darted around like the flight path of a hummingbird in search of nectar. The lead guard opened the doors and the trailing guard pushed Carlos inward, his legs unwilling to respond to nervous system commands. He crossed the portal and in his deepest thoughts hoped not for the last time. The sanctum sanctorum of Los Zetas now surrounded him in both space and emotion. He exhaled heavily and approached Zarilla's desk.

"Señor..."

"Sit." A smile slowly ran across Zarilla's features or what would pass as a smile if one were a pathological killer. "What brings you to me shaking like a jumping bean? Using the one time emergency number? What is this big problem? I think the big problem is yours, yes? Perhaps a trago of tequila to allow you to speak?"

Carlos nodded meekly. Zarilla opened his desk drawer and pulled out a bottle of Chinaco Negro Añejo, its black bottle matching nicely the ebony surface of the desk. One hundred percent agave, aged for five years, Zarilla spent ten thousand US dollars a year for four cases. He felt like he should keep it at hand for often it provided the final taste to the condemned.

José Jesús Dominguez filled two shot glasses with golden liquid and then motioned for Carlos to drink. The club manager slugged the potion down and returned to his seat. Zarilla tasted his as if it were fine wine.

"Now then, what is the problem? Take your time. I have all day even if you don't."

Carlos tried to form the words. His lips refused. Zarilla, at first amused, soon became impatient. Only the look of death that swept across El Patrón finally convinced the hesitant parts to speak.

"We've been robbed!" The words leapt from within like gas clouds from an explosion.

"We've been robbed?! I haven't been robbed. I've been sitting here. You mean you've been robbed of my money. The money we entrusted to you. Is that what you mean to say?"

The pitch and timbre of Zarilla's voice had increased with each syllable of the words formed as questions.

"Yes." The only word Carlos could muster.

"And this happened how?"

"I have proof. Here." Carlos slid the digital disc of the security camera loops across the desk.

Zarilla studied the images and stopped when one of the perpetrators held up the card with Carlos' name.

"What are we to make of this?" he swung the monitor around for Carlos to see.

"I don't know. They're framing me of course. But why I do not know."

"They're framing you? You don't know who they are but they're framing you? What if you tipped them off and they gave you up to split the money fewer ways. What about that?"

"No! No! That's not it. Why would I come here if I were part of it? I would run for my life!" Cold sweat ran into his eyes blurring his vision.

"Or-r-r, you would come here to get us off the trail and pick up your share later."

"I am not that loco. I know you are going to torture me but even then I can tell you nothing. I'm hoping at least the fact I know nada will save my family."

José Jesús Dominguez pondered the situation while Carlos' clothing became increasingly wet; some of the moisture the product of sweat. This hombre is either really good or telling the truth. Zarilla went with his instincts.

"OK. It is simple. Go back to Vegas. Find out what happened. You will have the assets of the entire organization. Los Halcones, Las Ventanas, Las Mañosos, Los Leopardos, and Dirección. All of them. If however, we find you are lying you will beg for death but not before you watch your mother and sister at the hands of our torturers and of course me. Do you understand?"

Carlos could only nod.

'Your mother and sister will be picked up and given a *holiday* until we find out who it is. They'll be in touch. When you get back you'll get a message where the new stash will be kept. I hope we never meet again for your sake. Adíos." Zarilla waved Carlos out of the room.

Carlos passed a male attendant hurrying to clean the area where the manager had sat. It wasn't an uncommon need after a session with El Patrón.

VEGAS

"Hey, Sam. What's up?" Wolfe and Daga swung around to see Sam arrive to a nearby bar stool. The pink faux leather caught his attention.

"Gotta love the décor at the Flamingo, huh?" Sam smirked while eyeing the chair backing.

"Come on Sam. It's Bugsy's Bar. What'd you expect? It's not going to ruin your sense of fashion." Wolfe and Daga acknowledged the joke between them with off-stage snickering.

"You're a funny guy. Hey, got some news. We lit a fire under your buddy Carlos. We should see something pretty soon. You two keep doing what you're doing.

"Anything I should look for specifically? More office traffic or him not at work?" Daga already wanted to get Carlos Juega, in her own way with her friend. The friend taped high on her thoracic vertebrae patiently waiting to sever an artery.

"Try to meet more of the other girls. Go out and have a few drinks. Be a good listener. See what they have to say after a few cold ones. Maybe they'll even think of you as a friend after awhile. Don't do anything to Carlos. He's going to lead us to the King Rat."

"I'm not going to do anything to him. Yet."

"That's what I thought. You're still itching from Aruba."

"Every itch needs a scratch."

"Just hold off awhile, Daga. Wolfe, when you're not playing at the WSOP head over to the Chocho and keep an eye on things as well."

Maria Villarena Lopez, professional name *Jaguar*, put her niña to bed in a small one bed apartment off of Craig road in North Las Vegas. She didn't have nor could afford a babysitter. She had made arrangements with the neighbor in the adjoining flat to just check on her from time to time. Hoping of course that the neighbor about whom she knew very little wouldn't sell her child while she went to work. Crack cocaine had that effect on people.

Everyday about this time she wondered how she ever got here. Her intentions and hopes had been grander. She would come to the USA, get an education, meet a nice man to share church and family. She met a hombre in Nuevo Laredo who said he would help her get across. She worked sixty hour weeks at eleven pesos an hour until she had saved up the money. The one thousand dollars constituted three years of deprivation. She walked fifteen hundred meters through flowing knee deep sewage hoping that in the dark pipe lit by only the coyote's lone flashlight she wouldn't fall in the river of filth. She heard voices, saw moonlight, and rejoiced in her arrival. Strong arms hoisted her up to ground level. The greeting party wore the uniform of the Federales. Had she gotten turned around?

She found herself in the company of *Zetas* posing as *policia*. The gang rape lasted for uncounted hours. Her last memory a final degradation as they hacked off her hair and left her for dead in the desert. The sun had awakened her and she stumbled blindly north. Somehow she hooked up with other *illegales* who gave her spare water and guided her to the small Catholic mission in the outskirts of Laredo that served as the modern version of the Underground Railroad.

She arrived in Vegas months later with her newborn child. Blessed with green eyes and small up tilted breasts despite her rough beginnings, she went from breakfast server, to cocktail server at the Chocho, to now a dancer. The last step requiring time spent with Carlos.

She didn't care. Ever since the rape she hated men. They were now only a means to an end. She had an otherwise worthless boyfriend who she tolerated for the purpose of protection in North Vegas. She caught the double deuce bus and nodded off thinking of the American dream.

CHOCHO ROSADO

Cheyenne Chandrika rolled into the parking lot just as Maria got off the bus.

"Hey, Maria what's up?"

Maria's spirits lifted somewhat. "Oh, hey Chey. Ready for work?"

"Only if you leave some of those mexicanos barrachos for me."

"I can't help it. They don't like Native Americans. Something about Geronimo and Cochise. Whites weren't the only victims of night raids."

"How you know all that?"

"Catholic monks and sisters don't only feed you but they demand you learn as well. It's where I got some of my English."

Daga and Wolfe swung their compact rental onto the Chocho's asphalt. Daga hurried towards the pair while Wolfe took his time.

"Hey girls! I'm Daga." She extended her hand. No hands were extended in return. " I'm obviously new here. I thought you two could show me some of the ropes."

"Which ones? How to make a living while you sell your soul or the ropes in Carlos' office?" An awkward silence for a few seconds broke easily as Wolfe walked up to the group. Cheyenne extended a fist bump. Maria quickly followed.

"I'm Cheyenne Chandrika. That's my real name. Means Cheyenne moonlight. I'm Cherokee though. Eastern tribe. Part of the Wolf clan."

"I'm Maria Lopez. Jaguar on stage." The green eyes flashed friendly, a thawing from moments ago.

"Well, she's Daga as you know. I'm Wolfe" More fist bumps all around.

"Wolf, huh. Got any Indian in you?" Chey's eyes danced even in their darkness.

"Is that a trick question?" The group broke into laughter.

"Heh, that's my man. You know." Daga rejoined in mock offense.

"You ladies get inside. I'll see you later. I'll be at the bar."

"Imagine that." Daga winked and hurried inside with the others. Wolfe waited and then opened the door a few minutes later.

Bobo stood just inside the door behind a make shift table and podium. "Twenty-five dollars cover."

Wolfe smiled. He didn't attempt to reach for his money neatly rolled in his front pocket. "I'm with Daga." More smiles followed.

"I don't know no Daga."

"Yeh. She's the new girl. I'm her independent security. You won't get a peep out of me unless you need help."

"I don't need help and we don't tolerate jealous boyfriends."

"Wouldn't expect you to. We've done this before. Trust me. Check it out with Carlos."

The name drop had its intended effect. "Go ahead in and I'll follow it up with the boss. Any bullshit and you're gone."

"Don't worry about me. I'm like a de-clawed cat." Wolfe headed to the bar while Bobo tried to figure out the simile. Not the word but the meaning.

The girls finished dressing or undressing depending on one's point of view. "Let's go screw some customers." Maria pumped her fist as she shouted her war cry.

"I'm here to dance. That's it." Daga hesitated at the door.

"No. No. She doesn't mean screw them as in sex. She means take their money and drink their booze. The old stripper saying is 'men come to a club to get fucked and all they get is screwed.' Get it?" Chey and Maria stared at Daga in disbelief.

"Hey. I said I was new. OK?"

"OK. Let's get'em." Maria hit the door first.

"Knob Creek on the rocks." Wolfe ordered from the burly Mexican behind the bar. Gang tats and lack of personality apparently were prerequisites for male hires at the Chocho. The drink landed unceremoniously not quite in front of Wolfe. He decided he might as well get things out of the way. "Is that drink for me?"

"You ordered it hombre."

"I don't know. I ordered a drink like it. But I'm sitting here and the drink is in front of the next seat. I thought you might have another customer."

"You some sorta smart ass, hombre?"

"No. Just a concerned customer."

"Twelve dollars." His name tag displayed 'Gordo'. Perfect, thought Wolfe.

"I haven't been served yet." Wolfe stared back.

Gordo moved the glass halfway between the two seats. Wolfe accepted the compromise.

"I'm Wolfe. Friend of Daga's."

"If that's the name of a dancer I don't know her. They come and go all of the time.

That's her real name?" Gordo seemed to be thawing if only a little.

"Kinda."

Almost on cue Daga slid in next to Wolfe. "Hi, baby. I'm on stage next. You ready?"

"I'm always ready. The question is are they ready?" Wolfe swept his hand around the bar and pointed at a table of losers. "You really think they are going to tip?"

"I just hope they don't have a heart attack first."

Daga climbed on stage and did the ubiquitous wrapping of the leg around the brass pole move. Must be in some training video, thought Wolfe.

She wore a loose fitting tunic similar to those of ancient Greek maidens although not historically accurate. Daga's consisted of Sea Island cotton trimmed with a real 18 carat gold leaf Greek key border and barely of the length necessary to protect her from charges of indecent exposure had she been in public. Of course, that was the idea.

She strutted her stuff for the first song, making pass after pass around the stage and pole. She did nothing too special except approach the front of the stage and demurely accept bills of all denominations in her matching garters.

The second song began and Daga stepped out of the tunic while using the pole for support. She wore a black leather thong with a pussycat outline sequined upon the garment where the most eyes would presumably focus. Starting at her right shoulder black leather strips three inches in width wrapped her body in an embrace of suggested sadism stopping at her waist. The money flowed onto the stage faster than Daga could pick it up.

When the third song began Daga attacked the pole as if it had done her wrong. While she twisted and writhed on the brass, articles of her costume came off slowly and individually. When the song ended, Daga stood with one leg stretched the length of the pole and her shaved chocho caressing the metal. The noise in the room seemed stadium-like. Benjamins littered the stage.

Customers stopped in mid-stride at the entrance. Bobo gave a standing ovation. Ludmilya Laparova stood seething at the service bar. She hadn't had a customer since Daga had begun her performance. Daga collected the money using her costume as a sack and left the stage.

"That's some girl you got there." Even Gordo's jaded eyes showed appreciation.

"What you saw there is how she meets me when I come back from out of town."

"I'd go out of town a lot." Gordo laughed at his own joke. Wolfe joined with him. Never know when you might need one fewer enemy.

Daga came over after dressing and hugged Wolfe. "How'd I do?"

"Great, baby. You..."

"Oh my God! Oh my God. Can you teach me that?" Chey hugged Daga like a long last friend.

Maria showed up as well. "You screwed'em good, baby." High fives all around ensued.

"Hey, when we close up let's go for drinks."

"Cool." From Wolfe's perspective it looked like Daga had some new BFF's.

"What do you mean 'cool, Wolfe? It's just the girls tonight." Daga stared at Wolfe.

"That's cool, too. Maybe I'll go by the Venetian."

Carlos came out of his office and spoke to Bobo. A small nod of acknowledgement in the direction of Daga served as his sign that any probationary period for her no longer existed.

Crlos drove to the new location for the money. West of the strip a few miles, Summerlin served as the upper middle class suburb of Sin City. It had been severely hit by foreclosures. Waiters, bartenders and dealers caught speculating in the real estate boom when it went bust left whole blocks of cookie cutter homes abandoned. One enterprising soul had been renting properties which he did not own. Squatters routinely moved from one property to the next rent free. One house seemed like the others but with key differences.

Carlos pulled off the road into the driveway. Decorative bars but bars none the less protected all glass openings from use as points of entry. He turned off the laser sensors with a key pad hidden in the plastic cactus to his right. With a glance over his shoulder, he entered. A little old man walked by with his dog. Carlos hesitated. He looked at his watch. The luminescent dial read 0400h. Pretty early for dog walking but those seniors don't sleep much. He closed the door.

VOODOO LOUNGE, TOP OF THE RIO

"How'd you do tonight?"

"Are you kidding? She hasn't had a chance to count it yet."

"I don't know. Pretty good. The drinks are on me." Easy way to make friends in Vegas, Daga thought. Buy a few rounds. Hell, easy way to make friends anywhere.

The drinks came. The usual stripper menu; Jaeger bombs, anejo tequila, purple hooters, and pink panty pull downs. "How long you guys been doing this?"

"Ever since I could. No education. Got a body. Might as well use it. No one says anything to boxers or football players when they sell their brains and spinal cords for money. What's the difference? My pussy ain't as important as my brain!" Chey raised her glass.

"Maybe it is. With your brain." Maria raised her glass.

"Smart ass."

"Does Carlos hit on you?"

"More than hit. You don't give it up you're stuck cocktailing. It's cocks one way or another." All three laughed at Maria's cynicism.

"How 'bout you Daga? How'd you and Wolfe get here? You two seem like you been together awhile. Not the usual recipe for a dancer."

"See. She does have a brain."

"We met in the islands. We match. I'm not easy and neither is he. The easy smile is only an easy smile. I understand."

"What about stripping? He doesn't care?"

"In the Caribbean, there are nude and topless beaches. He looks at it like at least I get paid for what I've been doing since adolescence for free."

"Seems like a good man."

"A good man. Not perfect. He plays poker and I dance. A normal family unit in Vegas."

"More normal than most." Chimed in Maria.

"Hey, would you two do me a favor?"

"Like what?" Signs of wariness crossed both girls' faces.

"If you see anything strange or hear anything strange especially when you're in the office, let me know."

"Why?"

"Maybe I can get Carlos to back off."

"Fair enough."

"Where'd Wolfe go?" Chey smiled innocently at Daga.

"He's over at the Venetian playing cash poker. Why? You like my Wolfie."

"Yeh, I do. I can tell he's good for you. Besides, us wolves have to stick together."

"Well, you can stick together but not too close together. I don't want to have to pry the two of you apart."

"Well, if you have to throw a bucket of hot water on us, go ahead."

"There won't be any warning."

"I'll try to remember that."

VII

VENETIAN POKER ROOM

Entering The Venetian beneath the massive vaulted
ceiling painted with copies of Italian masters, Wolfe could only
guess the rack rate for this modern faux version of the most
romantic city of the world. Francophiles be damned, in his
opinion Paris took a distant second.

The Venetian poker room consisted of approximately
eighty tables. If one were a day in day out grinder or tourist for
a two day stopover, this room provided the greatest variety and
most action anywhere in Vegas. Sure, the big game at The Bellagio with famous players and hangers on still had the largest
pots but it had become nearly a cartoon of itself. Wolfe gave
his name and immediately a chip runner escorted him to a 5-10
no limit Texas Hold'em game. His stake disappeared with the
employee and five minutes later five hundred in red and green
appeared in front of him.

He took a quick glance around the table. No one had an
alcoholic drink, light banter did not fill the air, and the player
in seat eight already had questioned the dealer if indeed Wolfe
could be dealt a hand. So much for friendly poker which Wolfe
knew as a very uncommon occurrence and more likely an oxymoron. The button occupied seat seven. Wolfe had seat six.
The cards and the destiny attached to them flew through the
air.

The player at seat ten tossed her cards in disgust. The
remainder of the table folded around to Wolfe. He called the

big blind. Seats seven and eight did as well. Nine checked his option.

The flop came 4-4-8. Action went to seat eight. They checked around to Wolfe. He had stayed with 8-6 unsuited in an attempt to get a feel for the players. Wolfe threw in a small value bet to see where he stood. The button, a young Asian male from LA, re-raised. The small blind called as well as Wolfe.

Fourth street hit the felt. Another eight showed which made a rainbow board eliminating a flush draw. Wolfe slow played his full house to get a read on the kid to his left and the calling station in seat eight. Wolfe checked. The kid took the bait and bet two hundred. Mr. Friendly in seat eight re-raised to four hundred. Wolfe scratched his head.

He didn't quite have the nuts. One of his opponents could have four fours. Luckily, Wolfe had an easy choice. The pot odds were in his favor. Most likely he would chop the pot with one of the others. Besides, all in takes the pressure off. The other two called.

The river came a six. Wolfe's six had nullified the fours on board. Now only four fours could beat him. Otherwise, the pot was his alone. Seats seven and eight checked it down.

The Asian flopped his hand. "Eights full of fours." Seat eight mucked his cards which probably meant fours full of eights.

Wolfe quietly turned his cards face up. "Eights full of sixes." Over seventeen hundred in mostly red and green chips came his way.

"Not bad for your first hand." The attempt at pleasantness came from the pretty middle-aged Asian female in seat ten. It didn't last long. Seat eight jumped right in the conversation.

"Bullshit luck. He had 8-6 unsuited "

"You let me have 8-6 unsuited." Wolfe responded in a low even voice followed by a weak smile. "Besides, both of you had weak aces, yours with a four and his with an eight. I saw his and what else could you have had? We're not going to rehash every hand are we?"

After the first hand, the remainder of the time Wolfe played bordered on monotony. Two hours later he excused himself from the table with a little more than the original seventeen hundred dollar pot. He walked over to the bank of coffee urns and poured himself a cup of very fresh java. When he turned away from the banquet table, the young Asian male greeted him.

"Hey dude. I never got your name."

"I know. I never got yours." Wolfe smiled.

"Oh, sorry. Tommy. Tommy Cho."

"Hi. Everyone calls me Wolfe. Just Wolfe." They shook hands warmly.

"Oh, I get it. One name. Like Bono or Cher."

"Kinda. Hey, you play a pretty good game. Where'd you pick it up online or at the Commerce in LA?"

"LA. How'd you know?"

"Dude sort of helps. Plus young and Asian. Very aggressive. Willing to lose large pots in order to win even larger ones. Poker is one of the few venues where it is still politically correct to profile people. What can I do for you?"

"Looking for some more action. That table died."

"You took all of their money."

"I didn't get yours."

"Imagine that. So what? You're grinding your way around town?"

"Yeh, my mom thinks I'm in med school. I don't have the heart to tell her. You know, the Asian parent thing."

"You guys always make it sound like such a burden. You know how many people wished they had parents like yours?'

"I know. I know. Anyhow, where to now?"

"I'm going home. I'm tired. You're not. Hit The Bellagio and the MGM. Don't stay too long and wear out your welcome."

"Cool. See ya back in here."

"Hey, wait a minute. Do me a favor?"

"Sure. You change your mind? Need a ride?"

"No. Just next time you see me let me know if when you're playing you're running into a lot of Latinos with gang tats and playing real loose. You know, a lot more than usual."

"How come you want to know?"

"That's not important is it?"

"Nope dude. You're cool, later Wolfe."

"Hasta."

NORTH VEGAS

Ludmilya Laparova sat up and rubbed her nose of the sting left from the coke. The shit kept getting more and more expensive. Fucking Amerikanskis kept screwing with the supply chain. What she got for time in Carlos' office didn't keep her going half a week. Now this newbie girl is taking some of her action. That will stop. She cut out a couple more lines and snorted. If this shit kept up, she'd have to go to meth and those asshole motorcycle guys.

Not far away, Carlos had other plans. Somebody had dropped a dime. A perfect anachronism, it had become a strange term since pay phones were becoming extinct and those that existed cost at least a quarter. Like a cop, he considered method, opportunity, and motive; MOM. He knew she associated with Russian gangs out of LA. Her drug habit controlled every aspect of her life. She could have followed him at sometime. In the whirlwind that becomes the mind of a person who fears for his life daily, the paranoia produces what seems a logical outcome as to who one's persecutor might be. Carlos picked up his phone and called some friends. Ludmilya was about to have a party and didn't even know it.

The knock came at her front door. Who the hell could that be? "Yeh, what you want?"

"Looking for Laparova?"

"Who's looking for Laparova?"

The verbal response to the second question never came. The door exploded inward. Two members of *La Dirección* rushed her. The third shut the door best he could and guarded it.

The other two slapped Laparova into submission, gagged her, and tied her to a kitchen chair. A handful of her hair lie on the living room floor in testimony to the fact she hadn't quit easily. The one guarding the door changed places with one of the muscle thugs and began the interrogation. Ludmilya knew she had little chance of seeing anymore days on earth. Her drug-addled brain raced to find solutions.

"Do you know who we are?"

"I don't care. You're going to kill me. Put me out of my misery. It's OK with me."

"It won't be that easy. We enjoy our work. We need information. Perhaps you can persuade us not to gang rape you, beat you until LVPD CSI can't identify you, and then kill you. What about that?"

Laparova's gambit had failed. Skilled interrogators look for body language like exaggerated breaths or looking down with a hang dog slouch. She resembled an illustrated version of the detainee handbook. The words came barely audible through tears. "I don't know anything."

"Wished I had a peso for every time I heard that one. Try again." The punch came quickly. The teeth cracked on impact, blood spurted to the floor, and the chair toppled. The assistant stuffed the gag again in her mouth while she cried in pain.

Like everyone being interrogated, the game consists of what can one tell them that will stop the pain and allow one to survive. This is why the most seasoned captives, ones trained in SERE, Survive, Evade, Resist, Escape, eventually talk. However, in many cases the objects of torture have nothing to tell so they weave a story. Anything to stop the agony is the goal.

"What do you want to know?"

"Who did you tell about Carlos' money drop?"

"I don't know about any money drop. He gave me coke for sex. That is what I know."

He lunged to strike her and then stopped. Laparova cow-ered like a child confronted by physically abusive parents. It, of course, had been a situation common in her childhood.

"You still hang around with the Little Odessa Russian gang out of New York?"

She considered her options."Sure. Sure. I used to work for them on my back."

"Did you tell them about the money?"

"I told them about the nightly cash at the club."

"Did you tell them about which nights were the largest drop?"

"Sure. Just talking in between blow jobs. I'd say how much I saw on his desk."

"So they could have followed him when he left the club?"

"I guess. I never checked. I never planned anything."

"Of course, you didn't." The leader replaced the gag and motioned with his hand to the other two as if offering a gift to a trusted employee.

The thugs bent the beaten Laparova over the couch, tying her hands to the front legs of the sofa and her ankles to the back. A knife flashed and the remnants of her clothing fell around her feet. The fact that the thugs lived without women in their lives and were in their twenties made repetition more often a given. In the midst of the fourth go 'round, the leader injected Laparova with a massive dose of cocaine in the carotid artery. Even he had his limits.

Leaving her as she died, the three exited the apartment and headed to the nearest dumpster to drop their black jump suits, gloves, and shoes. Sending a message meant making sure oth-ers heard about Laparova and thought twice about doing the same. With a crime scene so terrible, the media would provide the intended result. Eyes in the night acknowledged all of this.

Two *Halcones* had been in constant touch by radio trans-mission with Carlos and Zarilla. Watching the watchers, two members of the DEA joint task force had been in contact with their superiors. NSA satellites had picked up the entire set of conversations from parabolic microphones while a drone out of Nellis AFB recorded infrared photos. Sauria's op benefitted as the nexus of all this information.

BILL'S BAR –HARRAH'S

Sam seemed very happy even for Happy Hour. Wolfe and Daga bopped in off the strip. Wolfe's step seemed a little lighter after a good day at the Venetian poker room.

"What's with the Chiclet smile?" Daga got to Sam first.

"Had some new developments. We definitely kicked the sleeping dog."

"Got him up and moving?" Wolfe ordered a goose and soda even as he asked the question.

"Not yet but soon. Plus, I got rid of your problem. Two birds with one stone." Sam glanced at Daga.

"My problem!? I don't have a problem." Daga ordered Captain and soda.

"Not anymore. Remember Laparova?"

"The Russian slut hard ass?"

"Yeh. She didn't take too well to your show the last night she worked."

"How do you know?"

"A little birdie told......."

"Cut the crap Sam. You got somebody in the club besides me?"

"Yeh. Trying to protect you."

"And you don't tell me about it?"

"It's best you don't know. Eventually I'll tell you."

"I thought we were friends?'

"We are. That's why I didn't tell you."

"Are you two done? Have a drink."

"Sure thing Venetian boy." Sam smiled broadly like when one catches someone in an obvious error.

"How do you know I've been at the Venetian?"

"You both smell like burnt orange. It's the Venetian fragrance of choice. The locals call it the *Venetian smell*. It's in the soap, the lotion, and in the air. If you sit at a table for a short while you'll have the scent. Don't ever lie to Daga about where you have been if you've been at the Venetian. It's more of a giveaway than lipstick on your collar or Obsession perfume."

"We don't have that problem."

"Back to the Russian." Daga sipped her Morgan. New Orleans seemed a little further away in her mind.

"Oh, yeh. She quit."

"She's not working there anymore?"

"No. She quit breathing."

"You didn't..." Wolfe and Daga had gotten a glimpse of Sam's alter ego in Aruba, Wolfe more than Daga.

"Collateral damage. I needed someone to be guilty. She took Daga as a threat. I needed to misdirect the blame for Zarilla's, our target, bad luck. She filled the prerequisites. "

"Remind me not to forget your birthday." The Morgan went down smoothly.

"You already have."

"What's next?" Wolfe peered over his drink.

"Well, I'm hoping this latest episode has them thinking that they have nipped the problem in the bud. Once they relax, we'll kick 'em again." Sam looked up at Bob, the bartender and restaurant workers union rep. A real joker, the humor hid the fact he had once worn the Ranger tab. "Hey, can an old man get another drink?"

"Same as before? Strawberry daiquiri with whipped cream? Hey, Wolfe. You and Daga run with some real bad hombres."

Wolfe joined in the attack on Sam. "Yeh, I don't know what's worse, his drinking habits or his dressing habits."

Bob didn't let up. "Where'd you get the shirt? Sidewalk sale? Does it come with batteries?"

Sam's shirt displayed raging orange flames leaping from along the hem to waist level. The ubiquitous Viva Las Vegas lie embroidered across the left pocket. It literally screamed TOURIST! This, of course, fulfilled exactly the role that Sam wished. Sauria studiously sipped his frou-frou drink before answering with his own parry. "Jealousy comes in many forms. The ladies love it."

Wolfe didn't wait. "Sam, those weren't ladies. Those were trainies. Transsexuals and transvestites. You better be careful or you might find something in their stocking." The bar erupted in drunken guffaws.

"You never said anything. Why not?" Sam acted in mock dismay.

"I wanted to see if even trainies turned you down." The bar patrons repeated their exaggerated response.

As the drinks flowed and the laughter resonated, Sam cemented the idea in the minds of all that he was no more than another hapless visitor coming to Sin City to try to grasp some of the life that he had missed. He played the perfect foil to Wolfe's sharp barbs and created the cover persona that had served him well so many times.

VIII

WSOP

Wolfe walked down the long hallway in the Rio that led to the WSOP. From the buffet to the first poker room, it measured nearly a half mile, a half mile in beautiful inlaid tiles. As he passed the throngs of tourists, players on break or recently eliminated, and well known professionals stopped and signing autographs, he again saw small groups of gangstas, covered in tats, exchanging conversations and wads of bills as if they were all on a single bank roll. He decided at that moment to upset the apple cart.

With his familiar buy-in receipt in hand, seat and table number clearly marked and verified with the WSOP logo, Wolfe meandered over to table 222, seat 3. The dealer matched his photo ID to the name printed on the receipt and pushed three thousand in tournament chips toward him. Wolfe began the charade.

"Hey, wait a minute. I saw these guys out in the hallway talking. What are you guys buddies?" Wolfe pointed at the three Latinos covered in ink.

"Hey, man. What 'chu problem? 'Chu loco?" Seat seven hadn't looked to the others for advice or consent. Wolfe had the alpha dog.

"I want a floor man. Now! Come on dealer. I want to straighten this out before the cards fly." The worn out dealer, working long days during the WSOP, with a dire look followed by one of exasperation, signaled for a floor man. Since the tournament hadn't started, he arrived quickly.

"Who has a problem?"

"I do."

"Go ahead."

"These guys know each other. I thought seating had to be random." Wolfe used his best voice in the manner of someone wronged.

Seat seven jumped in the fray. "We paid for these like everyone else. No problem. The computer gave it to us.'

"See! See! He said 'we'!" Wolfe pointed at the alpha dog.

"Relax, sir. Would you care to go to a different table? I'll make a switch with someone. OK?

Wolfe had accomplished his goal. It was just a little something to get them wondering. "Sure. That's cool." Wolfe gathered his MP3 player and headed off with the floor man. Three pairs of eyes burned holes in his back.

CHOCHO ROSADO

Several hours later and one bad beat, Wolfe walked in the club and greeted Bobo. "Evening. Daga working?"

The Mexican brute waved his head towards the bar without a word. "Thanks. Saving your voice for American Idol?" Wolfe didn't wait for the response. As he walked towards the bar, there sat Sam chewing on Chey's ear.

"Funny to see you here. Where's Daga?'

"She's on stage next." Chey answered with a broad smile. She wore what could best be described as *stripper Indian outfit*. Rawhide top with loin cloth covering rawhide thong decorated with feathers, apparently played well to some of the customers' *pioneer-squaw* fantasies.

"Hey, Chey. How 'bout take the two of us into your teepee?" Sam started to get up from the bar stool.

"You mean where my campfire burns?" Chey could play with the best.

"Sam, that's kind of expensive. Private lap dances."

"It's OK. This one's on me."

When the threesome entered the private room, Chey set the music and started dancing. Sam started talking. "What do you know?"

"I think Carlos is off the hook. He seemed more relaxed, like he lost a load off his shoulders." Chey didn't miss a beat as she answered.

"Wait a minute. You work with Sam?" Wolfe couldn't believe it.

"Of course. This is a big operation." As she uttered those words, Chey dropped her top and sat on Wolfe's lap, her rounded breasts coming to within centimeters of his lips. Wolfe couldn't help but sneak a peek at her darkened areolae and erect nipples. "Don't worry. I'm working. Tell him, Sam. If I don't dance when I come in here someone will get suspicious. You're the beneficiary today. Usually it's Sam"

"Tough job. Somebody has to do it." Sam gave his best Cheshire smile.

"So you're keeping an eye on Daga?" Wolfe noticed a small birth mark high on her shoulder in the shape of a crescent moon. Cheyenne moonlight, of course.

"And now she'll be keeping an eye on me. Sam's about ready to stir up the herd."

"Is it just about the money and drugs, Sam?"

"No, Wolfe. It's more serious than people realize. There is one drug related kidnapping for ransom or murder on average every day in Phoenix. Phoenix, not Nuevo Laredo. I'm talking American citizens. The whole southwest is becoming the third world. Los Zetas are our local Taliban. This is as large a threat as any invasion or surprise attack in our history."

"I know. I know. You keep telling me. Seems that no one else cares."

"Yeh, not till their daughter goes missing from school or their son's body shows up nearly unrecognizable in the desert."

Before Wolfe could respond, Chey's long bronze legs wrapped around his waist in a hold as good as any Indian wrestler's, her breasts surrounding his cheeks, as her long, black braided hair fell along his back. "Time for a peace parlay."

"More like starting a war."

"I'm just working. Part of my cover."

"Or no cover."

LA COCA

High in the Andes near the Central and Northern ridge of these majestic mountains lies the mother lode of the drug trade. Lush green terraces of coffee plants soon give way to similar looking leaves of green. When compared to its cousin coffee, coca plants are much the same and if not for the deliberate process by which its purity is greatly increased would be likely just another form of breakfast drink.

Erythroxylon coca has been cultivated and used by the hardy inhabitants of Bolivia and Peru for centuries. Resistant to drought, disease, and needing no irrigation it thrives in this region for the same reasons cacti thrive in the desert. It can be harvested as many as six times a year. Coca, through the perfect logic and processes of evolution, has found its niche. Early on the indigenous peoples realized the stimulating effects of the plant and its ability to allow long treacherous treks through the mountains at altitude without the effects of fatigue. To this day, descendents of the Inca pursue their days with a wad of leaf in their jaws looking like out of place cowboy caricatures with chewing tobacco. Coca tea is for sale by street vendors. Again, the similarities between coca and coffee are hard to ignore. But here the human interaction with the two plants diverts greatly.

In the mid-nineteenth century, the medicinal effects of coca were discovered. It can be likened to how opium becomes much more dangerous as heroin. Through a process where leaves are crushed in a mixture of alcohol, gasoline, kerosene or really almost any solvent the alkaloids are released from the plant in solution.

Allowed to evaporate, what remains is crystalline. Dissolved a second time in hydrochloric acid, the same acid found in car batteries, the compound once dried is now sixty percent pure and no longer called coca but cocaine. Its new properties include local anesthesia, euphoria, and addiction. Prolonged, continued use brings first neurotic and then psychotic behavior. Sigmund Freud is one of the more famous sufferers of cocaine's properties.

A tumor in his jawbone demanding constant relief became the source of his addiction as he used cocaine at first as a local anesthetic. He then discovered its additional properties including those involving sexual activity. His body of written work can easily be divided into pre- and post usage including unusual treatments for sexual maladies and his descriptions of dreams. He was obsessed.

The deleterious effects of cocaine were recognized early in the twentieth century and its usage faded accompanied by the tightening of drug laws in the United States. Miami trade arrived in the eighties. The monster got out of its cave.

Smugglers once content to move bundles of marijuana realized how much easier and for far greater value one could move cocaine. This is the point at which Americans began shipping their wealth to South American narcos. With money comes power, with unlimited money comes unlimited power and generations of smugglers now look to the United States as the endless source of all money. This is how Zarilla does what he does.

SUMMERLIN STASH

Carlos pulled up to the house. It seemed much safer here. Summerlin suburbia made for a better neighborhood to hide millions of dollars in plain sight. He turned off the anti-theft devices, glanced as usual over his shoulder, and entered the dwelling. He went upstairs to the master bedroom walk-in closet. What his eyes saw his mind couldn't accept.

The money was gone. All of it except a single Benjamin with a note attached. 'Dearest Carlos, have a drink on us. Your friends.'

Carlos José Jueza sat down on the carpet and sobbed. His mother and sister would be horribly tortured no matter what happened to him. What could he do? A clear case of check, checkmate for Sam.

Up the side street a few hundred yards from Carlos, the two DEA agents talked over coffee.

"So, you think he's in by now?"

"Oh! Sure! He's trying to figure out his next move if he hasn't committed suicide yet."

"This guy running the joint task force op. He's pretty cold-hearted. Even if this Carlos slug comes over, you know his family is dead."

"Collateral damage. You heard the briefing. We're at war. These people sleeping in these houses just don't know it yet."

IX

LA FORTELEZA

José Jesús Dominguez took the news badly. Bobo and Gordo had delivered the message by phone. The conversation had been brief.

"We haven't seen him for two days. We figured he went on some kind of bender. Not even a phone call." Bobo wiped sweat from his brow even though two thousand miles separated the speakers. Please don't shoot the messenger approximated his mind set.

"Say no more. There are ears. The two of you will be rewarded. Run the business as usual. Someone will be in contact."

Zarilla hung up and picked up the secure line, the one that connected him by underground fiber optic cable to the head of *Dirección*.

"We've got a problem."

"Fifteen minutes."

"Make it ten."

Nine and a half minutes later Arturo Mateo Reyes, El Matador, El Jefe de Dirección and an efficient callous killer with or without help, walked into Zarilla's office. In his youth, he had killed for sport. Now he killed for money. Tattooed teardrops clumped below each eye like notches on a gun.

"We've got another problem in Vegas."

"I thought we took care of it."

"The manager is gone missing. Your muscle didn't have anything to do with it, did they?"

"No. Remember, you said to give him a pass."

"So we didn't grab him. He's either running from us or the DEA has him. If he's running from us, most likely he has something that is not his. Either way, go down to Cabo and visit his sister and mother. See what they know. Dump the bodies publicly in case he had help from the inside. Afterwards, I want you to personally head to Vegas. Everything you have needs to be brought online. I need eyes, ears, and enforcers. Check on the lavadero. I'm pretty sure it's not working. If that's the case, reload it and give those two pendejos a raise. Let the fat one have Carlos' job. Questions?" Even José used the code word 'lavadero', laundry in English, to signify the illegal money operation at the strip club. Criminals notoriously used transparent code words for their activities to the great delight of government investigators.

"I may choose my own methods?"

"As always."

POOL BAR-HARRAH'S

"Hey Tony! How about a beer for the troops?" Wolfe waved his hand toward the other three. Daga had been told about the addition of Cheyenne as part of their crew. Telling her had been planned anyway but when the boys came out of the private room at the club Daga had fired questions at Wolfe faster than he could consider answers. Sam had finally convinced her to be patient and all would become clear. She still wanted information.

"So what exactly is Chey's role?" Daga sipped her Amstel. No rum today.

"You've got each other's backs. You can warn one another at work if one of you sees something. I believe it's going to heat up quite a bit at the club following our latest little op. These guys are ruthless. They tend toward eliminating everyone if they suspect anyone. We've got you two together because you can keep an eye on things that Wolfe and I cannot. You guys have the run of the place."

"Well, the next time you need to pass information at the club, you and Wolfe can spring for a twofer in the champagne room with me." Daga stared at Wolfe who helplessly raised his arms in surrender. Cheyenne stared out at the pool.

"Fine, let's get down to business. It won't take them very long to at least become suspicious that first Chey and then Daga show up and nearly simultaneously their luck goes bad not once but twice. Try to keep your relationship at Chocho as it has been. Keep treating the other dancers like usual. No changes. Oh, and yeh, don't let Maria get too close. It's not safe for her or you. Remember, she's got kids."

"We've got it handled." Cheyenne finally sounded interested.

A bar back stocking paper products and beer had the practiced look of listening without looking like one eavesdropping. A newly recruited set of eyes and ears for the Zetas, he'd had no choice. In to a loan shark for ten large at ten points a week, a little harmless intel might get him out from under some of the nut. Of course, anytime someone compensates one for information, the outcome often isn't painless to the target.

A favorite tactic of money launderers, loan sharking distributed the cash from a central location and allowed the conspirators to get their claws into people who might normally not be disposed to be part of a criminal organization if only on the periphery.

After work, he went to an email address, and wrote a draft. He did not send it. Later, a member of the *Dirección* would read and then delete it, not sending it, and thereby avoiding the NSA Echelon intercept program and all of its siblings. All the two communicants needed were shared passwords.

The NSA utilized multiple super computers built by Cray which handled quadrillion operations per second. Its storage facility could hold two hundred petabytes which equaled all the printed material in the world. This allowed them to operate the TIDE operation, *Terrorists Identities Data list Environment,* from which the familiar notify list is derived. If someone on the list sent an email or spoke on a phone, it set off bells outside of Washington, DC.

Fortunately, for the good guys, FBI interrogators had become aware of the *draft* tactic used to hide communications and shared it with all agencies. Using *call chaining analysis* and *communities of interest* all agencies could backtrack and see who contacted whom. Leaving messages on the person's to be contacted draft file no longer qualified as secure. Sam knew about the breach in Zarilla's operational security within an hour.

The call came in to Sam via his STU-III secure phone provided by the NSA's Secure Compartmented Information Facility, SCIF, located not far from the South Carolina-North Carolina border. Los Zetas had some of the same equipment.

DIRECCION MEETING-VEGAS

In a non-descript clapboard house near the intersection of MLK Boulevard and Carey Avenue, where Latinos with gang tats drew little attention, El Matador spoke to begin the strategy meeting. The smallish living room served as a 'get to know' for one of the *Los Leopardos* and as a safe house when needed. Today, it served its alternative need. The occupant didn't mind. In exchange for a little inconvenience and service, the rent found its way to the landlord.

"We are under attack. We suspect by the gringo government. You see the photograph of one of our members being passed among you. If you see him and you are armed, you are to kill on sight. It's a go green light. If you are not armed, you are to leave a message at the number found on the photograph. The message will be current location and time and updated every fifteen minutes. Do not attempt to follow. He'll spook."

The full complement of Los Zetas powers were in attendance. Halcones, Ventanas, Leopardos, Mañosos, and Dirección, listened to additional instructions.

"Each of you will be given specific duties. All of you need to be suspicious. New faces, flashy money, too many questions at a bar, you get the idea. We believe the nucleus of this assault is at our club Chocho. We believe we know who they might be. Except for Los Leopardos, do not make one's self seen at that location. If it turns out to be solely a grab for money by one of our brothers, his family will suffer indescribable deaths. If he is found with our money, it will be worse.

However, if the Norteamericanos are involved, we will respond in our usual manner. We need to find and destroy our targets. At the very least they are attempting to interdict our Carretera de Diablo, between Altar and Tuscon. They will be stopped. Questions?"

Stone cold faces stared back at the speaker. The basic equation amounted to succeed or die. The group filed out of the house and into their cars. El Matador walked to the back bedroom to collect the occupant's share of the rent. She never paid the balance in currency.

As the members fanned out over the valley, sophisticated eavesdropping equipment zeroed in on Sam and his crew. The entire exercise reminded one of snipers peering at one another and then letting loose equally deadly shots. Sam knew about them. They now suspected him. What the opposing sides did not calculate amounted to the most significant reason for their being at this place and time, the survival of the United States of America as it now existed. Game on.

DEA OFFICES-FEDERAL COURT HOUSE

Carlos couldn't stop sweating. He had been given the star treatment since walking through the door and asking to speak to an agent in charge but even that hadn't ceased his anxiety. He knew these men had nothing but disdain for him and could turn on him in a minute.

The tactic might be something as simple as dropping him in front of Caesar's in a marked DEA vehicle which could mean his death sentence within hours, no sleep lost by either side. Once he had started to talk, information flowed endlessly from this scared little man.

Sam had been there for most of the second half of the interrogation arriving as he usually did by taxi. A taxi owned by the LVPD motor pool and driven by Sam served perfectly as cover. Entering at the below level parking garage any sight intel would be impossible. Just another pickup at the Federal building as far as any spectators, criminal or otherwise, could ascertain.

"So what do you want from us?" The DEA agent leaned in closely to the face of Carlos.

"I want my life."

"We can't guarantee that. You haven't told us anything we didn't already know," which qualified as a lie using the common dictionary as a source. Many interrogation techniques resembled negotiations of everyday life. De-value the opponent's position, cry inability to change the situation, inflate one's own position, and finally throw in the towel and make one last offer to close the deal. Most law enforcement interrogators would make great car salespeople.

"I don't know names. I am very low in the organization. We are compartmentalized so if one fails no one failure can destroy the organization."

"You disgust me. According to you, you've already traded the lives of your mother and sister and you still protect these people?"

Glancing at a two man DEA security detail standing at parade rest along the wall although no longer in the military, the agent waved his hand, "Take him back to his safe house. Don't let him out of your sight."

The two men slipped a blue jacket with DEA on the back in gold letters on Carlos's shoulders along with a baseball cap for his head and led him from the room. If seen leaving or entering a building, however unlikely, he would be recognized as another agent by others.

"What do you think Sauria?"

"I think he gave you what he knew which, wasn't much. The purpose of that scum is to attract Zarilla. His number two arrived in town yesterday and now has my crew under electronic surveillance. They have all hands on deck. We need to reply in kind.

Notify the LVPD and get the cops to harass the hookers that are working for Zarilla. Bust'em and squeeze 'em for information. At the very least, keep 'em off the streets where they can't see or hear anything. Go bust that little weasel bar back. Dream up something, a misdemeanor drug or weapons charge. Keep him out of circulation. I'll pick at Zarilla's open sore and see what happens."

Sam jumped in the taxi and headed out of the garage. From positions exactly calculated in the classic V-shaped ambush tactic, hundreds of rounds struck Sam's vehicle as he left the garage. With the shooters positioned at the base of the legs of the triangle and Sam as the target at the apex, no escape route forward indicated survival. On the floor and wounded from the initial fusillade, Sam drove back the way he came pressing the accelerator with his one hand while trying to steer with the other. One of the accepted methods of egress in an ambush, his car slammed into the cement column at the entrance to the garage. The hood popped but no movement stirred in the car. What remained of Sam cowered on the floor behind the engine block.

Smoke and the smell of cordite filled the canyons as pedestrians scattered with their M&M shopping bags and giant frozen drinks slung from their necks. Baby walkers rolled down the suddenly empty streets as mothers grabbed infants and dove for cover in fountains. Some took safety behind mobile billboards advertising escorts. Abandoned by their drivers, doors still flung open, the flatbed trucks caused even more chaos. Other vehicles, now stuck hopelessly in traffic, stalled or rolled onto sidewalks driverless.

After what seemed forever, US marshals poured into the street from the federal building. A few ran to the taxi nearly unrecognizable in its destruction while others began searching every square inch of the urban canyon. The ambush nests were quickly found. M4's and empty shells littered the ground. The weapons or the ammunition would never be traced back to anyone. Manufactured in the US, purchased legally with fake identification and social security numbers, then smuggled into Mexico, the weapons were another part of the underground economy related to the drug trade. The funny part of gun sales in the US, if the ID and social security matched and came back clean, the dealer had a legal sale. True gun control didn't exist. Like illegal pharmaceutical drugs, illegal gun sales were the unwritten dark side of the manufacturer's bottom line.

So much for the chamber of commerce's big pitch for the soon to open City Center, even Mayor Goodman would be challenged to explain this one. Los Zetas never played by the usual rules.

X

VENETIAN

Wolfe rode the escalator down to casino level and headed to the poker room. Daga and Cheyenne caught him before he got to the tables. Their faces told the bad news before they could open their mouths.

"What happened?" Wolfe blurted.

"They got to Sam. He's alive but wounded. We don't know how badly. We got a note under our door. Here." Daga thrust the paper in Wolfe's hand.

Wolfe glanced at the note. "Not much to go on. It's his handwriting or a helluva forgery. I mean 'been shot, in hospital, OK, will contact' doesn't do much. Any idea where he is?"

"There are seven hospitals in the valley. I started with the ones closest to the strip and worked my way around. University Medical Center seemed the most likely. No one admitted under that name at any of them."

"That's not surprising. Hell, we don't even know if Sam is his real name. Were they after Sam or all of us? We won't know until he gets through to us. We need to stick together so the two of you go to work and I'll show up for entertainment.

Cheyenne, I know Daga carries some protection. What about you?"

Cheyenne hiked her little black dress up to show a holster on the inside of her thigh, her long, lean thigh. She packed a Beretta 92L. The shortened barrel helped in concealment. Daga thought she kept the dress up for more than the necessary time to show Wolfe, unless she showed him something besides the gun.

"You can't wear that when you are dancing?"

"Well, I guess that's when I'll need Daga."

Daga stood silent. "Then we're all set?" Wolfe looked at both women.

"Sure." Cheyenne turned on her heels with Wolfe and Daga following.

Wolfe spoke to Daga as they trailed behind Chey's strides. "You got a problem with her?"

"Yeh. She likes you a little too much."

"Relax. Nothing will happen without you. If she hangs around long enough, she'll see we are hopelessly one. We're trying not to die. This stuff can wait. Sam may be out of commission. We need all three of us."

"I understand. I think I need some Mexicanos meurtos to satisfy mi cuchillo."

"I don't think you'll have to wait long."

As the conversation continued along the strip, Sam emerged from the sick bay at Nellis AFB. His survival anomalous to the scene outside the courthouse, his only wounds amounting to glass shards imbedded in forearms and legs, he looked no worse than a gawking tourist in a collision with a bicyclist. If having nine lives is not a myth, Sam now had one fewer.

CHOCHO ROSADO

The club rocked the night. Either the absence of Carlos or the presence of Gordo as El Jefe might explain it but, the money ran deep and green. Jaguar wore a good copy of Halle Berry's cat woman's suit at least for the first song. Cheyenne went on stage with a full length buffalo robe and when it no longer served its purpose a single tail feather at the base of her spine provided plenty of entertainment.

Wolfe sat at the bar jawing with the new bartender; Bobo. One could replace oversized doormen in Vegas as easily as needy girlfriends from the Midwest. Often castoff by their boyfriends once the men realize the size of the pool of beautiful woman available, bringing a girl to Vegas is like bringing sand to the beach.

Bobo's new position became his raise although he needed some training. Wolfe liked to say 'monkeys can make drinks but they can't be bartenders.' To the uninitiated, bartending looked like a cakewalk. Bar owners, many of whom had never tended bar, notoriously promoted people who couldn't count, came to work late, called off sick, gave away drinks, and had the personality of a rock. The owners saved themselves with airhead girls with 'D' cups who raked glassware through ice bins. Everything has tradeoffs.

Wolfe sipped his Soco as a familiar voice whispered in his ear. "They won't get us."

Wolfe swung around to see Sam's ashen face and a sling on his arm. "What the hell are you doing here?"

The largest smile Wolfe had ever seen appeared, "They had me dead to rights. That summer of playing in the woods at the academy working on evasion and survival taught me how to leave the kill zone. It's only a nick. All bets are off."

"Where the hell were you? We looked everywhere."

"Nellis sick bay. Figured they wouldn't look there."

"Neither would we"

"Get the girls over here. It's time to leave. We're forcing there hand and if necessary beginning a war of attrition." Sauria left alone after making arrangements to rendezvous.

Wolfe followed shortly with the girls in tow, both making different excuses about illness. They met at the foot of an access ramp. Sam led the three car caravan down Interstate 15 to the Strip

Later that night intruders entered the club. In the west, natural gas served as both heat and cooking fuel. While one unscrewed the coupling from the wall fitting but not completely, the other found half of a cigarette on the floor and re-lit it. He placed the cigarette next to the wick of a table candle at a perpendicular angle and then laid the base of the candle in a puddle of one-ninety alcohol from the bar. A good arson investigator might be fooled if the ensuing explosion dislodged the gas stove and fitting. All the materials came from the club. The two black bag operators left the way they had entered. There existed very little even microscopic evidence of their presence and that would soon revert to the ultimate in element recycling; fire.

Five minutes after the intruders' exit and before the club could fill with gas; the fuse neared the active phase. Using his key to the front door, El Matador casually walked to the middle of the floor and stomped out the cigarette. Check-check-no mate. Both opponents were worthy.

HARRAH'S

Usually sitting at a very public place insured a modicum at least of safety. Sam could no longer convince himself that in this situation it applied. He now knew, if he hadn't already, that his enemies were sociopaths in full bloom. People who are willing to shoot up a public place and carelessly endanger dozens of innocents in order to reach a single target fall into a very limited category. One does not capture these types of people. One does not negotiate with these people for nothing they say can be trusted. The only cure for a true sociopath is elimination. Killing anyone and everyone involved became Sam's new objective.

Cheyenne and Daga could no longer be seen in public with Sam. Somehow his cover had been blown so his role became less public and more planning. The three others had received STU-III phones as well and whether their covers had vanished had but one test. Continue on and see what kind of animals come to the watering hole. A nicer way of saying bait, the result might be the same.

Two Nordic looking men lingered at the sidewalk café outside Bill's Bar where Sam currently inhabited a bar stool and beer. They didn't stare. They engaged in animated conversation with frequent pointing and opening of brochures. A trained eye might have seen the weapons' bulges under their shirts and the loose fitting sizing attempting to hide the prominence. They were FBI agents selected using criteria not normally associated with Justice Department recruiting. Qualified as expert marksmen with a pistol rung, these agents were never going to be investigating white collar crime. The two men belonged specifically to IOS, Intel Operational Specialists, one of DHS's new weapons. They now operated as Sam's protection.

Sam liked to call them his Varangian guards, a reference to ninth century Vikings who had made a living as mercenaries in current day Russia. Big Ernie put another beer in front of Sam although one couldn't see the beer until the bartender let go. Sam's secure phone rang. It looked no different than any other telecommunication device a civilian might have. He answered anticipating a status report on the club.

"Hi. How's the weather?"

"Sunny and clear." This meant that both speakers should talk assuming at least one end of the conversation might be overheard by others.

"Hey, I threw that party."

"Oh, yeh. How'd it go?"

"OK. Everybody showed up. Even an unexpected guest or two. Just one thing."

"What's that?"

"The grill didn't start. So much for fancy gas barbecues. By the time the neighbor brought his over, people had gotten disinterested."

"There's always July fourth."

"Guess so. At least you didn't miss anything."

'I'll try to be there next time. Got to go. Later."

Sam slammed the phone shut. How had that gone bad? His conversations in *spook speak* allowed for plausible deniability in front of Congress. Not terribly different from *bad criminal code,* it always amused Sam how close the two worlds really were. In fact, some of the best field recruits often became criminals when their services were no longer needed or already were crooks which went a long way in explaining the danger of trusting anyone in this game. Varying degrees of sociopaths inhabited both sides of the tracks.

With little warning the bodyguards jumped from the table, threw money on the bar, and hustled Sam from the scene. Sam held his protests until they were back in the suite.

"What the hell was that?"

"We had a bet"

"A bet? What about?"

"Whether or not you'd still be breathing in five minutes."

"Don't run that witness protection crap past me. This isn't my first rodeo."

"Really? Maybe you should have the boys in Langley edit your dossier. You haven't played with these kinds of idiots before."

"Assholes are assholes."

"These are particularly nasty ones."

"What initiated my sudden exit?"

"Group of Latinos with Los Sueños tats gathering under the stairwell leading to Mickey D's. Might have been nothing. We couldn't take the chance."

"You guys are worse than my mother."

"We hope."

"You guys know that Vegas is crawling with gangsters and wannabes most of whom know nothing about this op."

"We know only what we need to know and we need to know you're breathing."

"How sentimental of you."

CHOCHO

Daga checked in with Sam using her new phone toy. She and Chey were up and running. Wolfe made conversation at the bar with Bobo and dancers looking to hustle drinks. A fair amount of intel could be gathered for a few shots of Red Bull and Jaeger Meister known as a Jaeger Bomb; relatively harmless as far as bombs go.

Daga came up on stage. She wore full body paint and nothing else. Painted as a zebra with the darker paint in strategic locations, jungle fever boiled to the surface in verbal grunts and wild eyed appreciation. Like robbing a bank in Columbus, Ohio during an Ohio State-Michigan game in the Horseshoe, Daga served as the perfect misdirection if one were so inclined.

As Wolfe swiveled his neck and his chair to keep an eye on things an unfamiliar face stared back at him. The person who owned that face became distinctive for more than a few reasons. The entire club males and females alike gawked as Daga continued her routine. This visage transfixed instead on Wolfe and it belonged to someone Rebelle did not recognize as having been to the club previously.

Yes, Wolfe had been rubbernecking often a sign of untrained people looking for information or up to no good, but it easily could be the movements of a curious sightseer in a strip club in Vegas for the first time. The man looking at Wolfe didn't have the build of a bouncer and he made no attempt to avert his eyes when Rebelle had noticed him. The club recently had lost Carlos so maybe this figure had been hired to replace him. Wolfe put the image of the face in front of his memory. It would be difficult to forget.

Arturo Mateo Reyes went back to the office and spoke to Gordo. The head of *Dirección* had some questions for his hapless underling.

"Who's the guy at the bar with his neck on a swivel? Average height and weight, he looks like he knows his way around a dark alley."

"Last time I looked it's the boyfriend of one of the new dancers."

"How many new dancers have you gotten in the last month?"

"Just two. That's fewer than normal. With the economy bad, we've had an uptick in applications and interviews."

"These two new ones, did they come in together?"

"Not exactly. Maybe a week apart."

"Do they hang around together?"

"Yeh, with the boyfriend, they're like the three amigos lately. He bought a dance from the Indian once. I just figured he's working on a three way."

"What's he do?"

"She never said. Like most guys with girls like her, he probably lives off of her income. With a shape like hers, he probably figures why work. I know he's in here a lot. Never causes any trouble which is nice when it comes to boyfriends."

"Keep your ears open. He's doesn't fit somehow."

Reyes walked out of the office and directly over to Wolfe at the bar. Wolfe saw him coming from the corner of his eye but made no move to acknowledge him as he approached. Reyes extended his hand once he entered Rebelle's line of sight.

"Hello. I'm Arturo. Hey, pendejo. Get our customer a drink on me." Reyes extended his hand to Wolfe while sneering at Bobo.

Bobo scooted over with a drink in hand. He even walked like a giant cockroach.

Rebelle took his hand. The feel seemed smallish for an average sized man; his hands hadn't done outdoor work for awhile. "I'm Wolfe. Guess you own the place or are you a manager?" Wolfe didn't like where this was going. It had a feel.

"I'm an investor in this business." He jerked his head in the direction of the bartender cowering down by the beer coolers. "Got to keep them on their toes". He looked back to Wolfe. "Gordo tells me that you're friends with one of our dancers?"

"Yeh, the super hot one in zebra paint."

Arturo turned to admire Daga at work. The normal look of appreciation in human female perfection that Rebelle had come to expect did not come to Reye's face. In fact the smile seemed cold and with effort.

"Lucky you."

"Very. You seem to know a lot for being new?"

"Not new. An infrequent visitor. Think troubleshooter. It's my job. What do you do while your girl takes off her clothes?"

The question came disguised as inoffensive, like asking some-one about their girl's favorite recipe. However, the asker's objective lay more deviously hidden. The query, intended to tweak the respondent's pride, caused most to give more infor-mation than needed to the questioner. Rebelle didn't fall for it but he did file it away.

"I play poker. We're in town for the WSOP." The best operational covers were the ones that were mostly true.

"She dances and you play poker. I've got to get that arrange-ment."

"Good luck."

"We'll see you around."

"I'm sure."

Daga finished her dance. The black paint mixed with sweat now ran like rivulets in the wilderness down the valleys of her body. Using her one thousand dollar leather bag by Coach and designed by Zoe, white nappa leather and painted zebra-like as well, she gathered the currency from the floor. Her choice of container to collect the appreciation of the audience perfectly closed out her evening as the money peeked above the edge of the overstuffed bag.

Two hundred fifty miles from Vegas in a neighborhood of Tempe near Phoenix, Zarilla's henchmen were at work.

XI

TEMPE, AZ

María Lopez Antonio could be mistaken for a younger Selma Hayek. Eighteen years old and a freshman at the nearby University of Arizona, she easily managed to be the most beautiful girl in any particular room. A communications major with a minor in theatre, she dreamed of a career in television broadcasting or acting. A goal no one had ever told her to be unattainable. Shy and conservative, she had very few boyfriends over the years and fell into that category of dazzling women too perfect to be approached by most men.

She opened the garage door and the early heat muscled its way instantly throughout the space. Always concerned that she may gain weight like so many of her relatives, she rode her bicycle to school even in the one hundred degree heat. Her daily routine included a shower and change of clothes at the university sports complex not far from her first class.

The door shut on the garage and she saddled up on her bike. The house, in the two thousand block of Fifth Street, held a value approaching two million US dollars. Along with their only daughter, the ranchero-style mansion fulfilled the American dream of her very religious mother Guadalupe and equally hard working father Luis.

In a perfect case of you never know who your neighbor is, Luis at first notice lived the life of a successful tile contractor with the Latino version of the Norman Rockwell family.

The beautiful inlaid façade of the house hid more than just the courtyard beyond.

María peddled out onto the street and headed to class. As she moved down the block, a black Escalade with heavily tinted windows pulled out of its parking spot near her house and began to follow her. She stopped at the stop sign and then continued straight ahead, her speed yet to pick up again as she crossed the intersection.

She had no chance. The SUV screeched to a halt in front of her causing her to lose her balance and fall. Doors flew open and in less than ten seconds María Lopez Antonio belonged to Los Zetas. Any bystanders and possible witnesses made an effort not to see anything as the vehicle sped away.

Picked by her kidnappers for her beauty and her wealth, she had been spotted while the gang members cruised wealthy neighborhoods looking for prime victims whose families would pay. Even gated communities had no defense for harmless looking landscapers and contractors who sold information to the gangs for money or drugs. Toddlers playing safely behind fences with their dutiful mothers nearby offered additional opportunity.

Something that the area chamber of commerce didn't tell people in Phoenix lately, it is the kidnapping capital of the US. The city and surrounding area averaged almost two abductions per day, so much for law and order Maricopa County.

Luis entered the house from the garage after work. Tired and dusty from a day with tile, his wife greeted him at the door ignoring the grime and giving a heartfelt hug and kiss.

"Get cleaned up. Dinner's almost ready."

"Where's María?"

"I don't know. She's a little late. She'd call if she had been delayed. I'll give her a call if she doesn't show while you're showering."

Fifteen minutes later, Luis entered the kitchen and grabbed a beer out of the fridge. "Did you call her?"

"Not yet. I got busy. Why don't you?"

María's phone rang. She did not pick up. Luis left a message about being thoughtful of others. The weeds surrounding her phone in an empty lot not far down the street didn't respond. Her cell had been the first thing thrown out the window after the thugs had snagged her.

"Let's go ahead. She can eat when she gets here. No need for us to wait. She's a college girl now."

"Luis you know I don't like that. I want us to eat as a family."

"I'll give her five minutes then I'm going to eat." Luis never did eat that night. The phone rang moments later.

The speaker's message seemed surreal as Luis listened. "Do not speak. Listen only. We have your hija. She is well. Gather one million dollars and be prepared to take it where and when we tell you. Do not call the police. We are watching and listening. We value money and our freedom more than her life. Do not do anything foolish."

"I want to...." The line went dead.

"Who was that, Luis? One of those telemarketers?"

Guadalupe knew the instant Luis looked up that sales had nothing to do with the phone call.

"Mi Dio, mi Dio. What Luis? What's a matter. Where's María?"

Luis explained the situation to his wife. The thick walls of the ranchero could not contain the wailing that ensued from the mother that had given the child life and watched her first breath. Luis prepared to take action even as Guadalupe slumped in his arms and then in a chair unable to bear the unimaginable.

Unknown to his neighbors and business contacts, Luis had once been a member of Los Nortes. Technically still a member based on the gang ritual of *blood in, blood out,* like the Mafia, one could not resign. Unlike the Italian version, most gang members were young men and with time many became regular citizens, very seldom having any gang contact with the new initiates.

Luis went out to the courtyard and dug at the foot of his favorite cactus. His effort produced a sealed plastic bag with a Glock nine millimeter carefully preserved. He checked the magazine, chambered a round, checked the safety, and then jammed it in the waist band of his jeans. In a gun state like Arizona, packing a concealed weapon almost qualified as jewelry or cell phone for the mostly conservative population.

Attempting to console his wife although he knew it to be hopeless, he informed her that he must leave and would be back shortly. He set the house alarm and kissed his wife warmly on the forehead. He hoped he would kiss her again.

Luis drove downtown eventually reaching the old barrio. Down in the thirties, where streets were numbered, one could find Latino gang members as easy as finding sand in the desert. Graffiti, the gang placazos, covered every square space once a traveler got anywhere near the neighborhood, acting as fair warning to anyone remotely concerned with one's safety. Luis drove straight to the corner of E. Chandler Boulevard and South 32nd Street near the 202 freeway.

He saw a group of young Latino men hanging in front of a liquor store, patted his weapon one more time in his waist-band, drove past them a block and got out and walked. Stopping directly in front of them could cause unintended anxiety on their part. If he approached on foot, they had time to get a feel for his business and how he carried himself. An urban tango framed by gang taggings on the buildings, it made everyone less jumpy.

Luis flashed a simple sign. He exposed the inner surface of his thumb facing his index finger, palm down. There on the connecting skin between the two digits, faded from age, three dots in the shape of a triangle occupied a small area. Gang tattoos are often elaborate but this one crossed over from gang to gang. Its meaning *mi vida loca* meant my crazy life and served as universal acknowledgement of gang affiliation.

A smallish member of the group, maybe not even a teenager, flashed back. Same location, but four dots in a row, served notice of home turf. *Mi barrio por vida*, an acceptance consciously or unconsciously that all of his days alive would be spent in this barrio unless incarcerated, defending the hood made for a full time job. The white flag had been waved and accepted.

"Hombre, you're not from around here. We don't like new faces."

"When I did what you are doing, I stood where you are standing. I need some information. I'm not a cop. I'm willing to pay but of course I carry no money now. If you can help, we can meet, exchange information and money and both are on our way."

"What kind of information?"

"Some gangbangers have something of value to me. I want it returned in perfect condition. For this favor, this act of goodwill, I will pay well. If however the goods are damaged, no matter how little, well I am an old man by good fortune only. I've stared into the cave of darkness. It is warm and comforting for those who don't return."

"And if we help you?"

"The money can be discussed when the information is discussed. You won't be disappointed. Call this number if you hear anything. Speak only to me. My street name is zanja. It is a place as you know where bodies can be found. Hasta."

Luis turned and walked back to his truck. In a period of a few minutes, all of the gang life he had left behind had returned as if only hiding just beneath his skin; waiting to bubble to the surface and infect his life like a long dormant virus. He cried uncontrollably as he drove back to his home. He had seen uncountable bodies bloated by gas and mutilated by bullets, struck down in their prime and he had felt nothing. But now this violence that he had helped procreate reached with bony fingers into his new life. The sins of the fathers come home to the innocents.

FIFTH STREET

The phone didn't have a chance to ring the second time. The caller spoke quickly. "You know your way around the barrio, heh? Then you should know better. We knew you were asking questions before they were answered. For this, the price doubles. It is now two million dollars. You have until tomorrow evening. We will call at that time and make final arrangements. This is business only unless you make it otherwise. Do not bother to protest. We know you have the money. Get it and be ready when the phone call comes."

Luis stood with the receiver in his hand motionless. His wife, curled into a fetal position on the couch in the early stages of a nervous breakdown, jumped to his side when the phone rang. She heard the speaker.

"What have you done? We don't have that kind of money. You've killed our daughter." She pounded her fists against Luis' chest. He felt nothing but the warm tears of his beloved Guadlupe falling on his bare arms, each drop another stab to his heart.

Luis spent the following day selling, pawning, and mortgaging every asset he had. By five in the evening he had the money. An entire lifetime rolled up in Benjamins in exchange for his daughter. He made his last stop at the insurance agency where he had done business for years.

The phone call came as promised. The drop instructions intended to protect the perps. "Bring the money and leave it locked in the truck at the entrance to South Mountain Park. Put your key under the driver's side rear tire. You will see a black barrio battlewagon parked ahead of you. On the front seat are directions to her location. Leave now. We're watching."

"I need proof of life. I want to speak to her."

"Papa. Help! Papa!" María's voice for sure.

"Good enough?"

"No. I want her to tell me the time."

"Six-thirty Papa.Hurry!" Fear in her voice.

"No more.' The line went dead.

Luis followed the directions exactly. As he walked toward the four-door Chevy Impala with air shocks and twenty inch rims he scanned the nearby trees for movement. He could see none. As he approached the car, the interior light of his truck flashed on. They had the money.

The note lay on the front seat as promised. It had scrawled upon it one word; trunk. He ran to the rear of the vehicle and the lid lifted without being unlocked. There, shaking and exhausting, lie the only good he had ever done in this world. His daughter, very alive with no outward markings of abuse, melted into his arms as he lifted her from captivity.

The ride home passed quickly. María, babbling nearly incoherent to her mother on the phone, her mother slobbering between words as badly, began to appreciate life and its ephemeral existence. Luis drove carefully but single-mindedly. He had his daughter. He now had other things on his mind.

With his wife and daughter reunited and their protestations pummeling him in stereo, Luis made excuses for his quick departure.

"I've got a few things that have to be done right away. I'll be back. You two enjoy each other. I won't be long." Luis waved his loved ones off and climbed in his truck. When he glanced in the rear view mirror the fleeting image he saw filled his eyes with tears, his wife and daughter walking hand in hand through the front door of the house he no longer owned.

The ride to E. Chandler and thirty second street passed without distinction, the actual objects his eyes fell upon never registered in his mind. He no longer inhabited the body of Luis Antonio. He became Zanja, El Norte gangster and proud of the street name which translated to *ditch,* where his targets usually came to rest later to be found by the police. It had been cops who gave him the handle.

When he got to his destination he came out blazing. By the time the cops arrived, two gangbangers and Zanja lay dead on the sidewalk, two others propped up against the building façade, wounded and bleeding out.

His wife and daughter would still have the house. All his loans had been covered with life insurance. His family would be taken care of financially and he had exacted vengeance.

The police blotter the next day faithfully reproduced in the *Arizona Republic* characterized the shootout as more gang on gang turf wars. A conclusion derived by the coroner and detectives who saw the gang tats on the participants. No mention made of the kidnapping, the defense of his family, the ultimate sacrifice, and the power and influence of drug lords with piles of money. All were unknown to observers or overlooked by authorities. Let them kill each other could describe the common law enforcement strategy in some cities.

Unfortunately within days, accountants for Los Zetas would report to Zarilla the receipt of two million dollars. Two million more dollars to be spent digging tunnels under the US border, bribing law enforcement on both sides of the frontier, and corrupting society throughout the Americas.

Open immigration or lack of enforcement depending on one's point of view, brought along with it smugglers and by extension a type of criminal whose acts of savagery stretched the sensibilities of even a violent society.

Those far from the borders or weekly church goers self-righteously suffering no guilt for this destruction of our ways supported this transformation of America. We hired cheap labor; the wages depressed by supply over demand, and ate in restaurants where the prices on the menu hadn't kept up with inflation because no one in the kitchen had a green card. We demanded nothing of our leaders except more money for us. We all wallowed in this greed and now Sam and his crew were left to clean up a small part of the mess.

Pandora's Box had been opened, and with the exception of Sauria and a few people like him, only hope remained.

XII

VEGAS

Sam picked up the phone and called Wolfe. "How's everything at the club?"

"We got a new player."

"What's he look like?"

"Latino, average height and build, mid-thirties maybe. No outstanding features, except his eyes. Zero emotion. Asked about Daga and me."

"What'd you tell him?"

"The truth. I play poker and she makes money. Maybe he's the new enforcer. Came in to see what the problem is."

"Yeh, he's probably the one that interfered with our party. Tell Daga about him when you get a chance then you go back to the poker rooms and sniff around. We're going to have to leave the club to the girls for awhile. See what they see. Talk to you later."

Rebelle rambled out of his room and down to the Harrah's parking garage. Cutting across the employee parking and then over by the Venetian back delivery entrance one could arrive at the main door of the Venetian without having ever walked along the crowded strip. Yet in spite of having taken that route, he had that feeling one gets when one has the sensation of being followed.

He stopped to gaze in the windows of the galleria shops along the approach to the casino proper. Gucci and Lagerfield were as common there as WalMart's in-house brand in Arkansas. Old field craft from the OSS predecessor of the CIA, windows of shops, especially high end stores whose clerks cleaned the panes daily, acted as excellent mirrors for checking one's six.

He saw her and she saw him see her. She held her ground not looking away or entering the store. Instead she acknowledged him with a nod of her head and a smile.

Dressed in a little black cocktail dress stretched to its limits as it cupped her round ass, she didn't have the build of most Asian women. D cups spilled aggressively from the neckline while defying gravity; a gathered stitch along the line of her seventh rib outlining the surgeon's handiwork. Petite in height, her body type could not be described as frail or thin. The word perfect entered Wolfe's mind. She stood on a pair of Nicolina pumps, Italian made. The heels lifted her only three inches, a discreet height for a woman of her size. A baby doll strap and open toe were highlighted with a single Swarovski crystal placed on the center of the upper. The leather, dyed dark purple, looked reptilian. A small tattoo unrecognizable at that distance by Wolfe decorated the back of her left shoulder

Wolfe turned and headed to the poker room. He found a seat at five-ten hold'em and got comfortable. A full table, the spot to his right sat unoccupied with a major stack in front of it. As he began assessing his opponents while waiting to be dealt a hand, a body dropped in to the empty seat.

"Yo dude. Where you been. Lose your stake? Wolfe. Right?" Tommy Cho had taken up residence.

"No, no. I'm cool. Been busy."

"I've been killing it. Cards are running hot. The dead money has been generous."

"Good for you. Most of the action here?"

"Pretty much. Hey, I did what you said."

"Like what?"

"Kept my eyes open. You're right. A lot of newbies with a lot of money from down Mexico way."

"Let's talk about it later. I'm buying. It'll probably be a short evening. I don't suppose you have the alcohol enzyme."

"Dude. Crash and burn. I do. I can drink like a white man. How do you know about the enzyme?"

"My parents made me go to school."

"Smart ass. I'm going to take your money."

Tommy played balls to the wall and Wolfe played conservatively. With Cho to his right, every time Rebelle had a possible play, Tommy would pile into the pot making it less than good odds to call. Wolfe got stuck waiting for actual hands, slow playing Tommy, and taking an above average pot from time to time. Rebelle's hands came with plenty of time in between. If it hadn't been for Cho's possible intel, Wolfe would have left earlier. Having invested enough time into Tommy's recruitment and his chips about where he started, Wolfe cashed out.

Wolfe walked over to the coffee machines. As he filled a cup and looked around the room, she entered. Without hesitation, she walked directly towards Rebelle. No smile, but a definite roll to her walk, her hips writing S curves in the air, the skirt and shoes did not go wasted. She extended her hand. Wolfe looked for a weapon.

"Hello. I'm Anna Lee. My friends call me China Doll. I thought we should meet formally first."

"Why should we meet?"

"Before we do what you are thinking."

What am I thinking if anything?"

"You want to be with me."

"What makes you think that?"

"You are male."

"Maybe I don't like women."

"Oh, you like women. You just like to be the decider. Our situation makes you uncomfortable. I can change that to comfortable if you like."

"What's that tattoo on your shoulder? May I look?" Wolfe touched her arm and then ran his finger along the outline of the ink. In proximity, the tattoo became a black widow spider with the under surface of the abdomen exposed, the red hour glass clearly delineated.

"Do you like my friend?"

"Very nice. But it doesn't make me at ease. After all, black widows kill their mates."

"Sometimes. Sometimes they keep them around for toys."

"I don't think of myself as a toy. More like a man."

"As I said, you're the decider"

"Maybe another time. You're very pretty."

"I'll definitely see you around."

Anna Lee walked past Rebelle brushing her breast against his arm and then looking demurely over her shoulder. The long black hair shimmered in the casino lights. The hips kept singing their song with a perfect rhythm.

Tommy Cho came up from behind. "Yo dude. That babe-ette is hot. Pretty nice fun bags for being Asian. You going to let that get away?"

"Who knows? Let's go get a drink."

Rebelle and Tommy squeezed into a couple of chairs at the main bar, the two grandmothers next to them never noticing as the video poker kept them in a trance.

"Alright Tommy, what you got for me?"

"Like you said. Money, money everywhere and they don't care. They treat it like it's Monopoly."

The bartender walked up. Just another dreamer waiting to take his money to the tables when he got off work, Vegas overflowed with guys like him. "May I take your order?"

"I'll take a Rumpie and a Sierra Nevada pale ale. I don't know what the old man is getting."

"May I have a goose and soda, squeeze of lime, please." Wolfe looked at Cho. "Old man? You're the one that looks like an egg roll."

"Poker is tough on my regimen."

"Your regimen? What's that? Wake up at two p.m., eat in room, shower, go play poker. If you win, blow a few bucks at a tittie bar, eat some more, drink, pass out, repeat.

"Sounds like you've done it before."

"Yeh, for a few days. Not as a lifestyle. Got a regular girl?"

"Yeh, I got a regular girl but not a girlfriend if you know what I mean."

"It's Vegas. I know what you mean. You want to make some extra cash?"

"Depends."

"See if you can catch any distinguishing tats. Maybe see what cars they're driving, license plates, out at the valet."

"Yo dude, I'm kinda laid back. I don't wanta do crazy shit that'll get me killed. What are you into?"

"No,no. I don't mean anything like that. You know, if you see something write it down. Carry a little pad. Make a note after they or you leave the area. I'll make it worth your time."

"I don't know..."

Wolfe put ten fresh Benjamins on the bar between them. "Make sure to tip the bartender."

CHOCHO

Cheyenne and Daga prepared for work. "Hey, what are you wearing tonight?" Chey had a natural relaxed way about her even now. She made it sound like they were going out dancing in a club instead of stripping down to their DNA for money while trying not to get killed.

"Basic black." As Daga dressed, Cheyenne smiled. Somewhat of an understatement to what most people might consider in the use of the term basic. Nothing could be basic on Daga.

The black leather seemed to be a part of her body, supple and soft like the skin beneath it. Designed like a Brando outfit from the *Wild Ones*, somehow her version made his look more conservative than a nun's habit. The chaps wrapped tightly around her, barely able to make the stretch. The only thing under them besides her brown legs smooth and velvet-like, a black leather thong played peek-a-boo with any observer willing to take the most casual of glances.

The halter top, made of similar material, had two flashing turn signals in the appropriate places. Both flashed green lights. Motorcycle boots completed the ensemble.

Cheyenne decided to dress for war. Battle paint straight from Cherokee, NC ran the lengths of her legs along the outside. More markings covered her discreetly with a leather rawhide thong matching her moccasins. A necklace of cascading layers of arrowheads, iridescent in shades of pinks and whites, hung down her front like multiple strands of pearls. A deerskin vest framed her unrestrained boobs. Topping the tribal tease, she placed a medicine man's wolf's head over her beaded hair.

"Ready to go to war?" Cheyenne looked at Daga.

"Sure. I'll take Route 66."

The two partners made more money than any other night they had ever worked. Each played off the other, the remainder of the girls either steaming or impressed with the pas de deux. After the doors closed and most of the dancers had left or were changing, Daga and Chey remained sitting at the bar with drinks.

Arturo Reyes smiled as he approached. He sported a crooked grin like when one has had too much tequila. "The two of you made mucho dinero tonight."

"So did you." retorted Daga.

Reyes motioned for Bobo to leave. He walked behind the now empty bar and started pouring shots of añejo for the three of them. "Chase the other ones out of the dressing room and lock the front door behind you." He yelled at the fleeing bartender.

"You want us to leave?"

"No. I thought we could celebrate."

Daga's blood began to simmer. Not in the way when she shared a bed with Wolfe but in the way when someone could get hurt. She made her decision.

"Let's go up and relax in one of the rooms."

Cheyenne, at first confused, figured it out. "Yeh, baby. You can count to three can't you?"

Daga pulled on his jacket leading the prey and Chey whispered in his ear. El Matador seemed more like El Borracho. He sat on the edge of the sofa, his head bouncing between Chey's naked breasts. Daga moved behind him massaging his upper back. As he wallowed in what most males imagined to be every man's fantasy, the swiftness of the attack came in a sudden swoop. Daga's blade separated numbers four and three of his cervical vertebrae before severing his spinal cord, the final signal to the brain one of disbelief. He slumped over and then fell to the floor. A small teaspoon of blood seeped like spilled sauce from his body. One of Daga's preferred locations of assault, neck wounds which avoid the arteries and target the spinal cord leave very little body fluid to clean.

"Girl. You don't play."

"He got off lucky. Imagine what he has done to others. Let's get out of here. Let me clean up first.

Daga soaked the SEAL pup knife at the bar sink in a solution of bleach for a few minutes, so much for DNA. It's not like he would be missed by the authorities or reported by his family.

"Help me move this guy onto the rug."

"Jesus, now I know what they mean by dead weight. He's not even that big."

"Back your car up to the kitchen door. Then come back and help."

While Cheyenne moved the car, Daga found a hand truck used to move beer. She took the requisite cheesy gold by the inch bracelet from his wrist, the Rolex, his wallet with money, credit cards, and identification.

"Here!" Daga stuffed a handful of hundreds into Chey's hand. "He won't need it. Besides, we want it to look like robbery. Get his boots. Use these." Daga threw her a pair of gloves from the kitchen.

When Reyes had been stripped of everything valuable, the two women struggled to get the body of one of the most feared men in Mexico on to the dolly. Finally, they were able to roll the body to the delivery door in the back of the house and with effort get the corpse into Cheys' trunk. Daga wiped down everything. One of the problems of working in Vegas consisted of the fact that everyone got fingerprinted who worked in the tourism industry regardless of criminal history.

"Wow. This is a blast. Driving around Vegas with a dead man in my car. You sure know how to have fun."

"Relax. Sam said it's war. I'd been waiting for a chance. Drive up into North Vegas." As Chey drove around North Vegas, Daga executed the rest of her hastily made plan.

The boots went out the window on a deserted street. Days from now, the LVPD would hassle some homeless person who found them and was wearing the hand crafted boa skin boots. She discreetly distributed the credit cards one at a time in a large quadrant of blocks. Those would be picked up by almost anyone and by the time the cops traced all those down they would have five or six more useless suspects. The identification she cut up and threw out in pieces.

"OK. Now head out US93 South towards Chloride."

"Chloride? What's that?"

"That's the name of a very small place out in the desert which you might gather is empty people wise. We're going to give this guy a dirt nap and hope the animals get most of his face and hands before the cops find him. We don't have to worry about his teeth. He's probably never been to a dentist or he's from Mexico. Either way he's a dead end."

"Have you done this before?"

"What? Kill an asshole?"

"No. Dispose of a body."

"No. But Wolfe and I talk about it a lot. We like to watch CSI."

"And you stayed at a Holiday Inn last night."

"Whatever. When you get home make sure the clothes and shoes you are wearing go immediately to Goodwill. We should be OK with the car. Not much blood. We'll stop at a car wash and vacuum the trunk."

"Great. Thanks."

Sam picked up the secure phone. "What's the deal?"

"The new guy at the club won't be a problem."

"What did you do with the package?"

"It's at the beach."

"Don't miss work. Keep me informed."

Sam rang off and called Wolfe. Now Rebelle definitely needed to keep his distance from the club.

XIII

LA FORTELEZA

José Jesús Dominguez sat at the head of the ornately carved ebony table with ten high backed chairs. The heads of all the other Mexican cartels were there. The hallway outside the meeting room had filled to capacity hours before with bodyguards and drivers. Marksmen ringed the rooftops for additional security.

"Why do we still kill each other? It serves no purpose. Our families and our great grand children's children won't be able to spend all of the money the Americans continue to send us. We have worked hard. Do we not want to enjoy the fruits of our sacrifice?" Zarilla, evil and sociopathic, never let bloodlust get in the way of good business.

Zarilla had taken control of the Gulf Cartel based in Matamoros, across the border from Brownsville, when the former leader Oriel Cardenas managed to be extradited to the US in spite of millions of bribes to Mexican authorities.

El Jefe of the Tijuana Cartel agreed. He, of course, also held the number two position behind Zarilla in the current alliance. A life time member of the Arellano Felix family tree, the AF ink in Old English script on his bare arm didn't stand for Abercrombie and Fitch.

"We don't fight for blood. We fight for money and for respect. Respect means more than life to a man." Vincente Carillo led a very tenuous union with the Sinaloa Cartel currently in a full battle with Los Zetas in the Southwest Texas corridor.

"We don't interfere with your business yet you come to our markets from Juarez and El Paso and when we don't melt like campesinos in the summer sun you try to destroy our livelihood. You've killed our mules, our whores, and our purchased authorities, policia and federales, for what reason? You don't make enough money?" Dominguez wanted badly to reach into the hidden compartment in the arm of the chair, grab the pistol, and shoot the idiot between the eyes. Push the bullet through his head is how marksmen describe it.

"We make money. You make more. What are we, second class? I risk everything being here. The federales want me more than ever." El Chapo spoke for the Sinaloa Cartel.

Zarilla responded. 'We have rifles, grenades, rocket launchers, and Kevlar vests. We kill more than we are killed. TNT is in our armory."

Shorty 'El Chapo' responded. "I believe we have something which can help both of us."

"I hope. We are running out of blood."

"Have you heard of PETN?"

"No, educate me."

El Chapo waved at the door. One of his henchmen opened it, the muzzle of a M4 flashed from the hallway. "Permit me to introduce you to a friend of mine. Dr. Basir Fahim."

Dr. Basir Fahim, educated in London, graduating in the top ten percent of his class, shuffled into the room. Young, handsome, and self-motivated he took his seat at the opposing end of the table from Zarilla.

"Good afternoon gentlemen. I am here on the invitation of El Chapo to describe to you a new weapon against our common enemies to the North. It is non-metallic, easily attained, anhydrous, making it very imaginative in the ways it can be put in places of soft targets. Bear with me as I lecture on its attributes.

It is called PETN. Pentaerythritol tetranitrate. A nitrogen based explosive, the most common ingredient in the Semtex plastic explosive. It is a crystalline white solid $C_5 H_8 N_4 O_{12}$. It melts at a very low point of 286 F. When it explodes it travels almost immediately at over 200 miles per hour.

In addition, it is used as a vasodilator making it available in many pharmacies around the world without prescription. You may remember its use by Richard Reid, the shoe bomber, in December of 2001, a near miss by my side. We attempted another action in August of 09 to eliminate the Minister of the Interior in Saudia Arabia. With the bomb secreted in his underwear, the martyr was stopped just actionable feet from his target. Only one hundred grams, less than four ounces, will destroy a car.

As a very young man I watched George W. Bush invade my country. At that point in time, I became a true believer. I understand that DHS and ICE are making your life more difficult. I'm here to help if you are willing to trade."

"They are making it difficult but we have enough people to still make money. What do you propose?" El Jefe AF smelled money.

"We supply the PETN, you smuggle us across the border. Our operatives are studying Spanish at the University of Mexico even as they study chemical engineering. A little sunlight on our skin, we become illegal immigrants."

"And for this we get what?"

"You get to blow up your enemies. The authorities will blame it on us."

"And you get what?"

"We get to blow planes out of the sky. Your families should travel by private jet which I don't believe is a problem for men of your stature."

It made a strange feeling. Zarilla wanted to kill the Americans who interfered with his drug deals but destroying over three hundred innocent lives on a single plane struck him as excessive although Pablo Escobar didn't mind mass destruction in order to eliminate one person. Somehow helping Al Qaeda didn't seem right. He wanted who ever had stolen his money in Vegas and soon El Matador would provide the intelligence.

"So what do you think? We have a deal?" El Chapo beamed eagerness.

The door to the outer room swung open and a gopher came to Zarilla's side. The word whisper stretched the definition as the messenger delivered the news in wide eyed agitation.

Zarilla held up his hand."We have a problem. My man in Vegas is missing. We've lost money twice, I believe another one of our men is in custody and talking, and now my number two is gone. We are under coordinated attack."

"With this material, you could blow up the entire building killing many policemen and your man with the loose lips." Basir wanted this deal badly.

"Sir, we will get back to you after further discussion. Please excuse us. We need to address these other problems. An arrangement of this magnitude cannot be agreed upon without due attention." Zarilla could hardly contain his anger resulting from the news concerning Reyes.

"As you wish. Allah Akbar" .Basir left the room and Dominguez exploded.

"I need every man the rest of you can spare put under my direct authority."

"Before we get to your problem let's address this new opportunity. What don't you like about the doctor's offer?" Now Faz Fuego of the Juarez Cartel spoke.

"Simply put it will bring too much heat. We might kill a few gringo cops but it doesn't make us money and might well cost us many of our smuggling routes. Right now we are treated as an unfortunate nuisance. If the Americans connect the dots and see that we are working with Al Qaeda while innocents are dying they may actually close the border. We have little to gain and much to lose. Remember we are here to make money. If some people are killed in order to protect our manner of business that is not a problem. However, it is obvious the Americans will not accept wholesale destruction and a disruption of their entire economy. These terrorists are driven blindly by their lust for American blood. We pursue wealth, a small consequence being the death of some. Once we help them how do we control it? We can't."

With this declaration, Zarilla displayed how he had parlayed innate intelligence and ruthlessness; controlled and calculated, into a multi-billion dollar operation.

"I agree with Dominguez. Why bring such a thing on our heads?" Essentially El Jefe had made his vote clear.

True to his usual ways, El Chapo disagreed. "I'm going to examine this more closely but I am leaning towards taking the doctor up on his offer."

"Si,si." Fuego voting with the Sinaloa Cartel came as no surprise.

"We will have another discussion of this important matter in the future. Right now, make arrangements to send every available asset to Vegas. El Jefe, send your number two man as my contact there. This meeting is over." As Zarilla adjourned the group, he made a mental note to eliminate both El Chapo and Fuego. Either by assassination or a tip off to the authorities, those two needed to be removed before they could ruin a very productive golden goose.

Perhaps the doctor might need to have an accident as well. Dominguez didn't need him around to stir the pot.

XIV

BUGSY'S BAR

Wolfe sat sipping Knob Creek on the rocks and passing the time at video poker. Technically a slot machine, it did allow for skill to be employed unlike the spinning wheels of random colors that were no more than lottery tickets. Of course, many people that played video poker had only a cursory understanding of draw poker odds.

Posted odds like those calculated for blackjack made the assumption that all choices would be made based on higher probability a supposition that defied reality. The calculated rake for the house in blackjack depending on the variation fluctuated between 1.5% and 3.0% but the real take approached 15% because of misplays and bad plays. That's 15% of every dollar risked. Don't cry for Vegas just yet.

The same distorted numbers applied to video poker. 99% payout implied a 1% house advantage but approached 20% in the books. Simple choices like drawing to an inside straight decreases the odds of hitting the straight by a 50% factor compared to an open ended straight. Drawing two exact cards for a royal flush are 2% times 2% or .0004 or 1/2500. The odds of being dealt a royal flush are 1 in 649,749. Paying out 800 times the original bet seems rather meager compared to the chances of hitting the hand.

When one has calculated the payouts, drawing to a four card flush pays four times more than hitting two pairs or better but is statistically only 60 percent less likely; 4:1 compared to 5:2. As long as one is paid more than 60% above the rate for two pairs one has pot odds. If one is dealt four to a flush and a small pair knowing the odds and following them improves one's chances in this instance by a maximum factor of 2.4 or less when calculating the possibility of the pair hitting three or four of a kind.

These numbers and many like them ran circles in Wolfe's head carefully tracked by Rebelle. That's when China Doll sat down beside him.

"Hello Wolfie." The afternoon hours drastically affected her clothing choices. Designer jeans clasped her thighs and ass starting just below a waist so small it seemed necessary organs wouldn't have enough room. She wore the low slung denim as the designer had hoped. No muffin tops could be glimpsed above the belt line. A simple white t-shirt either tailored to fit or manufactured for her body only, hung un-tucked but not too low on her body. Baby doll black canvas slippers completed her afternoon wardrobe. The hair hung low, long and black.

Wolfe did his best worst Travis Bickle imitation. The bourbon helped. "You talkin' to me?"

"If you want to talk first."

"No one calls me Wolfie."

"Sure she does. You mean everyone else?"

"Unless you read minds, you should be careful telling people what you think you know in contrast to what you have been told or know to be fact."

"A little protective aren't we?"

"We? We aren't concerned with anything. Where'd you get the name Wolfie?"

"Your name is Wolfe. I took a little license with the diminutive."

"I never told you my name."

"Your friend Tommy did. He needed some company."

Wolfe made a mental note to explain things to Cho. "With that matter cleared up, what brings you to the Flamingo?"

"My favorite poke-her player. I understand you like to play poke-her all the time" The emphasis on the second syllable didn't go unnoticed.

"You're wasting your time."

"You won't be wasting your money."

"My money? Not too likely."

"OK. No money. I think I like you."

Wolfe held back his laughter but only barely. "You know, the nice thing about being at best normal in one's looks, come-ons like your well practiced monologue have very little effect. I'm not thinking trust here."

"I think we have common goals. Why don't you buy me a drink and we'll talk?"

"The way you were dressed the other night, why don't you buy me a drink and I'll listen?"

Wolfe analyzed the situation as the bartender poured the drinks and China Doll pulled bills out of her clutch like facial tissues. The questions confronting Rebelle made playing three games of chess in the park simultaneously seem easy. The classic double agent, the provocateur, the honey pot, or just another player on the fringes trying to make a few bucks working both sides, this little hottie could be any one of the above.

Should he play the mark and pretend to be taken by her sensual being and in turn give her useless and misleading intel or fall for her manipulations of misinformation treating it as valuable knowledge and paying top dollar for it?

Might Wolfe become the alpha double agent soon trying to turn her, while pretending to come over to her side initially yet falling for the powers of truth and good in the end which only her help could give.? Might he run the false flag gambit, convincing her that indeed he worked for those who opposed the US government? His third choice; hardball, we have the bad guys in our sights; we soon will have you, would you like to be on the winning side? This evening had no markings of one that would end early nor easy. Machiavelli made good reading for those who played the intel game.

The difficult portion of one's interaction with possible recruits always rested on discovering motive. In any use of behavioral psychology, knowing the subject's objective made creating a strategy to exploit it attainable. The object of the recruitment if he or she is not already an agent is unaware of the manipulation. However, the operator attempting to recruit the recruiter is aware of what motive to display and therefore the possible strategies advantageous to defeating his opponent's goal.

Even good misinformation is filled with accuracies to act as verifiers to the one who might be checking. It is the one piece of false information after an extended time of good data that causes the receiver to self-destruct. Spot on information is occasionally ignored in the fear that it might be misleading, if these twists and turns through the mind of the other side sound familiar; they are. Some people play this head game in a less deadly form. The card version is called poker. This heads up match which Wolfe began to play with Anna Lee had a much larger risk versus reward ratio; everything or nothing, life or death.

"Let's not waste words. You and your girlfriend are working for a rival faction. You have access to money and tactics. You're part of a large crew well-organized. I believe there are people in this town that want you and others that work for you dead."

"Really? Who wants to eliminate a poker player and a stripper?"

"I don't know. I'm paid at a cash drop. The location changes every time. One day I arrived early and watched. He was careless and I saw him from the side and back. I think maybe Latino."

"What's the money for?"

"He gave me a picture. A middle age American white male. He dressed rather funny like a tourist. I found him at the bar at Harrah's. You, he, and your girl talked about something. I haven't seen the older guy for awhile so my new assignment is to follow you and any regular associates. Keep track of where you spend your time."

"So what do you do for money when strangers aren't paying you to be a junior private eye?"

"I'm a girlfriend escort."

"A hooker?"

"No,no, well yes. It depends. I provide a service to wealthy clients, very wealthy clients. They come into town and I am their girlfriend for three days. We go out to eat, shows, massages at the pool, and sex. Hookers are paid to leave after sex. I'm paid to stay."

"So why do spy versus spy?"

"One of my clients suggested it to me and since he pays so well I didn't want to lose him."

"A Latino?"

"Come to think of it, yes. Funny thing. I haven't seen him for awhile."

Probably Juega at the club, Wolfe thought. "So out of the blue you decide to help me?"

"No. I got scared. The amount of money they were paying caused me to think it was very dangerous. You know, you're in but how do you get out? What if I see something they don't want me to see?"

Wolfe stared into her eyes. Her gaze didn't leave him. Man, if she were lying, the acting deserved an award. Of course, people paid to do such things are very good. The perfect conundrum could be no better. As seven CIA agents discovered in Afghanistan, trusting a double agent might mean one's life. After months of feeding the Americans excellent intel, the Afghan double agent drove into camp one day and detonated himself during a meeting with the CIA operatives.

"OK. Here's the deal. You got to keep doing what you're doing. If you stop or run, they'll know. I'll employ your services, if you will, so we can be seen together."

"They'll think I'm plying you for information. That's cool. Like a Leopardo."

"Yeh, like a Leopardo." The word ran like a ball of electrons down Wolfe's back.

"You want to come over now?"

"Can't. Remember. Act natural."

Anna Lee stood and gave Wolfe a kiss full on the mouth. As she did, a player at the nearby slot machines got out of her seat and headed for the open doors. China Doll stirred a few hearts while the gawkers stirred their drinks as she left by the same exit.

Wolfe's phone vibrated; the one that belonged to Sam. Wolfe answered. "What's up?"

"What the hell are you doing?"

"What do you mean?"

"The hooker. Who the hell is she?"

"What the hell! You got eyes on me? Hey, she came to me!"

"Exactly."

"She wants to help us. She's scared."

"And helpless and beautiful maybe?"

"What if she can get us intel?"

"Alright, I wouldn't do this with anyone else. Go ahead and check her out. Don't go believing your own bullshit or hers either. Bring back what she gives you and we'll check it out. I don't want to be there when Daga starts slicing and dicing if you get too cozy."

"No. She's cool."

"So's Elena Bobbitt." Sam's phone went dead and Wolfe let Sauria's words sink to his gut.

Wolfe had pondered Anna Lee's use of the word leopardo subconsciously since she had used it. More than one double agent had slipped and used an awkward idiom or local slang with an otherwise perfect accent or story. Juega could have used that term when he recruited her for the tail. Maybe she heard him use it on the phone. Maybe she wanted Rebelle dead.

"Yo, yo, yo, it's Tommy Cho." Tommy slapped Wolfe on the back exactly at the time Rebelle stood to go to the Flamingo poker room.

"Hey, Tommy. How ya doing?"

"Dude, that cash you left? I built it to ten large. Ten G!"

"Good for you. Did I get anything for my money?"

"That Asian chick we saw. Asking a lot of questions. I didn't give her anything about you. I'm cool. Everything else seemed normal."

"I'm relieved. Look Tommy, somebody asks anything about me, you know nothing."

"I swear I didn't say anything important."

"That's cool Tommy. Let's go take some dead money from the retired guys that play here."

"They're not all retired. Sometimes small time local celebrities are bottom fishing here. It'll make for more action. The dinosaurs tend to play old school."

"Perfect."

CHOCHO

"You get the money."

"Why should I pick up the money?"

"Because you're in charge."

"Since I'm in charge, you get the money."

Military chain of command hadn't been introduced to Bobo and Gordo. They understood the threat of force and the use of force. Everything else became complicated. Technically, Gordo had to decide. Although the pair would never win team Jeopardy, they did know this much. Two separate men had been tasked with taking care of the rake and two men were missing. The details didn't clutter their minds. They understood very well how things worked.

"Look. A man called. He used the code. He said he would be arriving today. He's authorized by Mexico City. He gave me a location. I don't want to be the one that tells him we didn't do it. If you refuse, I'll tell him you refused. The bad side of that is I'll probably have to bury you. I don't mind that he kills you but that desert is like concrete."

The final argument convinced Bobo to follow instructions. He swore to himself if anything happened he'd come back here and kill Gordo if he could. He drove to another storage unit near the airport. Bobby Bonanza lifted the garage door. Three armed guards with machine pistols off safety greeted him. He made the pickup and the sentries stayed behind surrounded by millions of dollars in boxes they used as mattresses and end tables. The next time any unauthorized person tried for the money people would die.

Ernesto Cruz, El Jefe's number two, arranged the additional security after being briefed on the previous incursions. In town for only a few hours, he approached his job methodically. He looked forward to cleaning up this mess like he had Tijuana. His friends and enemies called him El Cruz or El Crucificador. His preferred method of killing involved precise attention to detail in replicating the Roman mode of execution, he rationalized that anything good enough for Jesus was good enough for mortals. Families of his victims if they were known always received a small white cross with the outline of a human skull carved at the intersection of the arms and the post.

He had decided en route that he didn't need to be at the club. The two pendejos could handle things and if the numbers started looking funny he would check it out. He figured that his time might be better spent analyzing information collected by the street level people. Trained in counter-intelligence in the Mexican Special Forces group, GAFE, he knew that with time and patience information coming out always led back to its origin. Once he had determined the source, El Cruz would teach whoever caused this problem some religion.

XV

Sam sat in his suite at The Venetian. Beautifully furnished, a mahogany armoire drew one's eye in the direction of the foot of the bed where a settee equally rich in color completed the elegant appeal. The room's separate sitting room, expansive and three steps down seemed oversized for one person but welcoming. The bathroom with double French doors dwarfed his boyhood bedroom he once shared with a brother. A shower with surround–you water jets gave clean a whole other meaning. Yet he couldn't enjoy it.

His wounds still ached but presented the least of his worries. Armed guards slouched outside his door serving as a rudimentary alarm for him. All that he had done so far and still Zarilla sat cozy in his lair. Sam more trapped than his target. He damned near had gotten himself killed at the ambush. Wolfe had a possible new recruit or he might already be dead. He hoped Daga had not started a killing spree.

He picked up the secure phone and called Cherokee. "Hey, Princess Minnehaha. Everything OK?"

"Everything is fine. We're kicked back waiting to go to work."

"Any new faces since you and Daga played in the sandbox?"

"Nope. Quiet over here."

"Keep an eye on her. I don't want her to get out of hand. Remember we want the Big Kahuna."

"Will do. Time to get naked. See ya later."

Sam hung up and stared at the wall. He had the feeling that something was coming from Zarilla and he couldn't figure what it might be. He didn't want to look up and find out he no longer attacked but defended. Waiting to respond didn't promise success only failure, a failure that could be permanent. While Sam sat puzzling about his next move or the strategy of his opponent, Los Zetas continued to make money that needed to be laundered in Las Vegas. Sam knew at least that much.

MATAMOROS

The drive north through Mexico usually passed uneventfully. Carrying forty tons of home appliances made by workers who earned less than ten dollars a day, a trailer full of washers and dryers headed to consumers in the US might signal to some that NAFTA had been a success. Trucks carrying consumer goods north received carte blanche treatment along the way from the Federales to insure timely delivery. Any trouble with Mexican authorities vanished in the face of packets of money. Like in many circumstances, the law of unintended consequences never seemed to be noticed until there were bad outcomes. Outcomes our leaders hadn't realized until now.

Job losses resulting when a Hoover plant closed in Canton, Ohio left a smaller negative footprint in the public eye and certainly less time on the evening news than the three tons of cocaine packed in the motor compartments of the appliances. The Department of Homeland Security and its arm ICE under the directive of the US Congress and George W. Bush had spent considerable time and money to build an impenetrable physical barrier at certain flow points along the Mexican border in an attempt to halt the movement of drugs and illegal immigrants.

Simultaneously, NAFTA had created a virtual endless train of tractor trailers moving north. So many that border crossings in an effort to be more efficient chose only a few carriers at random to inspect. After all, most ICE employees were busy driving along the fence.

This lucrative transportation system, *plazas* in cartel speak, financed in part by US taxes kept the drugs coming. Shipments of contraband that could not ever have been smuggled across the border now drove through the crossing at Brownsville-Matamoros with ease.

Although benefiting from the unintended largesse of the Americans, Los Zetas suffered from criminal problems common when one became too successful. First was, as always, what to do with so much money? Second, and nearly as important, how to protect one's business from pirates of the first order. Envy, greed, and mistrust are common traits among criminals. The same could be said for CEO's of major corporations.

The organization had taken steps to address the situation. Before the meetings like the one that had taken place at the Forteleza, internecine wars had nearly destroyed the cartels from within. Matamoros had been the flashpoint. The Tijuana and Gulf cartels had gotten the upper hand over the Sinaloa and Juarez cartels before a truce initiated by Zarilla allowed for cooperation among the four distinct groups. When the winners suggest negotiations most losers take the hint. His tactics then as now, ruthless and relentless, allowed José Jesús Dominguez to be El Padrino of the Los Zetas.

Zarilla had approached the problems as any well trained commander might. Airports, train stations, and major highways had eyes on them twenty-four/seven waiting for new faces that didn't belong. In order to have complete control over the city Zarilla made an offer to the police chief. Every day that the chief did not resign another policeman would be killed. As the total approached twenty, the chief resigned. Dominguez replaced him with one of the surviving cops already on his payroll.

Unlike the Mafia who avoided killing cops at all costs, being in law enforcement did not give one any additional protection from cartel killers. Zarilla issued orders that any attempt to interfere with his business by US agencies should be met with a full tactical response. The FBI got wind of this directive and notified the Mexican police and army. Late in 2008 three safe houses in the border town of Reynosa west of Matamoros yielded 540 rifles, 287 grenades, 2 shoulder rockets(LAW),

500,000 rounds of ammo, 67 ballistic vests and a case of dynamite. All US made, the weaponry had been purchased with the ill-gotten money gathered north of the border.

The difficulty of smuggling money south back to Mexico created the need for the laundering operation in Vegas. ICE had cracked down on southbound vehicles. Smuggling contraband *into* Mexico amounted to hiding in plain sight until an informant gave it away. Border Patrol agents found his body hanging from a cactus in the Sonoran Desert. DNA testing determined his identity and former gender.

At one time Zarilla had a safe house in Matamoros with forty kidnap victims held for ransom. All were family members of rival cartels. In one attempt to snag a teenage daughter, the father of the intended victim opened up on the Los Negros hit squad sent to grab her. The father employed by the Sinaloan faction, Los Negros by the Gulf crew, the opponents knew failure didn't pay. The shootout lasted forty minutes and included both shoulder and hand thrown artillery. These operations were aided in the fact that Dominguez could buy cell numbers and addresses from the local telephone companies used by his targets.

This powerful affiliation of military-trained personnel and all of the street people purchased to assist in human intel presented the greatest threat that Sam or the US government had faced in generations.

Zarilla had consolidated some of the most deadly sociopaths into an organization that rivaled the Chicago mob during prohibition. When gangsters stop killing one another and focus on others the authorities become overwhelmed. Only recently the authorities on the Mexican side had unearthed a killing field with hundreds of bodies. Most of them were mutilated before death. As we often forget, failure to remember the past causes one to repeat it.

The drug war has been going on for forty years yet we find ourselves in a 1920's Chicago déjà vu more deadly than the Roaring Twenties by a factor of one thousand. The same conditions that created Chicago on the northern border were now in play on the southern border. Smuggling is always a result of interfering with normal market forces i.e. extreme tariffs or illegality. The difference in severity solely a reflection of the lack of large amounts of official Canadian corruption compared to the Mexican version coupled with the modern criminals' absence of concern for killing anyone and everyone at anytime.

SAURIA AT THE VENETIAN

Sam grabbed his phone and called Wolfe. "Get over here. Bring a bottle of that bourbon you drink."

"Where's here?"

"Venetian at the Venezia tower. My boys will meet you at the elevator. The little guys built like jockeys. Third floor."

"Yeh, right."

The phone went dead. Sam had not ever called Wolfe in this manner. It sounded like a planning session, a meeting on how to eliminate killers before they wreaked their deadly dance on more innocents. Wolfe dropped his drink on the bar and headed out the door of Harrah's.

One arrived at the Venezia Tower by an elevator that only had one stop; the third floor. The two Varangian Vikings met Wolfe as the doors opened and escorted him directly to Sam's room. One guarded the six while the other opened the door only wide enough to allow Wolfe entry. Sam met him at the foyer with two glasses of ice in search of some bourbon. Rebelle poured them stiff.

Sam swallowed half the glass of Knob Creek, choked on it, and then motioned Wolfe down the steps into the well appointed sitting room with leather backed chairs and a full sectional couch in matching color.

"Nice digs, Sam. Apparently, I've been in the wrong line of work in my life. Should of gone government."

"Yeh , You might get shot one day but what the hell."

"I might get shot regardless. What's the deal?"

"The deal is we're getting our ass kicked. I can barely keep track of our ops in Vegas, a new face is hustling you at the Flamingo who we know nothing about, and then I get a flash message from DCIA and his boss Director of National Intelligence. The home team is losing.

As much as we have had them on the run here, our target is an organization as well organized as any military and more ruthless with untold mercenaries employed as well. Allow me to give you last month's scorecard, emphasizing this reflects the only the last thirty days, which I just received.

Twenty-six dead in Juarez, thirteen in Mexico City, ten in the state of Chihuahua, mostly Federales and citizens in Juarez, represent the tip of the problem. The authorities have a Mexican policeman's body sawed in half and placed in two separate Styrofoam coolers on the doorstep of his home. His high school daughter found it.

A tractor trailer full of frozen black tip sharks stumbled into a FDA inspection stop in El Paso. Four thousand kilos of cocaine in the body cavities of the fish represented twenty percent of the load. They wouldn't have been stopped but the manifest read sharks and one of the inspectors thought maybe they had endangered species. She counted the carcasses and did the math. The numbers didn't add up. They had endangered species alright, Americans who end up using the dope.

Six bodies were found in the trunk of a burning car in Tijuana. The bodies look like they may be American tourists. The cartel enforcement arm loves to dress up in policia uniforms and rob rich Anglos. Resistance of any amount is met with quick death if one is lucky. If you're unlucky, you end up like the suspected informant in Matamoros, they found his face sewed to a soccer ball the local kids were about to kick around the town square.

These are the people with whom we are fighting. One of the things you hate to do is to become your enemy. I'm getting that Gitmo feeling again." Sam finished the bourbon and poured him and Wolfe more.

"What do you need from me?"

"That's the problem Wolfe. I don't know.

"How's Daga? Our schedules aren't meshing lately."

"I know. She took out the chief idiot at the club. You can't go over there no matter what till it cools off. The other side has a new face in town and I don't think he's taking any prisoners. Therefore, we need to go on the hunt."

"Point me in the right direction."

"Go hang out with the little hottie. Don't trust her."

"Will do."

Wolfe left the suite, his steps down the hallway followed precisely by the eyes of the bodyguards. Sam poured the remainder of the whiskey in his glass and slumped in to the deep cushions of the sofa in near total resignation.

Sauria had always been successful throughout his career because of his belief that all problems were surmountable if one examined the situation relentlessly and through multiple prisms. What approach might not work in one occasion could very well be perfect for the next one.

This one however had become a conundrum of the first order. The area of operation struck Sam as more alien than if it were some two-bit dictator's backyard. He had operated in those theatres, he felt comfortable as the stranger in a strange land but Vegas like its games appeared unbeatable.

In the Third World, Sam could complete a mission, get on a plane or hire a driver, and be out of country before anyone suspected his whereabouts or activities. Here the spotlight shone more intensely and directly. Persons in authority usually gave their responsibilities the requisite amount of attention. Corruption and bribery made headlines.

If the media ever did its job and got wind of this op. who knows who would be sacrificed, figuratively or literally, in the name of national security. Fortunately for Sam, so far the journalists acted more like lap dogs to the politicians than any descendents of the Woodward-Bernstein gene pool.

As Sam fell further in to a feeling of hopelessness and Wolfe went looking for Anna Lee, Ernesto Cruz decided that he needed to find the puncture in the pipeline wherever it might be. He began his search at a point where a known problem existed.

XVI

The method of execution known as crucifixion served as testament to the imagination of humans in finding ways to destroy one another as cruelly as possible. Ernesto Cruz cherished these moments like others admired trophies of accomplishments or photos of special days. El Crucificador's *volunteer* sat before him bound and gagged in a plain metal folding chair. The eyes of the deer bright in the headlights of Cruz, the presenter began to speak to his audience. A group of employees scared and silent, thankful they had not been the target. If one hated meetings at work, this qualified as the worst.

Los Zetas employed hundreds of members of street gangs to do the dirty work. This particular one earned his street cred in MS-13 as a kidnapper and drug runner before moving up to a position with Los Mañosos, the arm suppliers for the cartel.

As commonly occurs, the man sitting in the chair in the center of the room had gotten greedy. Two thousand dollars a week didn't pay for his habits of women, cocaine, and poor gambling. He began to nibble at what did not belong to him. As any forensic accountant will tell you, cattle graze but pigs get slaughtered. The man became a pig.

What started as one M-4 assault weapon with two thousand rounds of ammo soon morphed into a case of rifles and one hundred thousand rounds. The man's bill had now come due and Ernesto intended to maximize the impression of his collection techniques on others who might consider such a risky route to wealth. Additional intel helpful with his larger problem might be gained as well.

Cruz's words flowed from his mouth slowly each syllable scraping the raw nerves of his audience as intended. The volunteer's eyes strained at their sockets as if trying to escape.

"As all of you can see, there is a cross mounted to the garage floor. It is known in Latin as a *decussata*, in the shape of an X. The Romans were very inventive in their use of the cross. A number of shapes existed. Like St. Peter I didn't feel that our friend deserved to die as El Salvador had suffered. After all, he is only a thief. I think."

The volunteer squirmed without benefit, causing Ernesto to be concerned that the man may die of shock before Cruz could enjoy himself.

"You see, the *Ingles* word for such pain, excruciating, comes from describing the suffering of the cross. The entire body weight is supported by the arms, shoulders and elbows fall out of place. It is in describing this process we get our word *en español,* insoportable. I hope the church goers out there are remembering their Latin.

With the rib cage stretched, the lungs cannot expand. Those finding themselves in this position would attempt to pull the body weight up and therefore cause more pressure on the upper limbs which resulted in additional pain. Eventually fatigue won out in spite of the pain and suffocation occurred.

Are there any questions before we begin the demonstration?"

Anyone in the room who in the past had trouble paying attention in class suddenly found themselves unable to do anything but be held in the grasp of this display. With the appropriate subject matter, anyone could be a good speaker. One should always remember his audience.

"Soldiers, please." With a nod of his head, four men came from the shadows dressed as Roman centurions. Ernesto did nothing without being vigilant of the details. They subdued the victim although not as easily as one might expect since he had been bound and gagged already.

The one to be crucified struggled vainly and eventually had been stretched across the X, bound not nailed. Nailing considered an unnecessary adornment, time constraints withstanding.

Ernesto approached the man. His gag had been removed. "Would you like *un trago* de tequila? I do not have any other sopor. I hope it is OK?" Ernesto poured most of the liquor down the man's face allowing just enough to be licked by the parched lips.

Cruz reached for an object on a nearby table. "This is a flagrum, a multi-strand whip with metal and bone shards attached. I do not want to use it. So I will ask only a few questions and depending on your answers you may live. That is an historical fact." It indeed was a fact that Romans had spared the lives of some of the crucified after the placations of relatives. It was not a fact that anything the man said would save his life.

"So far you are only a thief. But maybe you are a traitor. Convince me that I am wrong."

The fingers of the whip struck the man across the abdomen instantly opening wounds half a centimeter in depth. The blood flowed freely to the floor after first dividing in two equal streams down his legs. Cruz waited for the screaming to stop.

"Where is our money? Your entire family will die. What did you do with it?" The lash struck home again and again. The crucified never made any noise other than those associated with anguish. The word *no* repeatedly mouthed but never uttered.

Minutes passed and no better outcome resulted. Cruz had finished for the evening.

"Take his body out in the desert. Make sure you use enough lye. We don't want to make it easy on the CSI crew. If any of you know anything, contact me through Gordo at the club. Adios". He meant it.

"I don't think he is dead yet." As the words left the mouth of one of the men dressed as centurions, he wished he could grab the syllables before they reached the ears of El Crucidor.

"You may babysit him if you wish or lessen his pain with an early death. Regardless, bury him in sufficient lye, dead or alive."

A warm feeling washed over Ernesto Cruz. Though he could never be absolutely sure, any other employees contemplating theft no longer considered it and those guilty of it had recently decided to stop. Most humans innately understand risk versus reward and those that don't exemplify selective evolution. They die prematurely.

Unfortunately, no additional information had been forthcoming. Somewhere there was a leak and he had to find it before this treasure ship sank taking him down with it.

AMAZON ROOM WSOP

Wolfe had decided to find China Doll by allowing her to find him. If she showed up here, then she had been following him longer than he knew although how he would have missed her he couldn't guess. Rebelle showed his ticket and his ID to the dealer and settled in his chair. Another $1500 buy-in No Limit event hopefully would attract some of the same Latinos.

Before he could count his tournament chips Tommy Cho came in the room. He noticed Wolfe straight away and came over to his table.

"What's up dude? I just bought in with some of that 10K I made. I'd love to get a bracelet."

"Me too. Not to mention an easy buy-in for the main event."

"I'd rather have the bracelet."

"Everybody says that but you go in a pawn shop in Vegas and what do you find? WSOP bracelets. Gamblers are always looking for a free roll."

"Well good luck. I hope I beat you heads up at the final table."

"If we get heads up we can chop. You get the title and bracelet and I get first and second place money minus your buy-in."

"I need more than that, man."

"Like I said. Good luck."

Three hours of dead cards later and one unsuccessful all-in, Wolfe made his way back towards the main casino. On his way out he noticed Tommy still playing.

As he passed one of the benches that lined the hallway, China Doll stood up and hooked her arm in his.

"Going my way?"

"I see you're working the tournament. Please tell me you're not one of those floozies that hang around the final table hoping to help someone celebrate who just won a pocket full of money."

"You know the name Willie Sutton?"

"I'm surprised that you do but maybe not. He was the bank robber that when asked why he robbed banks he said 'that's where the money is'. That guy?"

"Yes him."

"Sorry. He denied saying it. Said it came from the reporter. Like political news. You know, make it up if it sells."

"Still a good rule to go by. They even teach it in accounting. If you're trying to cut costs go where the largest expenditures are. What business do I have hanging at Circus Circus trying to snag some salesman with three kids whose gambling with the mortgage and an overdrawn credit card?"

"Which brings you to me."

"No, no. You're different."

"Bet you never say that to anyone."

"Wolfe why are you so cynical?"

"I just read the cards. The world is cynical. It's not complicated. Tell you what. Let's go up to the Diamond Lounge and you can tell me about yourself over a few drinks."

"Don't take advantage of me."

"Wow, you don't stop do you?"

The pair caught the private elevator up to the bar and settled in on the sofas overlooking the topless pool, the skin all part of the Vegas experience. She ordered Stoli orange and OJ, Rebelle got a Woodford Reserve bourbon.

"OK. Tell me about yourself. Where you were raised. Where you went to school. The basics."

"And you need this information why?"

"I prefer living. Is that a good enough reason? You came to me. Not once but twice now. Convince me"

"Okay. Here goes. My parents raised me in LA. I'm a Chinese citizen. My father worked as the Science and Technology liaison at the Chinese consulate."

"He stole industrial secrets most likely aeronautics."

"Good guess."

'Not really. Go ahead."

"When the FBI closed the net, he left with diplomatic immunity. I stayed behind. I like being an American."

"What did he think of that?"

"Not happy."

"So to really piss him off, you became a high priced call girl? When they write these cover stories, they should try to be more imaginative."

"It's the truth. I can't change it to meet your expectations. I gave up my inheritance to stay here."

"Your education?"

"Hollywood High then UCLA. Languages and computer technology."

"How convenient."

"For what?"

"If you wanted to be a spy."

"Spies don't work on their backs."

"Some do."

"Not the operators with black passports."

There she went again. First Leopardos and now she mentioned the color of diplomatic passports. How many people know that fact besides high level government employees? Is she working a false flag op? Wolfe decided to do what he always did when he couldn't be sure of something. Step back and take another look. Play along like a fish hooked but waiting to breakaway at an opportune time.

"What can I do for you?"

"If I can help what you're doing, can you get me in the witness protection program when it's all over? I'm so tired of old men with bad breath and too much cologne. Not to mention my new employers might decide to get rid of me just for good measure."

"I have a friend who I can ask. I don't make promises."

"I understand. What do I do first?"

"Nothing different. When I need you I'll tell you. Changes make suspicion."

"Do you want to go back to my place now?"

"Sure." Wolfe chuckled to himself. The things he did for his country.

XVII

TOMMY CHO'S WIPEOUT

Tommy hadn't made it to the final table but 29K would cover his other bad habits for awhile. Cho, a 100% SoCal kid, did what most male natives of The Eureka state would do if they found some extra cash in Vegas. He went to a strip club. He chose one out of the phonebook, the one with the funny name; Chocho Rosado. Raised at the beach, bare chochos and chichis were considered an inalienable right.

A taxi dropped him at the front door and a missing link posing as a human collected the twenty-five dollar door charge, three drink minimum on top. Cho soon found himself enveloped in various sizes and shapes of breasts as he waved Benjamins around like buy-sell orders at the New York Stock Exchange. Cheyenne finished on stage and noticed the commotion. She managed to get close enough to be noticed and Tommy waved her over.

"*Aren't you* a coochie mama. What's your name?"

"Chey."

"I don't think so."

"No, Chey as in Cheyenne."

"Seriously dude. That's your real name?"

"Do I look like a dude to you? I'll prove it to you for a hundred dollars if you don't believe me."

"I'd rather spend a hundred watching you prove you're female. Get naked. Go for it."

Cho stuffed a bill in her top and settled in to his chair for the show. The drinks were arriving in regular intervals faster than anyone's liver could metabolize the alcohol. That's when Tommy started talking.

He pulled another dancer onto his lap and proceeded to brag to her about his money and how he spent it. Then he started talking about Wolfe. Cheyenne had finished but she lingered nearby listening without appearing to be listening. It always amazed her things people say when she had her back turned towards them as if her ears no longer functioned when she's faced away from the speaker. Not that Cho worried about being heard but most people will say all sorts of crazy things if they think only one person can hear the conversation. Tommy had become the only inhabitant of Planet Cho.

"Check this out. There's this dude I met at the Venetian. I think he's in his thirties. Kinda laid back for an old dude. He paid me to keep an eye on these gangstas. He's got a cool handle; Wolfe. Anyways, I parlayed the grand he paid me into twenty-nine grand playing poker and I need someone to help me spend it. You think we could hang out when you get off. Maybe do the horizontal bop?"

The girl in Cho's lap had very green eyes, a personal characteristic especially rare for a Latina. Maria Lopez's rent came due tomorrow. She had planned on being late again. Every strip club has a few, dancers who work off premises. Sometimes it's only stripping. Depending on the financial circumstances of the customer and the needs of the girl it may progress to prostitution.

Jaguar hated herself but she wanted the money more. She literally would do almost anything for her child. After three minutes of batting her eyelashes and rubbing her chichis on Tommy's head, she agreed to meet Cho at the Palms for a drink at the Ghost Bar. Gordo, standing in the shadows, had heard the entire conversation.

Cheyenne called Sam as soon as she and Daga got off work. "Sam I think Wolfe is in danger."

Sam rubbed the sleep out of eyes. "What happened? Is he hurt?"

"No, it's not like that. Some guy came in the club tonight running his mouth. Said Wolfe paid him to keep an eye on some LA gangsters. Gordo, the fat one, overheard the conversation and seemed very interested. That of course makes Daga a problem as well."

"Well we already talked about Daga. You and she are virtual conjoined twins. Rebelle's been told to stay away from the club. We know he's under surveillance and he and I are working on it. Not much we can do. Gordo is by now talking to someone I'm sure. Keep your head down and keep me posted."

"Will do."

Tommy Cho got to the Palms and hour earlier than the agreed upon appointment with Jaguar. He killed a little time at the blackjack tables located barely inside the main entrance. He didn't make any money and then went upstairs to the Playboy Casino on the second floor. The dealers were stunning but not any better at giving him winning cards. He hesitated to play poker because it required more time. As he came down the steps to the main casino, Jaguar popped in the front door. She wore what she thought would allow her to charge the maximum hourly rate for her company.

A single piece of cloth made of green silk the color of flawless jade started over her right shoulder and began to wrap itself around her curves. Except for a keyhole opening at her cleavage which showed the medial borders of her firm modest breasts, she had wrapped herself as a present for Tommy. Cho suddenly believed in Christmas.

Tommy almost tripped and fell on the final step as he looked up and saw the emerald eyes of Jaguar before moving his glance down her body to appreciate the dress and the shape it complimented. His clumsiness caught her attention. She sashayed over to Cho as her black stiletto pumps clicked on the polished tile counting down the seconds in Tommy's head until he could embrace her. Even as she fought to hide her true emotions from those who might see, she played well the part of one who enjoyed her vocation.

"How's my little kitten? You know it's the Year of the Tiger?" Tommy couldn't believe his good fortune.

"How about some cat nip before you try to get me to purr."

"Sounds great. Let's go up to the Ghost Bar. Ever been?"

"No. Should be a great view."

"It is. So is the club."

One gained access to the Ghost Bar via an express elevator that only stopped at the top of the house. A man the size of an offensive lineman waved Jaguar and Cho past the cordoned entrance to the elevator. All of Tommy's poker play had earned him VIP treatment at most clubs in town. The line for others twisted fifty yards back through the casino. Filled with beautiful people, more women than men, most males had dates that weren't their wives or were new found girlfriends while the unescorted women were looking for high rollers who might need some company. Jaguar fit the profile.

The elevator doors opened treating the passengers to an invigorating panorama of the Vegas skyline fifty-five floors above Flamingo Road. Bathed in soft blue light reminiscent of similar colors that are found in the palette of South Beach art deco, white lounges and sectionals dotted the floor inside at the bar proper.

As one continued toward the inspiring view first seen, the floor became a patio for outdoor partying. The DJ kept the beat going with rap dominating the selections. Railings four feet high kept any over eager Angelinos with too much of daddy's money to spend from taking a face plant.

"What do you think? Cool?"

"Yeh. Very. Give me some money and I'll go get us some drinks. Chicks always get waited on faster."

"Yeh, no shit. Let me have a Jaeger bomb."

Jaguar got up to go to the bar and Tommy stood to go over to the glass panel positioned in the floor that allowed one to

look fifty-five floors straight down. The unique feature mesmerized a few people while causing light dizziness in others.

Jaguar caught the eye of a bartender and made her order.
She turned to look around the club when uncontrolled female
screaming filled the space. Everyone shuffled toward the outdoor dance floor and many were leaning over the railing to see
something. Small groups of people huddled among themselves
and mostly females hid their faces. Jaguar paid for the drinks
and then more disruption began. Huge security types ran in
the bar from the elevator lobby. Soon they were pushing clientele back toward the entrance. Jaguar looked for Tommy but
couldn't see over the crowd.

She bumped in to another girl standing alone. "Hey, what
the hell is going on?"

"I think somebody jumped."

"Jumped? Like suicide? Did you see it?"

"I was right there. I didn't see shit. I just heard someone
say it. That's when I bent over and looked."

"How do they know it was suicide?"

"I don't know. It just kind of happened."

"What did the person look like?"

"I heard it's a young Asian guy. Black on black clothes."

Jaguar got that strange feeling in her gut which usually
meant her night just got terrible. She still hadn't seen Cho.
With her head on a swivel as she waited her turn to take the
elevator, a set of hands grabbed her from behind at the waist.

"That was fucked up." Tommy visibly shook in his shoes as
Jaguar craned her neck to see him.

"What the hell went down? I couldn't find you."

"I don't really know, dude. You left to get the drinks and
I got up from my seat. Some other guy sat down as I left but
space wasn't a problem so I was down with it. I checked out the
viewing glass and all of a sudden I heard screams. Very cree-
pazoid. Then after the initial shock I go over and look down
and the body on the pavement is dressed in all black like me.
Then I hear somebody say the leaper was Asian. Double cree-

pazoid. Let's get off this carnival ride. I want a refund for this spook house. I'm ready for something normal like sex with a hot chick."

"You're still in the mood?"

"Hell yeah mamacita. I'm ready for the tangled tango."

"It's going to cost you."

"No kidding. Free is the biggest bullshit word in the English language."

Tommy and his date caught a cab at the front entrance to the Palms and if Cho had his way he'd be a little poorer and a lot happier by the end of the night.

ANNA LEE'S DOLLHOUSE

Wolfe found himself sitting on a red love seat the back of which very much resembled silicone injected pursed female lips, a designer's caricature of Botox bimbos. China Doll inhabited a chair shaped like an oversize version of a woman's pump covered in purple velvet. Her nicely shaped bum fell deeply into the chair as a foot might with a well-fitted shoe. Her bare feet alternatively pointing to and fro then back to Wolfe keeping time to a melody only she could hear. He felt surrounded and outnumbered by her and her gal crew of furnishings.

"Would you like some wine?"

"Sure." Rebelle's index finger went to his lips in the universal sign of *be quiet*. "I'll turn on some music." Rebelle found some Wagner and cranked the volume to maximum. Anna started to protest but Wolfe signaled silence again.

He walked to the sink and turned on the faucets. He placed a cast iron skillet below the stream of water creating a sound like rain on a tin roof. He grabbed China Doll and moved her near the wall speakers. "Now we can talk. There's no reason to believe that your apartment isn't bugged. These guys pay attention to details."

"Okay. Okay. But I don't think so."

"You're not supposed to. Listen. You're a very beautiful woman. You've got yourself in a pickle. You won't get out by seducing me. What we need from you is to feed them misinformation. Incorrect information from a valued source if suspected of being worthless but unable to be determined as to its veracity can freeze a spy agency with a trillion dollar a year budget. Think Aldrich Ames."

"I don't know who that is."

"He ran the Soviet Union desk for the CIA during the Cold War. Sometimes he fed us good information. Sometimes he didn't. He personally ruined over one hundred CIA ops."

"I need to know this why?"

"Because if you were telling me the truth earlier today then you want to be a double agent as well, in an effort to be an agent supposedly trying to help my cause. This we shall soon find out. A word of caution. Being a double agent does not promote trust or spending time with one's grandchildren. I will do everything I can to protect you but if we find out that you are working both sides your final disposition is over my pay grade. Are we clear?"

"Agreed, I guess. Now how about some fun?" As Anna Lee began to peel clothing, Wolfe shut off the faucet and turned down the music. Rebelle made it to the door before China Doll could stop him.

"Thanks." One last shout-out to the microphones just in case anyone had been listening.

CARTEL SAFE HOUSE

Ernesto sat on the deck smoking an Arturo Fuentes maduro torpedo. "OK, fat boy. You think we got him? What does that mean?"

"Flat as a tortilla. Our guys said he fit the description. He entered the club with the puta from Chochos." Gordo's shirt dripped sweat onto the back of his hands and then finally on to the hardwood.

"Do you have any idea how many Asian hombres are in that club at any one time? If that piece of shit pops back up the two pendejos that did the job are your responsibility. You will get one more chance. Then you can join them?"

"Si, si, I understand. I will not fail again if needed."

"I know. By the way, how is your family? Your two niñas?"

On a desert evening where the ambient temperature reached well into the nineties early in the morning hours, midnight more of a memory than a time marker in Vegas, Gordo shivered even as his shirt soaked him through and through with his own fear.

Cruz continued. "Send some people for the girl. I want her able to talk. Whoever grabs her can have her when I am finished. Bring her to me. Go. Oh, by the way, one of my sets of eyes saw the girl leaving The Palms with an Asian male."

Gordo turned and hurried from the house, his shoes making sounds like wet sandals at the pool.

Maria Lopez checked on her little girl. Curled in a fetal position sucking her thumb, the baby child meant everything to Jaguar. Her precious niña always the one thing she had done right in this life. Her birth, given by God as a gift to Maria, occurred in what she thought a divine manner. She got back to her apartment after leaving Tommy Cho, paid the neighbor for babysitting and now enjoyed being home and finished with the evening. She cracked a Sol beer and thought about all the events of the day.

The door burst open in a shotgun blast of metal hinges and wood splinters the only thing not seen or smelled being the actual cordite. Two members of MS-13 holding a police issued door entry ram encompassed the entire space at the kitchen-living room junction. The muscle grabbed Maria and her child. The leverage that a threat on a baby could provide did not have an equal. Momma would talk freely to save her offspring.

The door to Cruz's private elevator slid open and Jaguar tumbled to the hard cold tile. Perhaps a preview of what awaited her. The baby screamed siren-like in a vain attempt to find its mother's arms. The muscle held her at arm length. Ernesto couldn't stand the sound of screaming babies.

"Enough. Let her have the baby. Wait in the other room."

Maria grabbed the child from the large arms that held her and collapsed back to the floor holding the baby close to her chest. She looked up at Ernesto. He stood motionless and without expression waiting for her to quiet the crying niña.

"Thank you. Thank you. They wouldn't let me have her."

Ernesto stared back silently. Now in possession of her dearest creation Maria's situation became clear. Clear in a manner she hadn't considered.

"What do you want? I don't know you. I haven't done anything."

"You have information that I desire. If you provide it without withholding important details I will take care of you."

"What information do I have? I know no one. I work. I go home. I take care of my baby?"

"Perhaps you know more than you think. Please take a seat. Would you like something to drink?" Maria crawled onto the sofa hiding her baby's face with her hand as if to shield it from evil. One of the men appeared instantly and poured two Chinaco Negro tequilas, no ice.

Cruz handed one to Jaguar. Like any good stripper she could handle her liquor even while holding her baby. Ernesto played the good cop routine even as he wrestled in his mind to decide which final methods he would use for his own enjoyment.

One drink down and another to replace it, Cruz began the questioning. Funny thing, the CIA had spent millions in the 1950's to discover a truth serum and the best one already existed; alcohol.

"You were at the Palms tonight with a young Asian man." A statement not a question, the inflection of the voice suggested as much. "Why? Who is he?"

"I was on a working date. I know him only as Tommy. He's from SoCal living here. He's plays poker. That is all I know about him."

"You're a hooker. I see." A small smile came to Ernesto's face. Knowing that she hooked and stripped helped him decide what to do with her. "What did he tell you about a friend he had met? Someone wanted him to keep an eye on people?"

"Yeh, he bragged about making a lot of money at poker and meeting this gringo who did some kind of following people around. Like a private detective. Wanted Tommy to help. Said it would be easy."

"Did he mention a name? Where he worked?"

"Tommy said he met the guy at the Venetian Poker room. Said he was older than Tommy."

"So this Tommy, he decided to help?"

"Yeh. Said all he had to do was play poker and keep an eye on some Latinos. Keep track of how many."

"What kind of Latinos?"

"I don't know. I figured some gangbangers."

"You have been very helpful."

"Can I go now?"

"Not just yet. But I promise you'll be gone before the morning light."

The two thugs entered the room. One tore the sleeping baby from Maria's grasp while the other pushed her back down into the cushion and in a single motion practiced over time sealed her protests with a strip of duct tape. Her eyes seemed to be escaping her skull as she tried to follow the child's whereabouts and resist as well. A few more sections of tape later and she lay bound with her hands behind her and her feet crossed on the sofa.

Cruz began to spread plastic sheeting on the floor. The cruelest death is often the one that is anticipated not instant. Maria had no false allusions concerning her fate. Like most mothers, her mind wandered to her child, even as the two men constructed El Crucidor's 'X' in the middle of the room.

A few hours later and the entertainment complete, Maria Lopez began her final journey. The open sands of the desert awaited her as it had many before her. No one would report her missing, just another stripper gone wild. The landlord would cuss her when the rent did not appear while maggots and scorpions feasted on her remains. The child would be gone as well. The assumption when garbage men found the body in the dumpster that another meth head momma had killed her baby.

Behind the bright lights of the strip, describing Vegas amounted to using words synonymous with death and despair covered in an abundance of greed. Yet fresh dupes arrived every day. Incomprehensible to those entrusted to making Vegas inhabitable, the cartels had upped the ante in the highest stakes game in town.

XVIII

SAM'S SUITE

"Please introduce me, Wolfe. I'm dying to meet your new friend." Sam had relented in allowing Rebelle to bring Tommy Cho there. It represented a complete break in security procedures but Wolfe's plaintive tone had convinced him.

Tommy didn't wait for the introduction. "Dude, I'm Tommy Cho. I'm the one the bangers tried to kill. I mean I'm all laid back chilling with this mamacita and bodies start doing the cannonball dive from fifty-five floors up minus the wet part."

"Only one body, Tommy." Wolfe corrected. "He's a little excited, Sam."

"How do you know they were trying to kill you?"

"Dude. We were like twins. You know, we all look alike to people from the brown and white bread factory. People ask me if I'm Japanese. What are they smoking? They got the wrong guy."

"It could be only a coincidence." Sam, like all employees of OGA's, Other Government Agencies, had been trained to never except something as a coincidence although the suggestion often worked with civilians. If one made three stops during the day and the same car appeared in the rear view mirror or the parking lot assuming it was random seldom turned out well for the one who might have been followed.

"Well, unless he was doing what I was doing, they fucked up the burrito."

"Yes, Wolfe explained you were helping but not really. I mean, you told him what? A few more Latinos playing poker?"

"I've been bouncing that board off a few curls and I remembered something. I had a few drinks at a strip club and...."

"Which one?"

"Oh, it had a massive cool name. Chocho Rosado. Pink pussy. Is that killer or what? Right on the street. Nobody says nada. You can't throw f-bombs at poker tables but pink pussy right on the highway and the school busses go by every day full of Spanish-speaking kids."

Sam glanced at Rebelle and Cho caught the look.

"What? What? I went in some mob joint? I thought Vegas was over all that backwash. Just another bad movie."

"You were saying? You went in this club?"

"Yeh, I took the money Wolfe gave me and ran it up to 29K. So I went partying and my mouth got out ahead of the break. Crash and burn, hey wait a second. You guys aren't a bunch of kooks are you? Do I need to take the doggy door out of this mess?"

"What did you just say?"

"Sam, he wants to know if we are fuckups. Does he need to exit immediately?"

"Thanks for the translation, Wolfe." Sam squirmed in his seat. He thought they taught English in California.

"Hey dude, don't be a hater." Tommy glanced from Sam to Rebelle. "Wolfe, if this is not cool.....

"Relax Tommy. You probably should take the Boulder Highway out to US95 down to Interstate 10 at Blythe and then over. I know it's longer but just in case they're sitting on Interstate 15."

"What? They know my ride? What am I, seafood? How do I make a living?"

"Tommy, you know and I know there are poker rooms all over Cali."

"Yeh, I'll play great looking over my shoulder waiting for some natural born killer to blow my brains out."

"You watch too many movies."

"I'm from California dude. What do you expect?"

ANNIE LEE'S

Ernesto knocked on the door. China Doll peeked through the lens, exhaled, and opened the portal. The curtains separated to begin the performance. Ernesto pushed his way past her and settled on the sofa.

"You had a visitor?"

"Yes, yes, the American. The one you wanted me to watch."

"Convenient."

"He knows nothing. He's only a whore monger. His girlfriend is a stripper. That's how I got him here."

"We may need you to bring him to a location in the future."

"I have him wrapped around my finger. He's like most men. Only one thing guides him."

"Make sure he keeps you on the menu. We need information and in spite of what you think he or his girlfriend knows something. We'll be in touch." Before China Doll could reach the door, Cruz let himself out. He had his answer.

Annie Lee stood in the middle of the room and tried to quiet her heart beat. She felt like she had passed the test. Only one person would be giving the grade and failure equaled death, a slow death.

CHOCHO

"Have you seen Jaguar?" Cheyenne pulled on her war bonnet. The leather thong always went on last.

"How would I know? I'm not her papa." Gordo liked to hang around the dressing room for cheap peeks. One would think that he'd seen enough on the floor.

"Are you still the jefe?"

"I guess. Carlos took off."

"If you see Jaguar let me know. Now go do something useful."

"If I get this job permanently you're out of here."

"If you lose a hundred pounds you won't be fat. Fuck you."
Gordo shuffled out the door like a dog whipped with a newspaper, so much for macho.

Daga came out of the head. "Is he gone?"

"Yeh, what an asshole."

"No idea what happened to Jaguar?"

"I know she needed the money for her kid. She wouldn't
leave unless she had a better gig. Why? Do you think they did
something to her?"

"No idea. Sam will tell us. Let's go take their money."

Cheyenne and Daga left the dressing room. Ernesto Cruz
sat on the corner stool at the bar watching. Part of his job in
working for the cartel concerned intel, human intel. He liked
to say he could smell a rat in a sewer. To his eyes, very distinctive were the silent characteristics of a snitch.

"What's the deal with those two?" Cruz stared at Bobo and
then motioned his head in the direction of Daga and Chey. In
spite of the body heat in the room, cold described his particular spot at the rail.

"The two chicas? I think they're attached."

"You trust them?"

"I don't trust any of these putas. The Indian one is an idiot."

"And the mixto?" Mixto referred to Daga's mixed heritage.

"Not a lot of words. Makes a lot of money. I'd like to show
her mi capullo."

"Why? So she can laugh? Where's her boyfriend?"

"He doesn't come around so much anymore."

Cruz got up and walked over to Daga. "When you're done
come see me at the bar."

"Who are you?"

"Your boss."

"I don't think so. Gordo's the jefe. I pay to work here and
I make the owners plenty of money."

"He got a demotion. If you don't want to have a bad day,
I'll be at the bar." Ernesto turned and walked back to his seat.

"Cheyenne. The guy at the bar wants to talk to me. Says he's our boss. Keep an eye on me. If I give you the high sign, come over and interfere with his game plan if he has one."

Daga fingered her friend faithfully taped to her upper back beneath her hair. Maybe this guy was stupid too. She sauntered over to the bar taking her time in her classic passive resistant behavior when confronted by authority. "How may I be of help?" Daga's ability to be sarcastic oozed between the two.

"Gordo tells me you have a boyfriend?"

Daga stared at Ernesto. What she saw touched a warning button somewhere in her reptilian brain. She fought the reflex to fight or run. She turned to the bartender. "Gordo get me a Cruzan dark rum with soda water and lime." She did not look back at Cruz until she had her drink in hand. A stage prop always helped.

"On again, off again. Right now I'm with Cheyenne."

"He must like that. Why doesn't he come around?"

"WSOP and cash games. Plenty of them this time of year. He's busy."

"Tell him he's welcome here."

"Thanks. Sorry about earlier. I trust very few people. I'm Daga."

She extended her hand. Ernesto's skin felt like cold vinyl. A small portion of a Santa Muerte tattoo peeked beneath his cuff.

"I understand you got some red hot chili pepper in your blood but I'm on your side. Go make some money."

Daga turned and sashayed over to a cocktail table. Three minutes later guys were handing her money.

MOJAVE

Sam had enjoyed snakes since his childhood. His CIA field name literally translated to Sam Lizard. With his two guards accompanying him but at what they considered a safe distance, not for him but for themselves, Sam had a snake hook and collection bag looking for some of the local inhabitants. The guards preferred human targets. Something they understood.

The Vegas area provided habitat for a large number of reptiles, all of them cold-blooded but some walked upright on two feet. It occurred to Sam that the targets of his searches were all venomous snakes and lizards regardless if they crawled out of a desert hole or sat at a bar. Sam preferred the ones living under rocks. They were more predictable.

Today halfway up Mount Charleston which ringed the west side of the valley, he searched for two particular species. The sidewinder or horned rattler and the Mojave green. Each had attributes which he would find helpful in the near future.

The sidewinder with its two protrusions on either side of its head and exotic motions through the sand provided the element of terror. The Mojave green, smaller and seemingly less dangerous, carried some of the most potent venom in the US. It provided the coup de grace.

In an arroyo shaded on the east bank by the sun's early position the distinct S-curves through the sand led Sauria to an outcropping. Protected from the direct rays of the sun, the area beneath the small ledge made an ideal habitat for any animal escaping the intense heat of the desert. As he approached, the distinct sounds of a mature rattle permeated the relative silence of the wilderness. His Varangian guards pulled their guns.

"Put the weapons away. I want it alive. I can see her. She must have just given birth. No eggs from these snakes. It's into the breach straightaway for these little buggers."

The two men holstered the handguns and rolled their eyes on cue. The thought of riding back to town with this pissed off momma in a bag in the back of the SUV didn't seem like a good day. One of the men ventured a question.

"Hey boss. What are you going to do with that thing?"

"Are you trying to angle for an assignment in DC? You don't really want to testify before the Intelligence committee, do you?"

The guard and his companion fell silent except for the kicking of stones while Sam wrangled the snake. Testifying before Congress usually got one a security assignment guarding the front door of CIA headquarters in Langley with Barney Fife as one's partner and a bad uniform.

One snake down and one to go would complete Sam's hunt. Green snakes as one might imagine inhabited the sparse areas of the desert with a limited growth of greenery. In a low point where the water collected for a few days on the rare occasions of rain, Sam found his other friend. He now had the tools he needed.

Riding back down into the valley, Sam considered the details for his use of the snakes. If this didn't bring Zarilla out of his fortress more extreme measures would be needed. How excessive did Sam plan on being? To himself, he had one goal, reach into Mexico City and grab Dominguez without the target knowing that he had been grabbed. The objective would deliver himself to the lion's den. Any method required to make this happen qualified as acceptable. The gloves were off. Sam pondered the possibilities.

Before they reached the suite, Sam called Cheyenne. "You awake?"

"I guess. What's up?"

"Still working on how to roust my target. I think he needs some more motivation. You got anything to report?"

"Yeh, a new guy. I got his name. Goes by Ernesto. Says he the boss. I guess Gordo qualifies as a temp. He rattled Daga. She said he seemed kinda dangerous and you know she's no sissy."

"Put Daga on."

A few seconds of sounds passed as Cheyenne woke Daga and told her Sam wanted to talk. The moaning and cussing that invariably followed only what Sam expected. Daga picked up the receiver.

"Yeh, Sam."

"What's with the hibernation?

"What do you expect? I work till three and I haven't had sex with Wolfe for a week. That's like dog years for us."

"Poor baby. Tell me about this new guy."

"Empty eyes, that's what I remember, the kind of eyes that can put you in the ground in pieces and be eating a rare hamburger two minutes later. Had a tattoo as well. A Santa Muerte on his forearm ringed with tear drops. I couldn't see how many drops but the ones I saw were at least eight and I'm thinking there were more."

Sam understood. Each tear drop equaled a kill like the Wild West version of notches in the pistol grip. If the new player had that many he most certainly had been and might be a chief enforcer.

"Good eye. Don't you or Cheyenne go anywhere alone with him. No matter what information you think you can gain. If he gets pissed off make space. Put Cheyenne back on."

Daga handed the phone back to Chey and cocooned herself into the duvet.

"Chey here."

"OK. Here's the deal. I want Gordo. With him out of the picture it'll force the new guy's hand. I'll run a computer search for that tattoo and body location. See if he's ever been a guest of the US government. Meanwhile, you entice the fat boy. I don't care if it's you or Daga or both. Use the usual honey pot gambit. Rent a room at the Summer Sunset Motel near the convention center. Call me when you have him there."

"What kind of place is that?"

"The kind crackheads and conventioneers rent by the hour."

"You want him alive?"

Of course, I want him alive. I need information."

"Can we have some fun with him?"

"You can have some fun but don't overdo anything."

"What do you have planned?"

"You ever see that show *Venom in Vegas?*"

"Yeh. I walked by it one day down on the strip. Why?"

"Nothing. You're not afraid of snakes are you?"

"Depends what they are attached to."

"These are attached to fangs and venom sacs, Wonder Woman.

"Sam, you're showing your age."

"You're showing your butt. A nice one at that. Kinda wasted on me. Save it for a guy who can do something about it."

"I've got one picked out."

"What? A guy or an ass?"

"Both."

"There's hope for me still."

XIX

CONVENTION CENTER DRIVE

Sam entered the room. No doubt the paint on the wall had seen births, deaths, and the top five felonies in the Nevada Revised code. A small bathroom to the right greeted one entering the space with its odor before it could be noticed with one's eyes. On the far wall although in this case far served accurately only in a relative perspective, yellowed curtains once white now stained with nicotine framed the windows. Brown polka dots of blood splatter, the maid's bleach ineffective in their removal, added a strange depth to the pea green walls. A second door leading directly to the parking lot completed the picture.

Sauria turned and secured the door. This required three different mechanisms in addition to the metal plate added by management to prevent uninvited guests with lock picking skills. Chey and Daga sat on the edge of the bed watching TV. Gordo took up the remaining area of the mattress. He didn't look as relaxed as the girls. Sam sat his bags on the floor. A brief rattle emanating from the one canvas sack harmonized briefly with the background noise of the program.

"You don't look comfortable. Maybe I can help." Sam didn't move. The fat one had been strapped on his back, spread eagle on the bed, naked with a ball gag in place. A blindfold completed his helplessness. Animal noises along with drool were all Gordo could muster.

"Now ladies, you didn't do anything to hurt our friend did you?"

"No Sam, not at all. He said let's get our swerve on. Well, he got us. I think there might have been some confusion on the part of the consumer. We asked him if he wanted to party with us and he said yes. Maybe he should have asked more questions."

"Well Chey let's find out if he can help himself." Sam approached the fat one. "Señor Gordo. I'm going to remove your gag. If anything but answers come out of your mouth I will replace the gag and attempt other methods for achieving what I need. Nod yes if this is agreeable." Sam's voice oozed control but in a soft tone. The intention of which is to give the captive hope of survival. It makes the victim imagine that perhaps someone normal has arrived. This desperate grasping at ethereal handholds to pull oneself from the abyss is precisely the intended purpose.

Sam removed the gag not the blindfold. What a person in this submissive situation could imagine without being able to see always would be worse than the actual sight. Gordo's mind flashed back to some of the cartel interrogations he had seen just as Sauria expected. The personal terror level for Gordo presently moved to red.

"Who is the new boss?"

"I don't know"

"That's not a very promising start. I can replace the gag and leave you with my tigresses?"

"Please! Pretty please! That would be perfect for our birthday presents." Daga played the part well.

"I don't know. He came to town after our other guy took off. He's from Mexico City."

"And a member of what gang?"

"I don't know about any gang."

"Daga, you might get your wish." Sam turned back to Gordo. "You are covered in gang tats, Hermanos Pistoleros, and you give me that answer? Please do not waste my time. Tell me what you think and I'll decide if it's possible or bullshit. Now, the new boss, what gang? Is he a Los Zetas?"

"I think he started in Tijuana. He's got that kind of accent. You know, spanglish when he forgets to hide it."

"Now we are making progress. Very good my friend. And his role here in Vegas?"

"I think we have a leak. Money went missing. Mucho dinero. He's here to plug it."

"His name? Not his handle, his name."

"Ernesto Cruz. I think he's like a troubleshooter."

"Excellent, my fat friend. OK, ladies you can go. Thank you for your help. Use the back door. The security camera is on the blink."

"Gotcha. See you Sam."

Until that moment Gordo thought he had a chance. But when the mixto bitch said his interrogator's name even if it were a cover, he knew the jig was up. Sam watched him struggle against his bindings until he reached exhaustion.

Sam removed the blindfold. Eyes stared back at him protruding as if they were eggs in a carton. Sauria reached for a bag. The rattle responded in kind. Carefully, gently, Sam placed the sidewinder on the bed. He watched as the serpent whipped its body along the mattress until it snuggled tightly against the warm body of Gordo at the armpit. Not surprisingly, the fat one lay frozen in a sculpture of fear. He tried not to breathe but of course found it soon impossible. Then the coughing reflex seemed to arise in his throat. He held back as best he could and like a confluence of two events that seemed perfectly timed depending on one's point of view, he sneezed and coughed. The strike would not have been seen with the human eye.

The fat one writhed in terror and pain while another dose of venom entered his system prompted by the thrashing of the warm-blooded animal in the snake's presence. Strictly biology, the serpent didn't think, it responded to stimuli. This horned rattler could pick up a change in temperature as little as .5 degrees Fahrenheit. It had been content to warm itself until the movement it interpreted as an attack precipitated the strike.

Sam sat silent on the chair, his snake hook at the ready should he become the target. Death would come in hours not minutes as in the movies. The shock came immediately. To hurry the process along, Sam captured the sidewinder and returned it to its bag. He then removed the Mojave Green.

Smaller and more aggressive, the green didn't need any provocation, its venom calculated in multiples of potency greater than the sidewinder. The pit viper slithered straight to the back of the knee where blood vessels ran close to the skin surface. The neurotoxins began their enzymatic destruction, first of Gordo's dendrites and axons, then his life.

Sam called the cleaners. They would arrive through the unlocked back door and find the body. Per his instructions, they were to dump it not far into the desert but outside the city limits. The restraints used by Chey and Daga were stand-ard issue OGA. Designed to distribute force along the limbs and therefore more like medieval leather forearm cuffs, signs of struggle against a ligature would be unnoticeable.

The coroner would get the cause of death correct, poison-ous snake bite, but not the manner of death which of course was homicide or patriotism depending on one's assignment. Minus an extreme interest in herpetology or local fauna the medical examiner well could describe the manner of death as *a misadventure*. A naked body with multiple fang injections from local species, lying in the desert, certainly didn't appear to be a well thought out evening.

The winds that blow at night out of the mountains scrubbed clean with fine granules of sand the hard surface of the body dump site explaining the lack of footprints and tire tracks. The fat one's preliminary resting place, like many others before him, fulfilled the basic requirements of a body disposal.

The desiccation caused by the dry desert air would pre-vent post-mortem toxicology. Body fluids long gone into the atmosphere or devoured by scavengers made processing solutions unreliable even if attempted. The doctor would have proof of the injection sites and that made for a swift conclusion. Another drunk wandered out into the desert, passed out, and fell in the one place he shouldn't. Case closed. In Mexican slang, *cae bien,* literally fall well but the true meaning meant drink responsibly. The corpse had done neither.

As Sauria's Varangian guards drove him back to his suite, he thought about his entire career. Throughout, death by snakebite, especially in third world countries or directed upon third world citizens, had proven to be his go to method over the years. His childhood hobby served him well. Now he considered what response this would elicit from Cruz.

Sam now had his name. The distinctive tattoo as an easy identifier and Gordo's death should bring Sauria's target out of the shadows. He figured that Cruz wouldn't accept the misadventure ruling by the coroner. When El Crucidor contacted Dominguez in Mexico City about the bogus death, it should be enough to bring Zarilla to Vegas.

VENETIAN

Sam got comfortable in the thousand count sheets of Egyptian cotton he wrapped about himself in his king size bed at the Venetian. A hot shower and a nice glass of Rosemount Syrah with its pleasant full bouquet and finish of pepper with blackberries helped wash away the nastiness of the day. It had to be done as distasteful as it had been. He had no real stomach for wet work as the KGB used to call field assassinations but this crew of murderers and narcos had no limits and stopping them required the same.

As Sam settled back to enjoy some mindless TV, the satellite phone with only one other human link operating under the title of Director NCS, flashed an LED and then rang. This couldn't be good.

NCS, National Clandestine Service, absorbed the CIA HUMINT operations in 2005 under the restructuring of the intelligence community. This created the Director of National

Intelligence as well. The DCI no longer sat atop the intel community. Sam's bosses had changed.

The man on the other receiver came into this world the son of Boston bluebloods.

Barnsworth Donovan Bailey, a legacy at Yale like his good friend W, became an employee of the CIA upon graduation and H.W. Bush's election. The nonsense of the Skull and Bones Society had proven well worth it.

Quite content to be in an office, his mentors instead insisted he join the Army Reserves and train as a Ranger at first opportunity. Really not his cup of tea, he somehow muddled through at the rank of Captain while failing twice the three day survival course in the Georgia swamps. He now had the necessary credentials.

Fresh from his training, he garnered an assistant directorship for SOG, Special Operations Group, which managed the paramilitary part of the directorship of operations back in the day. Grenada, Panama, and Colombia all helped build the resume from a safe distance and out of the line of fire of wayward shrapnel that might spill his martini. His promotion to SAD, Special Activities Division, shortly after his friend's ascension to President, sealed his reputation at the agency as a fast riser.

Part of Dick Cheney's new hit squad to hunt down Al Qaeda's leaders and cut the head from the snake, pilotless drones had made him the beneficiary of timely technology.

Tall, thin, and disinclined to physical exertion not required while blessed with the requisite metabolism, he wore turtle shell glasses and what Sam liked to call *professional preppy office*.

Blue oxford shirts with patterned ties finished his upper ensemble with khakis completing the look. His blond hair parted at the left and longer in carefully staged neglect than what one might expect of one in his position, wrapped a nonexistent chin. Blue eyes peeking from beneath the canopy of hair seemed careless like is often the persona of one who is given much.

This last characteristic played to his homosexuality which he took little care to hide. He had never worried about blackmail because he didn't live a separate life. Sauria had studied all of this profile in an attempt to be able to work with his new director. Sam would now see if it had done him any good.

"Sauria. What the hell is going on out there? The murder rate in Vegas is going up. Do you know how hard it is to make the murder rate go up in Vegas? That's like making meth usage go up in Missouri."

"Sir, it's not us. It's why we are here. Like their friends in Matamoros, Nuevo Laredo, Reynosa, Cuidad Juárez......."

"I got it. I don't need a geography lesson of the southwest border." Actually, he did but he needed to maintain his position of superiority more. "The reason I called is that Mayor Goodman gave W a call to see if anything could be done."

"He's no longer president, right? W? Why don't you tell the mayor that when we're done with what we are doing, the FBI is going to start looking into RICO charges concerning some high profile Vegas politicians. Tell him the US Attorney is all on board."

"Why can't you play ball?"

"I do play ball but not with mob hangers-on looking for a foot up. Look, when we are done the crime rate in Vegas will drop so low the police will complain about layoffs and lack of overtime. They'll be so bored they'll start arresting hookers and johns. I wouldn't be surprised if the escort card guys on the Eastside of the North strip get snagged for littering. Hell the Fremont Experience might get a ticket for attempted show."

"Easy Sam, I get it."

"Do you?" Sam had no patience for politicos. Men died and rotted in the desert because somebody had an agenda legitimate or otherwise. His military training forced him to follow orders but he had enough time in rank under his belt to give his point of view.

"So our target? What's the status?"

"The cheese is under his nose and his whiskers are twitching. It is only a matter of time. Subconsciously, he probably knows better but his narcissism demands he assert himself."

"How much longer?"

"By the time the summer is over, he should be as well. Maybe sooner."

"Keep me posted."

"I'll give you a heads up when I need you. Go play golf till it's over."

"Are you trying to lose your pension? I'm still your boss."

"I'm sorry, sir. Please go play golf until it's over, SIR!"

The sat phone went dead and so did any chance of Sam having a restful night of sleep.

XX

LA FORTELEZA

Zarilla picked up what he thought was his secure phone connected by underground coaxial cable. However, Sam had changed the game. When Sauria read through the collected intel the FBI had gathered from Carlos Juega, he became aware of the underground cable. A tactic of Sadaam Hussein during the Gulf Wars, the use of cable prevented interception of messages by satellite and microwave. This method, considered very secure, did have a single failing. If the listeners could physically find and splice into the cable, they would receive real time information un-garbled and unadulterated.

In order for that to happen, the interceptors would have to enter the country undetected. Something one of the SOG teams attempted without success in Iraq, a result of poor intelligence concerning location. But cutting into cables had been met with great success during the Cold War including eavesdropping on the Soviet Union during message delivery via transoceanic cable to its KGB officers in the Far East. Another coup had been the joint operation between the Brits and US where underground cable leading from the offices of the DDR Stasi secret police became a superior source of pure intel. Both of these operations were destroyed by the American citizen spying for the Soviet Union, John Anthony Walker.

Like football defenses improving tactics to overcome offensive strategy and then football offenses changing to meet the challenges of the new defenses, the NSA had gotten better at finding cable. The NSA, National Security Agency, had at one time been known as No Such Agency, among those who used its product. The NSA serves as America's eavesdropper of all kind of conversation and information. If the computer geek who went to school with you hasn't been heard from for awhile, he's likely working for the NSA.

The *street sweepers* picking up litter outside of La Forteleza were employed by the NSA. In the sacks on their backs and the poles used to capture trash before it flew away, were ultra-sensitive metal detectors. The path of the coaxial cable had been located and intercepted from a position not covered by the security cameras. All of this led to Sam being able to read transcripts of Zarilla's conversations in less than twenty-fours after transmission.

"What do you want?"

"It's Ernesto. I wouldn't have called if it wasn't important."

"Go ahead."

"We've got another problem in Vegas."

"Do I have to guess?"

No,no. Lo siento. They found the body of another employee in the desert outside of town. The doctor said it was snake bite and *borracho*. I don't think so. We can't be that unlucky."

"Are you sure this isn't one of the other cartels trying to take over our operation. The last meeting we held wasn't exactly in total agreement. Maybe some of the others decided to take things in their own hands."

"I don't know. What should I do?"

"Kill anyone you suspect. If in doubt, send them to God. I will be there when possible. No more bad news. Understand?"

"Yes." The phone went dead. While Cruz considered his options, the NSA began to transcribe the conversation. Although Ernesto disliked being castigated, his reward for making the difficult phone call materialized as an open season on killing, something he could appreciate. He began to make his list.

This mirrored exactly Sam's wishes as it concerned the cartel members. Like an animal caught in a leg hold trap that chews its own leg off in order to escape, Sauria had managed to get one of Los Zetas premier killers to take aim at any and all possible rats on board his own ship. The drawback asserted itself in that any known associates of the enemy were fair game as well. While being targeted was usually not a concern for Sam when dealing with foreign governments, Los Zetas did not concern itself with such restraints. This time those criteria would mean Wolfe, Daga, and Chey became targets. Sauria called a meeting.

BILL'S BAR

With the Varangian guards near the doors seemingly immersed in a time share sales pitch, the showgirl model trying her best to engage them, Sauria felt safe enough to have a few drinks with his friends at happy hour. Wearing as usual his Jimmy Buffet evening attire, Sam had outdone himself. His shirt and hat both fresh from the Parrot Head store at the Flamingo, were in hues described by the designer as sunset and mango. Dressed like a cruise passenger on a Caribbean shore excursion, how Sam had gotten past every pitchman between the bar and the Venetian demonstrated street skills never taught on the Company's Farm.

Bob had the bar and Sam sipped from a strawberry daiquiri. Wolfe walked up from the direction of the escalator, Daga and Chey came off the street as if coming from the Mirage. The foursome took up the chairs closest to the guards.

"What brings you out Sam?"

"Trouble. Cruz just got the hit notice. Eliminate everyone that could possibly be a rat. That includes the three of you and anyone else you've picked up along the way like the two Asians. I had hoped it would only be his guys, you know kill all the rats even if you're not sure, but this sounds more like an extermination. Think three degrees of separation are not enough."

"About the two Asians, one got in for the money and the other got in to get out. How are you so sure he's targeted them or us for that matter?"

"What two Asians?" Daga wondered.

"Wolfe is becoming quite the recruiter. He's got a male and a female for helpers. A few more sets of eyes on the street."

"The girl better be ugly." Daga ordered a captain and coke from Bob.

"We've got ears on the main man, El Jefe Zarilla. Look Wolfe, I'm not blaming you but you enticed the kid, a known gambler, with money and the other one well she was just desperate."

"So we should do what? Get lost?" Cheyenne meant it as a question not a sarcastic aside.

"No. But the three of you need to go see our local dentist."

"I don't like dentists. My teeth are perfect." Daga had very few fears but the sound of a dentist's drill qualified as her greatest.

"Look if he gets his hands on one of you, the first thing he'll take is your phone. We need to know where each one of you is at all times. If he's going to kill you, we at least want to catch him in the act.'

"That's comforting." Wolfe smiled. He knew the next line.

"Well, yeh. Worst case scenario kind of thing. Anyway go see our dentist. He'll put a cap on one of your molars that contains a GPS chip. It's simple enough. You'll like the guy. He's a former local that lost his ass gambling and borrowed from mob loan sharks. Now he's in our witness program. The only teeth he works on currently belong to federal employees. They hid him in plain sight outside of town at Nellis AFB. Those flyboys have some of the best teeth in America thanks to him and if they go down behind enemy lines, we know where they are if their radios are confiscated and beacons destroyed. It's a win-win.

Keep your eyes open and space between you and other employees who might be first on the list. It's a collateral damage sort of thing. There will be a gate pass waiting for all of you as individuals. Tell the AP guard you're coming in to see Doc Holliday. Yeh, the wit sec boys like to get cute sometimes when they think they can get away with it. OK. Get to it. Cheers. Oh, one other thing. I left passes for the other two. Tell them when you see them. Only need to know basis."

Sam lifted his near empty glass and turned to order another from Bob. Facing the bar helped him hide the concern on his face.

As Sam's crew separated in their respective directions, a familiar face caught up with Wolfe on his way back to the Venetian. Dressed in blue jeans and yellow baby doll blouse with a scoop neck, she had even lost the pumps and instead wore matching yellow Converse old school basketball shoes except for the fact they were bright yellow.

She had waited till he had passed but Wolfe had caught a glimpse of her motion as she stood from a sidewalk table. Study almost any animal, staying still is great defense if the adversary is human. The *Homo sapien* eye evolved to notice movement not detail. It's why camouflage works. He walked normally waiting for her to catch up.

"Hey! Wolfie!"

"Yes Anna Lee." Wolfe neither slowed nor turned to greet her.

"How do you know it's me?" She finally got abreast of Rebelle.

"I saw you stand up to follow me. I assume you weren't trying to be discreet or you would have worn something besides yellow."

"OOOh, you're the tiger in the jungle. I hope that applies to the bedroom as well and not just a crowded sidewalk?"

"I need you to understand this *is* a jungle full of very dangerous animals. Don't let their stripes confuse you." Wolfe found ignoring China Doll's repeated come-ons increasingly more difficult.

"Come on Wolfie. Let's play." She stuck her hands in the back pocket of his jeans like a high school cheerleader on a date with the football captain.

"I've got a better idea. Let's go have a drink at the Champagne Bar over at the Palazzo." Anna Lee didn't remove her hand and Wolfe didn't ask her to do so. They walked as a couple down the string of restaurants that connect the Venetian to the Palazzo gazing at the menus posted outside the entrances and passing the time as many others might as well.

"Oh my God, Wolfie. Look!"

"What?" Wolfe tensed as Anna took off jogging. What had caught her eye and that of many others encompassed nearly half the entrance to the Palazzo. A giant stuffed tiger lounged indifferently in filtered afternoon sunlight from the skylights directly overhead.

Wolfe finally arrived a moment later. "What's the big deal? It's a stuffed toy, so what?"

"You're such a *guilao*."

"A what? Speak English."

"Of course master. Chop, chop for me." Anna Lee imitated her best or worst pidgin English depending on one's perspective. She paused to stare at Wolfe for affect. "A guilao, literally a ghost or a ghost guy. It's Mandarin slang for a white person who is culturally ignorant or insensitive to other cultures and specifically Chinese. It is right up there with white eyes as far as ethnic insults go."

"And how did I become a guilao, I may ask? I'm here with you."

"Having sex with beautiful Chinese women doesn't count as being culturally expansive. Sex is only about sex."

"I haven't had sex with you."

"Yet. Now as far as being ignorant culturally, I'm sure you have noticed that Asians as an ethnic group gamble in greater proportion than their representative percentage in the population whether you are counting worldwide or in Asia."

"Sure I see that all the time. They also gamble at higher stakes."

"Exactly. So they are very welcome in casinos. The Palazzo has taken that in to account and put this display here because

2010 is the Year of the Tiger in China, a very positive year for gamblers. Each animal of the Chinese zodiac has attributes one of which is the motto. This year the motto is *I win*. So you can see it is perfect for risk takers. The gemstone attribute is diamond and the polarity is yang. Also, it is all about sex. A very positive year is predicted. "

"I believe you made up that last part. Keep it up and I'll strap into a lie detector."

"O-Oh, straps. I like that. What? You can't believe me? Which part, the positive part or the sex part? Let me guess, the sex part? What's the difference? Isn't sex positive? No really. Why do you think I mentioned the tiger in the jungle?"

"Because you're crazy?"

"You'll like the kind of crazy I am if you give it a chance."

"I think we both need some champagne"

"Men need it. I want it."

"Jesus. You don't quit do you?"

Wolfe and China Doll made it to the bar and as he sat, Wolfe felt sweat beading on his forehead in sixty degree air conditioning. John, the bartender, hurried over to take their order.

"Wolfe. How ya doin'?" Somewhere between NYC and Jersey had spawned his accent.

"Great, John. This is Anna Lee. May I have a bottle of your Bollinger Grand Anneé Brut 1999."

"Sure thing 007."

"What?"

"That's what James Bond drinks. You didn't know that?"

"No. I just drink it because the casino comps it."

"Gotcha. Man, I thought you were up on all that."

"Nope. Kind of plain vanilla."

Rebelle and Anna Lee finished off the bottle in less than thirty minutes and Anna Lee excused herself to use the bathroom.

"Yo, Wolfe. That's your new babe?"

"No. We work together."

"Yeh right. I know how you work together."

Sometimes it is easier to allow someone to fall victim to an active imagination than it is to convince him otherwise. No matter what Wolfe would say John would not have changed his mind so Rebelle played the man game.

"John you know Daga is my girl. There's nobody else." Like anything in life, the more one protested innocence the less one succeeded in convincing someone. Wolfe was telling the truth and it sounded like a lie.

"Man, I saw her looking at you. If you're being straight with me you better keep your distance from her. You want me to hit on her?"

"How thoughtful of you."

"What are friends for?"

"Thanks but no thanks. Hey, why don't you give us another bottle of Bolly."

"That's the spirit."

John poured fresh glasses full of the bubbly and left to wait on other customers. Where the hell is Anna Lee, Wolfe wondered.

At that exact moment Anna Lee cleaned what blood splatter she could readily see from the white tiles in the bathroom. The attack had come unexpectedly, only a glance in the mirror at the most opportune time had saved her life. Unlike Louisiana where magnetometers prevented concealed weapons in casinos, Nevada had an open carry law and the legislature had written in a clause preventing local governments from overriding it. In essence, one could carry anything with a permit.

The weapon, a 22 caliber five shot revolver with a silencer, had been the point of struggle. A Latina, probably a gang mama, had burst from the stall and tried to shoot. During the wrestling for the weapon, the muzzle had gotten under the Mexicana's chin and when Anna Lee got her finger inside the trigger housing the round entered the skull and bounced around for awhile before being fatal to the chica.

Anna Lee got the body back into the stall and sat her on the toilet spread-legged. She wiped down the gun with toilet tissue and dropped it in the bowl water in an attempt to ruin any fingerprints and give investigators pause to consider a possible suicide. Maybe she lost too much money. China Doll closed the stall door, locked it from the inside and crawled out under the door just as another patron entered the room.

"Lock jammed. That's about how my luck is running today."

"I hear ya." The woman entered the stall farthest from the body. Anna Lee's luck still held.

She knew her clothes were splattered with blood and brain matter. Fortunately, she had a light shawl in her bag she used as protection against the air conditioning when needed. With her top turned inside out and her shawl gathered at her shoulders with her hand, she straightened herself the best she could and hurried back to the bar hoping along the way that there were no security cameras in the woman's bathroom. Historically, there were none but lately in American life security cameras sprouted almost anywhere and in greater numbers. Mushrooms don't pop up after a rain as quickly as cameras have since 9/11.

"There she is." John trumpeted to anyone in hearing distance, exactly what she did not need.

Wolfe swiveled on his seat and saw from her face something had not gone well. Waiting for John to move to the other side of the bar, anxiety brewed in his stomach.

"What's up?" The champagne made Rebelle's question seem lighthearted to listeners. His eyes said otherwise to Anna Lee shielded to all but her by his head position.

"Time to go."

"I'm not drunk. I know something is wrong. What is it?"

"Not here. Let's go."

Wolfe slammed the last glass and left John a chip for a tip lacking any cash. Anna Lee already had a ten yard lead.

"So much for good luck in the Year of the Tiger."

"Shut up Wolfe. We're under attack." There it was again. A phrase, a slip of the tongue, but something rubbed Rebelle wrong periodically when Anna Lee talked under stress. It compared to poker players asking questions of one another. Tension caused information to be exposed in spite of one's best efforts, silence the best policy. Miranda v. Arizona came into being to allow citizens to actually utilize the Fifth Amendment, namely not to testify against oneself even if were accidental.

China Doll hurried them along until they exited out into the Venetian near more restaurants. "Where's your room?"

"That's your game? You went through all that to set me up?"

"This is not a setup."

"Well, if it's not, why do you need to go to my room?"

"I have somebody's blood splatter on my clothes. Trust me."

Even for a cynic like Wolfe, no one he knew joked about such things. He headed to Harrah's with Anna Lee in tow.

BOOM BOOM FOR BOBO

Sadly for Bobo, his recent promotion to bartender didn't seem to have any legs. Bartending held the enviable position of being a union job in Vegas. Employers had to follow seniority rules, post open positions, offer retirement plans and health insurance packages. For these reasons and others bartending had many applicants for each opening. Filling an open bartender position or for that matter, an open bar back position offered many choices for anyone doing the hiring.

There were even classifications of bartending. The top class and compensated the best were the flair bartenders, the ones that put on a show rather than make your drink. Ernesto Cruz didn't go to bars to be entertained by the bartender while he waited longer for his drink. He felt it to be a waste of his time and employee time. He wouldn't be alone in that assessment.

The next lower classification were the ones that knew all the recipes of popular drinks and/or understood fine dining perhaps working as a sommelier on some shifts. The lowest

classification were the ones that most people liked and bar-
tended because they enjoyed the money and most of the customers. Having a good bartender was as important as having
a good mechanic who was honest. That would be these guys.

Bobo inhabited some space below all of these in the bartender hierarchy. He had child support payments garnisheed
from his paycheck so he needed a job that compensated him
mostly in unreported tips. How a woman had laid still long
enough for Bobo to impregnate her filled many hours of bore-
dom with laughter among the strippers.

He drank on the job putting most of the drinks on drunken
customer's tabs and practically extorted the dancers to give
him a larger share of their shift tips than he deserved.

Bobo drove a 1995 Ford Explorer, which at some point in
history had been red but now a shade of pink. It matched the
color of the club's décor compliments of the desert sun. The
design of the SUV made crawling beneath it and accessing the
undercarriage a simpler task.

An Angelino member of MS-13 crawled beneath the vehicle. He had learned his trade like most good bombers do, in
the military, in this case in Iraq defusing IED's. One of the
least advertised unintended consequences of the simultaneous
wars in Iraq and Afghanistan concerned gang members. The
Pentagon had lowered its standards concerning felony convic-
tions and some of the gang members had taken them up on the
deal. We now had military veterans who were trained in all the
arts of war including designing bombs since disarming a bomb,
required knowledge of the engineering. The Joint Chiefs of
Staff probably haven't informed the large city chiefs of police
about this new development.

Car bombs in Vegas during the mob years predated the car
bombs during the troubles in Belfast. Both became the weapon
of choice for ridding oneself of pesky rivals or rats. Those early
models were detonated by weight changes when the driver sat
down or electrical charges when the ignition engaged. None of
them were like the one being attached to Bobo's car.

This bomber's trademark or handle could be traced back to the Iranian Revolutionary Guard. It utilized both a tilt fuse and a cell phone. The tilt fuse consisted of a small vessel similar in size to a ten milliliter test tube one end of which contained mercury. During the usual stopping and starting of driving, the mercury would wash forward and a contact situated on the test tube plug would complete the first circuit allowing the bomber time to exit the blast zone and flexibility concerning the time of detonation.

The first circuit attached to the guts of the cell phone and when called the second circuit became complete and detonated the bomb. Once the car had been driven the bomber had free choice concerning activation place and time.

Bobo exited the club earlier than usual. Mid-week sometimes could be slow. He had three hundred dollars in his pocket that the bloodsucking mother of the child didn't know about. He always referred to her as the mother of the child rather than the mother of his child because he hadn't gotten around to DNA testing. He was sure that bitch was screwing someone else when she got pregnant. One of these days he planned on getting rid of them both, but not now.

Now he felt like some poker. First he needed to stop for some gas and a quick bite to eat. He headed down the access road between the strip and I-15. Approximately fifteen minutes after he started his engine and Ernesto saw him leave, his SUV became two thousand pounds of twisted steel and not only did his job not have legs neither did Bobo, not that he would need them.

In spite of himself and unknowingly, Bobo had managed to do good. The fact that many grammar teachers over the years had repeated ad infinitum a mnemonic phrase to help their charges remember the proper usages of good and well, the words *superman does good, you do well* seemed apropos.

Bobo had done some good if not well. Decapitated and mangled, his funeral box a sculpture of steel reminiscent of modern art in a garden, Bobo had managed to achieve a higher purpose in death if not in life. The mother of his child and the niño would receive social security checks for twenty years thus sparing them the sins of the father and sparing the gene pool the burden of more Bobo offspring.

XXI

HARRAH'S

"So what did this woman look like?"

"Before or after her head exploded?"

"No not her, the second one. She might have been part of the deal."

"Latina. Short. Slight build. She had some small tattoos on her left hand."

"You just described seventy-five percent of the females in the Western Hemisphere."

"I'd recognize her if I saw her again."

"You won't see her again. When she goes back and tells them her partner didn't succeed they'll eliminate the witness to the attempted hit. That is of course if she even goes back. She may get the hell out of Dodge."

"So what do I do?"

"Hole up here for awhile but they'll definitely give it another try. We need to get rid of your clothing. Everything including your shoes."

"I knew you'd finally see it my way." Anna Lee began pulling her blouse over her head.

"Hold it right there."

With her face still obscured by her blouse and her arms over her head Anna Lee looked funny standing in the middle of a hotel room talking through her clothes. She had not bothered with a bra. "Oooh, what's this all about? Something kinky?"

'It's nothing kinky. Go directly to the shower, touch nothing including the curtain, and disrobe in the shower itself. I'm coming to help. Be patient. I'm going to be a minute." Wolfe opened the door to the hall, glanced outside, saw what he needed, a maid's cart, and ran to get a large garbage bag hanging on the side of it.

He hustled back in the room while China Doll grew increasingly impatient."Come on. I'm freezing." Wolfe reached across the stall and turned on the water. He didn't try to avert his eyes. Trying to do so would have been futile. She had a perfect little body as her nickname suggested.

"Put all your belongings in this bag and hand it to me. Then wash your whole body twice including your hair. When you dry off, put the towel in the bag as well. Nothing leaves the stall but to go directly into the bag. What size are you?"

Anna Lee pulled back the curtain. Standing in the classic nude pose imaged by artists and photographers alike she looked perfect. "What size do you think I am?"

"I'm not guessing. What size?"

"Zero or one. My shoe size is a six."

"OK. Get busy. I'm going to get you some new clothes. Don't answer the door for any reason and don't get out of the stall until I return."

"That sounds like fun. I could use some help washing my back."

"Whatever."

Wolfe headed down to the boutiques in the lobby. God, she's tough to ignore crossed his mind. Rebelle so far had managed to stay focused but other parts of his body weren't playing along. It had been awhile since he had seen Daga and Anna Lee must have sensed the same and delighted in rubbing his nose in it.

A few quick purchases later, Wolfe returned to the room. Anna Lee had done as he told her. "Ok, hand me the bag. We're checking out. We are going over to the Venetian. I think we should all be under one roof."

Wolfe called Sam to relay what happened while China Doll got dressed complaining the entire time how she hadn't been able to clean her dirty back. If Wolfe had to guess, she probably could equal gymnasts in her flexibility. Thoughts like that kept popping up in his consciousness much too often than he wanted.

The pair cut through Harrah's garage and in the side entrance to the Venetian. By the time they checked in their room and got to Sam's suite, Daga and Cheyenne were there. When Anna Lee entered the room practically on Wolfe's arm, the guttural sound that escaped Daga's throat matched well the flared nostrils and piercing blue eyes. The voodoo princess wouldn't need much convincing to break out her mojo.

Wolfe picked up all the body language immediately and moved quickly to embrace Daga. The wrapping of her arms about Wolfe seemed more like a bear hug meant to break bones than a heartfelt reunion. Her pupils, tiny pin pricks against a background of sky, seemed capable of burning laser-like through Wolfe's brain. Sam interceded with his agenda.

"OK. Things are going to move quickly. Bobo just became marinara sauce down by the club, probably some of Cruz's work. Zarilla is making plans to come to town. It's exactly what we've been hoping. I'll be working on our strategy. We want to act not react if possible. It wasn't just Bobo who got targeted. Wolfe and Anna tell them what happened."

When they finished relating the story Wolfe knew Daga believed him but didn't like meeting China Doll after the fact. The icy atmosphere between the two women warmed noticeably as Sam laid out plans and put them up for consideration by his crew. When a commander has excellent people in his charge, not utilizing the talents of your subordinates including alternative points of view, failed to maximize unit strengths for success. Sauria had never suffered from that common ailment of failed officers. Besides, when one is putting others at risk, it is a good idea to have them onboard with any near future tactics.

"Any questions?"

"When I do get to sleep with Wolfe?" Daga smiled as she said it, realizing a little late how strange it sounded. Wolfe turned a few shades of red while basking in the badly disguised approval.

"Same as before. I've got a room for you and Cheyenne. You two are like Eng and Chang, conjoined twins. Maybe for another day or so. Wolfe and Anna Lee are in-house same as the rest of us. When you go to the casino, attempt to be in large public areas in full view. Now I know all of you are skilled street people but I gotta tell you, what these yahoos lack in tactics and training, they compensate for it in ruthlessness and lack of concern for collateral damage to civilians."

"Allow me to give this warning. A few months ago Mossad hit one of the leaders of Hamas at a luxury hotel in Dubai, broad daylight, middle of the day. They figured out his room number by following him up in the elevator and one member of a two man crew followed the target down the hall acting as if he were lost and confused about the location of his own room.

The second operator stood at the elevator bank to delay any possible witnesses to the reconnaissance. Once they had the room number, getting a key from the desk, unfortunately for the target, became a simple matter. The two agents were dressed in tennis outfits.

How do we know all of this? The entire episode had been captured on hotel security cameras yet the whole hit squad got away clean with false passports and disguises confusing investigators about who had actually checked-in at the hotel. I say this because our adversaries may be quick learners. If a person or persons suddenly runs to make the elevator press some more floor numbers, get off on a random floor, if they follow, return to the elevator mentioning how you must be on the wrong floor. Do not enter your room with another person in the hallway; don't mention your room number in public, and hang your Do Not Disturb sign permanently on the door handle. Anyone can steal a maid's uniform or room service black and whites .You can make do with what's in the room and if you need more towels or soap steal some from the maid's cart. No one is to be alone, ever. I'll be in touch. Good luck. Fair wind and a following sea."

Wolfe and Daga hugged some more and he kissed tears from her cheeks. Amazing, a voodoo girl that could put you in the ground in less than a breath, but her heart belonged to Wolfe. The duos were staying in separate towers, the girls in the Venezia while Wolfe and his partner walked to the Palace.

Daga's blood boiled only slightly less than if she were in zero atmospheric pressure, no social constraints able to modify how she felt. Like juvenile males who thankfully take out most of their testosterone driven aggression on playing fields and courts, allowing the rest of society to co-exist peacefully, whoever encountered Daga in these last days of the operation would suffer greatly for her needed release of billowing tension.

Why the hell couldn't she stay with Wolfe? She knew Sam had a plan but he had been trained to follow orders and she had trained herself to be independent. Both were strong suits, equal in positive outcomes. All of the rum from the mini bar barely put her to sleep. Let Sam pay for it was her final conscious thought as she fell into her alcohol induced slumber.

BENITO JUAREZ AEROPUERTO, MEXICO CITY

Zarilla entered the passenger lounge at the executive airport not far from the one used by common visitors. The GS-II Gulfstream awaited him just beyond the glass, the air steps leading to the passenger compartment inviting him forward, the shape upwardly curved, reminding one of a pretty girl's beckoning finger.

José Jesús Dominguez, El Jefe, El Zarilla, the names weren't important only secondary to his work, settled into the butter soft leather seat and ordered a drink from the stunning Latina working the cabin.

"I need to speak with the captain." In spite of a pre-flight checklist only partially completed, the pilot appeared in front of Zarilla in seconds.

"Captain, have you filed you flight plan?"

"Si, as you requested. John Wayne Airport, Orange County, California."

"Excellente. When we enter the Estados Unidos, I want you to declare an air emergency requesting the nearest airport which will be Tucson. The authorities will allow you land regardless. This is correct?"

"Si. But I could lose my license if the FAA realized it to be untrue."

"Losing one's pilot's license in comparison to more valuable assets is relatively minor. You will be very well compensated at the appropriate time. Agreed?" The last question was only a polite gesture to calm edgy nerves. This plane and its high value passenger would land where Zarilla wanted it to land.

"Of course, I'll think of something."

"Report an engine flameout. It's not that unusual an emergency."

"As you wish" The captain walked back to the cockpit with his hands trembling so badly he might need the co-pilot to takeoff.

Dominguez always entered the US in this manner. A false passport, an emergency change of flight plan in case authorities were waiting for him at his scheduled destination, and ground transportation at the far end of the runway where all emergency landings are directed for safety reasons. Any agency tracking his flight would not be able to make adjustments by the time he landed and disappeared.

This time however his conversations had been intercepted and although Sam expected him to go to Orange County, the final destination remained the same. Somewhere in Las Vegas in a luxury suite under a false name Sauria would find one of the most dangerous men in the hemisphere.

XXII

CRUZ CONTROL

Ernesto currently found himself in a cold-blooded
killer's frenzy. He would in the future be the perfect subject
for forensic neurologists that believe violent criminals carry
a genetic propensity for their behavior and it manifests itself
outwardly in the abnormal anatomy of their brains. Forensic
psychologists battled one another to interview killers like Cruz
although the likelihood of Ernesto being captured alive could
be estimated in a probability near zero. His criminal profile
fit the general description of a sociopath but his murdering
ways didn't drive him to an uncontrollable climax as much as
the psychological soothing he received when it made him more
money.

He had no desire to be captured as is often the case with
pure serial killers. No, Cruz was about business but he enjoyed
going to work. Think of him as the killing version of Bernie
Madoff. Both did the work they did in order to make inordi-
nate amounts of money and that served the primary drive but
the secondary benefits, torture/killing for Cruz and stealing
from rich New Yorkers and Jewish charities for Madoff, made
how they passed the time much more pleasing.

Today seemed a little different. He had or rival gangbangers had wiped out any possible rats in the rat nest except for
that Asian chica, the two strippers, and their boyfriend. The
attack on Sauria had come from Los Zetas at the very top and
Cruz didn't know anything of it. Those four targets that had

gotten away ate in large portions at his psyche. He had planned to lure the strippers somewhere once they were at work but before that happened they had vanished. Missing China Doll in the restroom qualified as bad luck.

Other thoughts raced around Ernesto's mind. Had El Jefe put him on this assignment because Zarilla trusted no one else and if so did he trust Cruz? Did Zarilla plan on eliminating Cruz when he got to town? Should Cruz strike first? All criminals suffer from varying degrees of crippling paranoia because they don't trust themselves which makes trusting others problematic. Ernesto continued to spar with his thoughts as Zarilla checked into the Rio. All of Sam's eyes had missed him on the way in to Vegas from Tucson. Black Escalades with heavily tinted windows were as common as losers in Vegas.

Wolfe took the elevator down to the poker room with Anna Lee for what looked like just some guy with eye candy on his arm but she actually served as another set of ears. She would sit as many other girlfriends did alongside the table as Rebelle played. Cash games floor men allowed this small courtesy although technically against the rules. If someone at the table complained, China Doll would have to sit at least as far away as the next empty table. The casinos permitted girlfriend seats because in many cases when the girlfriend couldn't accompany her man they both left. Their jobs this evening consisted of listening and watching fellow players hoping for a few bits of intel. Anna Lee would strike up conversations with other women and men spectators while Wolfe worked the players.

Wolfe found a 2-5 game and he and Anna Lee walked their way to table #23 after stopping at the fresh coffee urns for two cups on the North side of the room. Wolfe settled in to seat six and Anna Lee pulled up a chair. Wolfe bought in for five hundred and as he counted his chips to verify the proper amount a voice from the past permeated his concentration.

Wolfe stared in to his coffee as if he had been drugged. "Yo,yo yo, it's Tommy Cho." Tommy slid into the empty seat at number ten.

"What's a matter bro? You don't look glad to see me."

"What the hell are you doing here? You just wiped out and you don't even know it."

"Forget about me. The action is here. I see you ended up with the china doll? I knew it. You couldn't resist. You know what they say about Asian women? Once you go china there's nothing any finer."

"Tommy this isn't a strip club or a video poker bar. You owe her an apology."

"Oh, man. I'm sorry. I'm kinda on a bitchin' wave right now. Got a poker high going. "

"You still haven't apologized to her. Thank you for apologizing to me."

"Man I'm way sorry. Miss Asian babe, I totally took a Neptune Cocktail on that one. I'm just amped."

Anna Lee had ignored Cho the entire time, caught up in a conversation with another Asian female.

"She accepts your apology. You still haven't told me why you are here?"

"I'm here to catch some monster poker waves. Shuffle up and deal."

"Suit yourself. We'll talk later."

The table held an eclectic compilation of human characters. Besides Cho and Rebelle, the seats were filled with people only one's imagination could make possible yet they existed in real time and space just across the table from Rebelle.

Seats one and two were occupied by a couple of college kids convinced that their feeble attempts at collusion were going unnoticed. Rebelle tipped his hat to Tommy to gain his attention then straight forwardly said within earshot of all players and the dealer that seats one and two were good friends. The bow shot went over the heads of the frat boys who eagerly agreed it to be so.

Seat three lived in a cabin in rural Nevada three hours west of town and spent most of his time smoking dope and had written a book about how to utilize modern horticulture to improve the potency of his favorite medicinal weed. He had one bet, all in, and the caller better have the nuts.

Seats four and five were conventioneers happy as hell that they were finally out of the house. Of course, they played and acted in that manner. They were determined to drink two hundred dollars of cocktails in order to cover their losses. They were well on their way.

Seat seven had been one of the first safari guides in Zimbabwe and regaled the table with stories of point blank stare downs of rogue elephants and man killing lions. He didn't shy from big pots with less than the perfect hand as poker likely seemed tame compared to bush hunting in Africa.

Eight and nine seats completed the compliment of out of town businessmen taking a tax deduction. One sipped from a three foot plastic container of frozen margarita. No one had told him that the rules change from basement to casino along with the predators. Cho had the enviable position of sitting behind this dead money.

The cards were in the air. Tommy had the button. Everyone folded to Wolfe and he couldn't play with a 2-9 off suit. Safari man called and Cho raised two times the big blind. Seat one folded and seat two called. Big guns made it three.

The flop came 2-4-5 diamonds. The table checked around to Cho and he raised the pot. Wolfe couldn't figure if Tommy had bluffed, was on a draw or hit the flop. Seat two went all in and Safari and Cho called. Wolfe turned to comment to Anna Lee about the hand. Her empty seat stared back at him.

"Tommy, where'd Anna Lee go?"

"Wolfe, I'm in a hand. Shut up."

Wolfe jumped from the table and sprinted to the nearest restroom. China Doll met him as she exited.

"Are you Okay?"

"Am I Okay? Why wouldn't I be Okay? I went to the bathroom."

"Right! Nothing ever happens in the bathroom."

"Sorry. How are you doing in the game?"

"First hand. It looks to be pretty hinky. It's a big pot. Somebody's going to get hurt."

Wolfe got back to the table and Cho's chips were there but he was not. He showed up a few minutes later.

"Hey Tommy, where were you? What happened?"

"What are you, my papa san? The safari guy and I both hit a straight and chopped the pot. Seat two went to re-load I guess. No big deal."

"Do me a favor before you leave again, let's go have a drink. Deal?"

"Sure. No problem."

A few hours later and enough coffee to twist his stomach, Wolfe got up from the table virtually even. Tommy and safari man had wiped out the college kids a couple of times, the only pots the frat boys won were against each other. Cho played a few more hands and then collected his chips. The threesome walked over to the video poker bar at the sports book.

"What is on your mind Wolfe?"

"You were very lucky last time. I thought you took the hint."

"Dude, the cash is here. Don't worry I won't be going up to any outdoor bars at the tops of hotels anymore."

"You're playing out of your league. They'll use another method. You'll never see it coming. They don't like being unsuccessful. The girl that you were with that night has not been seen since."

"She's a fulltime stripper and part-time hooker. What do you expect? Hell, she got scared that night too."

"Usually when one leaves town, one takes one's clothes, cleans out the work locker, and cancels utilities to get the deposits."

"You know those kind are capable of leaving in a matter of minutes if a better deal comes along. Some sugar daddy wants her to be the maid for his mansion. Wear a backless French maid's outfit with no panties. Whatever."

"Fair enough, I hope you don't catch a sand facial. It will be permanent. Remember I don't need you anymore. If you stay, you're staying for Tommy. Good Luck."

"Cowabunga."

Cho left the bar and Wolfe turned to Anna Lee who had sat silent the entire time but listening closely.

"They tried to kill him as well?"

"Yeh, being around me is like being Dirty Harry's partner. Not much of a retirement program."

"Is he going to make it?"

"I doubt it."

Cruz wanted this one for himself. It would fill that hollow space in his gut. He hadn't thought he would get another chance but fate intervened. One of his leopardos had called and given Ernesto enough time to settle in a sniper's nest. The shrubbery in front of the faux roman statuary that dotted the landscape in front of Caesar's Palace provided great cover including seclusion from cameras. Cruz stood on a short ladder virtually inside of a shrub facing the sidewalk in front of the Imperial Palace across the street. He had a description of his target and where he may be headed.

Wearing maintenance overalls he could have been anyone if a drunk stumbled his way. His weapon of choice, perfect for urban warfare, needed comparatively less training to become proficient. Crossbows have been around since late BC. Even in those times the bolts could penetrate defenses. As the technology improved by the Battle of Hastings in 1066, crossbowmen were some of the most feared of medieval warriors. Singlehandedly, peasants could defeat the expensive armor of the king's knights.

Curiously in the history of the United States, crossbows were never included in weapons laws. One could transport, own, use, and never register a crossbow in all fifty states. One needed a license to hunt with one but not a license to own one. Ernesto found this curious about the US but much to his liking.

He had a Durango model which shot 400 grain arrows made of carbon. Gold tipped, they traveled 340 feet per second delivering 103 foot pounds of force into an area the size of the tip. Most targets would be penetrated through and through.

Alone, the target made the curved corner of the sidewalk at Harrah's on the east side of the strip. Early in the morning, street sweepers and security guards outnumbered the drunks stumbling back to their hotels. By his body language, he appeared to be in good spirits. Walking briskly, arms assisting, the mark either wanted to party with some drunken brides-maids or catch a poker game full of bachelor party Vegas virgins full of Jaeger bombs.

Ernesto took aim resting the crossbow on the top step of the ladder for balance. He slowly pressured the trigger after exhaling. He withdrew. The mark had stopped to talk to a group of girls with balloons shaped like penises floating above their heads. Cruz waited. The girls moved on.

The target stopped at the driveway access to the Imperial. An advertising truck passed on the strip between Cruz and his target, *Strippers anywhere, anytime.* The message screamed in lighted letters the size of a billboard. The truck continued up the strip. Frustrated, Ernesto looked again. Unbelievably, the mark remained in place, his progress delayed by a cartoonish stretch Hummer limo entering the driveway.

The bolt entered the chest cavity just below the diaphragm pinning the mark to an advertising sign with a giant arrow on it pointing in the direction of an on-strip bar with two for one drink specials. Tommy Cho never felt a thing.

Uniquely or at least not common in other cities at 0400h, drunks began to crowd the corpse. It still stood lifelike with a dazed look on its face. Some of the partiers confused it with a really cool way of advertising. Who was the dude who thought of using a wax figure that looked so real and then leaked red fluid which resembled human blood like in the movies?

Cruz's empty feeling had been satisfied with this surfin' safari.

XXIII

NELLIS AFB

"Permission to come aboard?"

"We drive planes here not rusty sinking tubs." The E-9 AP probably had been doing this job or one like it since Tan Son Nhat airport in 1976. The three up and five down chevrons on his arm patch with the diamond in the blue field made his dealings with all things civilian or officer a major pain in his ass.

"I'm here to see Doc Holliday."

"Smile for the camera." A not too discreet warning that one's photo had been recorded, the temporary vehicle pass handled by the sergeant landed unceremoniously on the driver's side dashboard. The hardboard AP checked the ID against his approved visitors list and waved her on through. Cheyenne drove through the gate following the signs to the health clinic building.

"Hi. I have an appointment with Doctor Holliday. 0900h."

"Honey, it's Doc Holliday. It doesn't matter if you're new or a regular." A big-boned secretary, red hair piled high with a voice to match, spent her days dealing with all forms military. Capable of handling every person who entered her lair from full bird colonels to E-2's, she ran interference with a southern drawl that dripped barbecue sauce as she spoke.

"OK fine. I'm here for Doc Holliday and the Earp brothers. I don't suppose he calls his office the OK Corral?"

"You're close. Welcome to the tooth ranch. Now you're in the saddle. Go on in. New patients don't wait."

Doc Holliday didn't have tuberculosis but his hacking cough from years of chain smoking in sports books made for a good imitation. If he had tried to have a worse comb over it would have required the skills of a Hollywood hairdresser. Flat brown eyes encircled by tiny rivers of broken red capillaries completed the first impression.

Upon a more complete perusal, cowboy boots capped with brass tips and made of exotic ostrich leather peeked from beneath the cuffs of Wrangler jeans. A cowhide belt cinched with a dinner plate buckle did little to hide the pot belly extending over the legs so thin they seemed incapable of supporting even his small-boned frame.

A dental chair with the usual auxiliary equipment dominated the middle of the room. The doc stood by his desk off to the side searching the internet for the morning's opening sport lines, a gray felt ten gallon Stetson capping the computer monitor. Sports gambling was the original habit that had brought him to where he now worked and lived. Fortunately, his collection of addictions didn't include illegal substances. Alcohol filled his anesthetic requirements when it concerned his emotional pain. A little nitrous oxide on the side topped off the night from time to time.

It appeared to Cheyenne that all this urban cowboy get up sufficed as a meager attempt to hide the insecurities of a degenerate dentist who crossed the line with the mob. She chuckled discreetly. How in the hell did the native tribes lose to the pony soldiers whose descendents spawned this white man remained the unspoken question she wanted to ask.

"What's so funny?" Apparently Chey's laughter had carried farther than she thought.

"Oh, nothing. Our mutual friend Sam sent me."

"Here for one of our little beauties are you? They are very helpful in finding dead bodies."

"So I hear. I wouldn't want to get buried off the reservation."

"Make yourself comfortable. I'll be with you in a moment."

"Take your time. I don't want you working on me while you're thinking about starting pitchers."

Soon Doc Holliday managed to tear himself from the screen and begin prepping for the GPS insertion. He placed the GPS chip in the underbelly of the cap and protected it with dental adhesive. It would withstand normal daily routines including highly acidic liquids such as orange juice. In its location sticky foods and gum could not dislodge it. Anyone peering into the mouth would not find it in a normal search.

Designed to facilitate prisoner rescues and avoid hostage situations, its usage in the coming years might include anyone living and working in hostile territory or countries known for rebel groups demanding ransoms from corporations in exchange for the safe return of employees. The New York Times had utilized it with foreign correspondents since one of their employees had been beheaded live via the internet witnessed by Al Jazeera subscribers.

He leaned over the chair coming uncomfortably close to resting his hand on Chey's chest. Chey pushed him away.

"Doc. Put the cap in and you're done. Try that again and I'll personally request that you be taken off the wit sec. After I kick your ass."

"The what?"

"Jesus, you're in it and don't know what it's called? You know, witness protection."

"They had some other long name for it. Why is it all you military types have these acronyms and abbreviations?"

"Most people have short attentions spans so it helps with communications and paperwork. Anyway, don't try getting frisky with me."

The dentist completed the procedure quickly and Cheyenne stood up from the chair. The whole thing had taken less than five minutes.

"Hey, would you like to go to the officer's club with me. Maybe have brunch and some mimosas?"

"I thought you were a dentist? What about other patients on your schedule? Besides, you don't take hints very well."

"I figured we got off on the wrong foot is all."

"Don't worry. I've already forgotten everything. I'll be sure to tell the others how friendly you are."

Cheyenne left the inner office and walked past the secretary who kept busy polishing her nails. Chey wondered to herself how slow days went for the secretary with that drunken hound dog in the other room. No matter, it wasn't her problem.

The curious part of the equation involved the secretary being so glad to have her job considering the current unemployment rate. Not since 1982 and 2006 had deficits and unemployment beleaguered the American economy so badly. Adding to it the ridiculous state of the Las Vegas real estate market, did the economic numbers help explain the secretary's patience with the mad dentist and his secondary role of depraved witness to the mob.

Over time each of the other members of Sam's tribe visited the dentist, each time coming away with the type of confusion experienced by Vietnam vets stepping down from an air stairwell in San Francisco. Confronting war protesters spitting on them, wondering if this is what the chiefs want, this is what they get, but why me?

Sam called Wolfe. "Come on down. Don't bring the china girl."

"How do you know I'm in the hotel?"

"Remember? You visited my dentist."

"So I did. I don't suppose I'll have any trouble passing through airport security?"

"They scan coffins but you won't know the difference."

"Funny guy."

"Hurry up and get down here."

Wolfe walked in the room. Sam already had the bourbon out and poured into the glasses. His face told much but not everything. For Rebelle, deciding who had become the object of bad news mimicked picking a winning horse but not the race you were watching and certainly not holding the correct ticket.

"What happened?"

"Your surfer dude Asian buddy took an arrow, *AN ARROW!* You believe that? Right on the strip outside the Imperial, pinned him to the wall right through his chest."

"I tried to warn him. Hell, he'd already gotten out of town alive once."

"Greed, the great motivator."

"So it seems."

"I'm putting the paramilitaries on Cruz. There job is only to capture him. I have sole control over him once he is delivered to me. I'm going old school on him plus a little Gitmo. I should get what I want with enough effort and time."

"You know where to find him?"

"He's at the club some time tonight. It'll be his last fun time. I think he either ordered the hit on Cho or handled it himself. All of us are on his list no doubt. You want to come along?"

"Who's driving?"

"My watchdogs."

"Good, pour me another Woodford Reserve."

CHOCHO

Ernesto Cruz felt satisfied. He had pinned that chink kid to the wall at sixty-five meters and there were no witnesses. Not as much fun as the cross, but the kid still got nailed. He had a few more targets to go and Zarilla would be pleased. He, El Crucificador, would run this whole operation, laundering money for the cartel and keeping all these chicas calliente company.

Ernesto squashed the adrenalin rush with tequila and VIP room time. He knew Zarilla had to be in town by now but no phone call had been received. It didn't matter. He could report progress in his assignment. He looked forward to more killing. It's what he did in the same manner musicians like music.

With a half of liter of tequila in his gut and a few rounds of couch time with one of the new girls, he walked out the back door of the club to his Escalade parked nearby. The rain of bullets started shortly thereafter. Sam's team hadn't even locked and loaded when the first round hit Cruz's bullet proof windshield.

Sauria couldn't believe what he saw. His pickup team hadn't even come out of the camouflaged jump point behind the fence when the shooting started. Then to add to his disbelief, his men were firing on the position of the incoming, tracers giving Sam an idea of the situation.

The uninvited gangbangers were well-armed for thugs but no match for M-4 assault rifles, body armor and night vision monoculars. What the operators had for equipment represented only standard gear. The Angelino gang members had come out blasting like a drunken cowboy in Dodge City. They had not expected any real return fire. The silenced firefight had lasted less than a minute. The sounds of the lead bouncing off metal making more noise than the exploding gunpowder. Bodies lay strewn about in war wagons, old impalas and buicks, refurbished with new paint and suspension, now sinking slowly to the pavement as air escaped from the oversized tires. Ernesto still cowered on the passenger floor of his SUV.

Sauria's team, once control had been established, called for transportation and El Crucificador got a free cab fare to an unknown destination.

"What the hell just happened Sam?"

"We saved Cruz's life so we can use *enhanced* interrogation methods on him. Zarilla must have put a hit on him and we crashed the party, so much for cartel loyalty. This is perfect. We took out some gangstas, we have them trying to kill one another, and I have my catch. I'd say this qualifies as a good night's work. Of course, we have the matter of Ernesto Cruz to keep us entertained the remainder of the evening. Plus I'm sure I'll be getting a call."

"What about?"

"The mess we have here. I mean our people will put out a story about a gang shootout over turf or somebody's stripper girlfriend. But the rounds are high-velocity military-issued and we'll have to go see the coroner sort of like *Men in Black*. It has a comical touch to it except that medical examiners aren't known for being anything but straight arrows. It will eventually get to the mayor's office and my boss will get another phone call from Mayor Goodman about bodies piling up in Las Vegas, the sweet innocent town he wants it to be.

The current mayor is all about appearances not reality. He doesn't quite see the long term benefits much further than the quarterly reports from the chamber of commerce. I mean his check says he gets paid by the city but the business owners, the largest of course are the casinos, pretty much call the shots."

"What's that have to do with you?"

"My boss has an affinity for the mayor and his politics and he doesn't have a liking when it comes to me."

"Something this important and there are politics involved?"

"My dear, dear Wolfe, I didn't think you were naïve about anything. I have been proven incorrect."

"How so?"

"Do you think we invaded Iraq for WMD's? Really? That occurred because W wanted the oil and revenge for Hussein trying to kill his old man. I will repeat something that I often tell people, when it doesn't make sense follow the money. Even this drug war is about cheap immigrant labor and our puritanical perspective on drugs. Think about how much less alcohol would be manufactured and sold if citizens could use other less harmful drugs legally? It's all politics."

"So why do you do what you do?"

"Working with the system insures more success than bucking it. That doesn't mean I'm always pleased. At one time, I lived in a bubble of naiveté. When one reads the newspaper or watches the evening news, one should remember one of the best movie lines of all time, 'pay no attention to the man behind the curtain'. It is almost always about politics and in turn money."

"Right now however, we have man's work to do. Ernesto awaits his fate and we need information."

Cruz had been sedated the moment the operators had gotten their hands on him. When he awoke, the stage setting put him ten thousand miles away in an Eastern European dungeon. In reality, he sat a mile and a half from the main gate of Nellis AFB. Bright lights shone in his eyes blocking any ability to see beyond the semi-circle corona illuminating the immediate area.

Block walls dripped tea-colored water while mortal screams echoed from beyond hell. The air, a crisp but not fatal fifty degrees F, tended to bring any wayward senses by the detainee into focus.

The Pentagon used Hollywood for reasons many would never guess. After 9/11, the intelligence community had queried producers and writers about what might be the plot of the next terrorism movie thus providing insight into what one's enemies may be planning. One's enemies' imagination can be the defenders' worst scenario.

Hollywood's talents are so respected the internet to this day runs rampant with conspiracies about the 1969 moon landing being only excellent stage props built by the movie industry. Keep in mind the wizards of movie magic are capable of almost anything. The refueling scene at the end of *Casablanca* took place on a sound stage with a miniaturized plane and a crew of midgets. To make Ernesto Cruz believe he had awakened in a medieval dungeon in Eastern Europe approached only the level of apprenticeship in the eyes of those who had built the set.

Sam went out of his way to make the surroundings a little more familiar for his captive. The roman cross in the shape of an 'X' dominated the center of the room not yet in Cruz's range of sight. Sauria slowly walked toward the sole source of light where Ernesto sat, additional lights illuminating Sam's path as he approached and exposing the cross to Cruz's barely contained horror. A trained soldier in resisting interrogation, he couldn't hide his deepest fears though he tried.

"Good morning. I hope you enjoyed your flight? Probably not nearly as bad as you imagined." Cruz, already in a state of confusion, fought Sam's attempt to confound him more.

"Bullshit. I can't be that far from Vegas, pendejo."

"Really? What day is it? What time is it? Hell, just give me latitude or longitude either one." When one is deprived of all modern conveniences that allow one to determine with accuracy the answers to such seemingly simple questions, the correct responses become nothing but a guess. No cell phone, no watch, no windows, artificial temperature environment, all added to Ernesto's sensory deprivation and frustration.

"Why didn't you just shoot me?"

"We were never shooting at you. We saved your life. Looked like it to me that your El Jefe tried to get rid of you. Those were Angelino gangbanger bullets bouncing off your car. Bullet proof glass and armor are the only things that saved you from the opening rain of lead."

"You can't ever be too careful."

"Exactly, so you understand that we find ourselves in that same sort of predicament? We can't be too careful. The cartels are completely out of control. Home invasions in the Southwestern US are up two hundred percent. Kidnappings for ransom and shootouts with cops are now daily occurrences. You may think that is business as usual in Mexico but that's not going to continue in the US. We had to teach the Russian criminals and now we will teach you. That is where we enter the picture."

"You don't have a chance. As long as gringos need drugs we will supply them. No public employee, even American Federales, can resist corruption when the amount of money is the right price."

"Funny you should say that. The price is right but not how you think. More accurately said it would be the cost. When it involved gang bangers killing each other, selling drugs to each other, or raping each other's women, we really didn't care. But like most criminal enterprises, greed got in the way, you couldn't control yourselves. So we find ourselves here." On cue a male voice coming from another room could be heard screaming to be killed in Mexican Spanish.

"What do you expect from me? Information or you will kill me? From the time I joined a gang I expected to die. I have been preparing for this moment since I grew a pair of nuts. Do you see the scars on my face? They are not scars to me but medals of honor for me and my brothers." He purposely traced his index finger over disfigurements large and small running from ear to chin even fingering a missing ear lobe on the opposite side of his head.

"Oh, we won't kill you. Well, not directly. We're Americans for God's sake. Dying is easy. Dying fast is very easy. We're thinking more like an extended stay. Diapers and bedsores come immediately to mind."

Everyman has an unspoken fear. Ernesto couldn't hide it. Cruz had no fear of dying. He trembled though thinking of himself helpless in a bed, a blob of tissue of no use to himself. At that moment, Doc Holliday stepped from the shadows wearing a lab coat and holding a syringe used for inter-spinal injections. Hand bicycle pumps were about the same size.

"Allow me to introduce Doc Holliday. He's sort of like our 2.0 version of Hannibal Lecter although admittedly not nearly as skilled. He is getting better with practice however. Aren't you Doc?"

Holliday stood motionless his red-rimmed eyes partially concealed by geeky old school lab goggles.

"He doesn't look so bad?" Cruz attempted to reassure himself that he could take whatever came his way.

"You are correct. He isn't. However, the compound he will inject into your spine is a new one that he has helped us to design. It dissolves the synapse receptors on all of your motor neurons leaving the autonomic system neurons alone. In other words, your heart and brain will work but you will be unable to move even your jaw. Doctor Holliday, are you ready? Remember Ernesto you've been preparing for death not this. You won't even be able to kill yourself."

Big, bad El Crucificador began to scream much like many of his victims had done. When he no longer could scream he began to talk. So much that Sam soon had all the information he needed and Sauria left others to drag additional tidbits of value from the quivering man.

Sam left the interrogation set and entered a connecting room. Doc Holliday sat at a table slamming vodka shots. "What the hell, Sauria? We don't really have that kind of stuff, do we?"

"Of course not. We don't need it as long as you're willing to work off your debt to the public with this cameo part from time to time."

"Remind me not to piss you off ever."

A few days later the body of Ernesto 'El Crucificador' Cruz fell five thousand feet from the open cargo compartment of an Apache helicopter. The body bounced on impact a few times and then lay still. The dust of the Sierra Madre Mountains west of Chihuahua soon began to claim it though a coyote pack returned more than once over the days.

When the remains were discovered by authorities the bones were the only items resembling human origin. A routine post-mortem examination by the coroner of Chihuahua puzzled the examiner greatly. No markings where bullets creased bones, no crushed hyoid from strangulation, but nearly every bone recovered had suffered from some sort of collision.

If the good doctor had known the manner of death, sudden stoppage at terminal velocity approaching one hundred and thirty miles per hour, he may not have signed the death certificate with the notation 'high force trauma, misadventure.'

Cruz had enjoyed thirty seconds or so of true flying. Sam didn't think Ernesto had ever prepared to die like a bug colliding with a windshield.

XXIV

VOODOO WARPATH

Daga rolled over on her stomach and looked at the flat screen. Cheyenne stared straight ahead in the general direction of watching the program but appeared to be asleep with her eyes wide open.

"Hey squaw woman."

"I know you don't know what that means."

"I'll bite. What does it mean?"

"It means vagina. The word squaw literally means vagina. Basically, it acknowledged their most important role in the tribal hierarchy. Make more braves. It's like me calling you cho-cho woman."

"Sorry. Didn't know."

"Most people don't. Too many bad cowboy and indian movies. Do you know how far you have to go to find someone that knows the word indian is derived from indigenes? You know, like we got here first."

"Hey, you got the casinos?"

"Even casinos can't make the kind of money that has been taken out of our native lands."

"Yeh, people from the Caribbean Islands don't exactly celebrate Columbus Day."

"Hey, Daga. You get the feeling we're just sitting here while Sam and Wolfe are handling things?"

"All the time. I'd like to know what that little Asian bitch is trying to do with my man."

"I was thinking. As long as we stay in touch with Sam why not go out and see what we can see. You know, more eyes."

"You heard Sam. They're looking for us. Every person we pass could be a possible enemy."

"Come on Daga. From what Sam told me, you got an itch that needs scratching."

"Ah, como no. Why not? First, I want to talk with my ancestors. Drop some hoodoo in their lap. Then I'll be ready to go."

"Go for it."

Daga went to the closet and pulled out her luggage. Inside she found her joujou bag, full of doll-like images of her favorite loas, voodoo deities. Her two favorite she set on the ledge of the window. A petwo loa, known for being aggressive, while hot and restless as well. The other, Papa Legbe, guardian of the crossroads would help her decide her path. She placed incense in a Cruzan rum bottle and lit it. Soft, lazy smoke drifted upward as if in prayer to higher beings.

"What the hell is all this? I thought you wanted to meditate or pray."

"Maybe Sam didn't tell you. I'm a mambo, a voodoo princess. Please don't interrupt me again. I'm chanting a hoodoo, a spell, and non-believers may cancel any benefits I may derive from my efforts."

"Cool. When you're done I'm going to hit you with some Indian shit you ain't ever seen."

Chey went back to bed. The television had been turned off and the remote nowhere to be found. What pot of crap had she stirred up? Lying motionless, Chey watched as Daga entered the spirit world.

In front of her loas, Daga prostrated herself, her hair fallen over her face. Suddenly, she jumped to her feet contorting her body into shapes Cirque de Soleil performers couldn't imitate. Sweat beaded quickly on her skin, her hair wet and draped on her shoulders, clinging like moss to an oak tree after a rain storm.

The chanting had begun when she jumped to her feet. The sounds now emanating from the voodoo queen changed to a steady guttural series of grunts, the spoken words if any unrecognizable to Cheyenne. As suddenly as it had begun, Daga slumped to the floor, breathing heavily, her eyes wide and staring into infinity.

Then silence as the energy seemed to leave her body, collapsed and looking as if in a deep sleep. Cheyenne leaned over the figure; she could here steady breathing so she didn't dare touch her. It reminded her of when her grandfather, a Cherokee shaman, would fall into a deep slumber after traveling with the spirits.

A few minutes passed and Daga began to stir. Cheyenne visibly showed relief on her face.

"Are you Okay?"

"Si, just a little tired. I hope I didn't upset you."

"That was some kind of show. You should do that for a living."

"It is sacred and not for entertainment. You were allowed to see it because we are about to travel together towards evil."

"I understand. Well, my Cherokee ceremony is tame compared to what I just witnessed. My grandfather, a didanawisgi or medicine man, taught me many things. One is the Sun Dance. It is the right time of day to begin, nearly dawn. It symbolizes a new beginning and fresh start to what paths lay before the individual. When in doubt, unsure of oneself, always follow the sun. It goes something like this."

Cheyenne faced east, her legs crossed in the ceremonial manner. She chanted the sacred words that would help guide her on her journey. The ones from the earth birth story when the sun shone on the path which her people would follow to their lands to become the great Cherokee Nation.

She got to her feet and danced the circle symbolizing the great ball of life in the sky. Cheyenne could now face what would come.

THE RIO

Zarilla's bodyguards ushered the room service waiter into the suite never more than an arm's distance from the very intimidated server. He set El Jefe's table and breakfast. Hurrying from the room, he nearly ran as if nature demanded immediate attention.

José Dominguez had a problem. He had eliminated any possible rats, the last one Cruz, but it had not gone as planned and he had no explanation as to why. Cruz was gone; no doubt about it, but the club's parking lot contained most of the Angelino hit squad. Had some survived and carried Cruz's body away? If not, than who?

A queasy feeling began to interrupt his meal. Did the DEA have Ernesto and this very minute they were gathering intel on Zarilla? He had work to do. He needed to get this operation back up and running. Dirty money continued to flow his way and he absolutely required Vegas as a place to launder it for the purchase of guns for exportation back to Mexico.

José Dominguez made a few calls and finished his food. Everything would be all right. After all, he was El Jefe.

Daga and Cheyenne caught a cab over to the Rio. They were dressed for the pool underneath their warm-ups. Wolfe had talked about seeing so many gangstas there and they figured to give it a try. They had devised a simple plan for the day and decided to put in to immediate operation.

The pair opened the back doors to the casino that led out to the pool. If one didn't characterize it as a grand entrance it at least qualified as worth a glance. As they hit the pool deck, the jackets came off revealing why neither one had any problem using stripping as a cover story. They stopped at the nearby towel stand and picked up an armful of linens while the cabana boy nearly choked on his slurpy.

They walked to their right in order to sunbathe at Paradise pool, one of the four pools at the Rio, it allowed topless relaxing. Males were charged a fee to enter while females got in free in order to insure the proper mix of spectators and eye candy. Cheyenne had never seen a girl buy her own drink at this pool. Of course, the pool might run the risk of having a very brief history if a number of girls happened to solicit some under-cover LVPD vice.

When the pants came off as the two situated their chairs to the sun, most male activity came to a screeching halt. Even drinks seem to fall from the mouths of partiers, drinking becoming increasingly more difficult with one's jaw hanging down to his chest.

Daga wore a suit in a shade of mango. Her fruit displayed for the picking. The contrast between the color of her skin and the Brazilian bikini perfectly complimented all things female on her. The top soon became a casualty while Daga slowly rolled to her stomach stretching like a cat just awakened from a nap. Moans, literally in concert, escaped from the males who had noticed the performance.

Cheyenne became Act II. The audience hung on every but-ton, snap, or zipper. The cool water helped to prevent too much embarrassment. Her skin, a deep brown with rose undertones, commended the pinto horse motif of her maillot. Displaying this one piece with legs cut all the way to her pelvic crest, she settled on the chaise longue and began rolling the top down to her waist in the manner of the French bathers on the Riviera. Stopping periodically as if she had forgotten something in her bag, even some of the mesmerized men looked away briefly, suddenly aware of being indiscreet. Most overcame their man-ners and continued gawking and giggling like school boys.

From behind oversized straw hats and sunglasses, sipping on frozen drinks as part of their disguise, the pair surveyed the water and deck for possible targets. It didn't take too long to find a deserving fellow.

"You see the one over by the waterfall with all the girls hanging on him, buying all the drinks?"

"Sure do. You want me to go hit him with some Spanish?"

"Oh, that's good. Let's give him a little while we see if we pique his curiosity."

"Let me know." Daga rolled over on her back. The target looked up as Cheyenne watched. That was easy. Girlfriends do it all the time. If a woman sees a male in whom she is interested, she'll find a way to walk through his line of sight. Most men will wait until she passes to stare at her at which time her friend can see whether or not he showed an interest or simply glanced. He had shown above average attention by ignoring one of the girls draped on his shoulder, time to make their move.

The double-headed attack came smoothly like strippers surrounding the big spender at the bar. He had no more of a chance than a wildebeest at the watering hole looking around and finding itself surrounded by a pride of lions. The difference of course with the humans involved the fact that he wanted to be caught.

He waved the college girls away and spread his arms to welcome these new women. Gang tats covered most of his upper body making him nearly impossible to mistake for someone else because of the uniqueness of the ink. The grunts on the ground in Iraq had taken to putting replicas of their dog tags as tattoos on their trunks, in military slang as meat tags, in order to improve the chances of being identified after an IED went off. The gang bangers had done the same with entire body tattoos, without realizing the assistance they inadvertently gave the cops.

"Hola guapo. You want to party?" Daga straddled his lap and put his head between her bare breasts. His ears came out of the introduction looking like a beginning boxer's, red and puffy. Before he could respond, Cheyenne settled behind him on a step. She reached around his waist and jammed her hands down his pants while pressing her chichis against him like canned ham.

"Hey, Daga. I think he's ready."

"I don't think so. Maybe he's a show-er and not a grow-er."

"Uh,uh, would you ladies like to come to my private condo attached to its own pool area. It's about fifty meters from here through a private entrance." It had been awhile since this guy had been at a loss for words around aggressive women. He'd wait to get them alone and then he'd make good on theirs and his fantasies.

"Do I get a name?" Daga wiggled harder into his lap.

"They call me El Corpulento. Just call me Corpe."

"That sounds perfect, don't you think Daga?" Coming from the same Latin root for body, Cheyenne thought the nickname apropos for what they had in mind.

"Can I bring a friend?"

"You won't need one." Two on one would make him easier to control.

"Ay,ay,ay, una casa de tres. Mucho calliente!" The threesome strolled as one over to the unremarkable door just to the side of the artificial waterfall. Security, dressed like a tourist, checked the room card and opened the door. By then Cheyenne and Daga had covered up but the guard still couldn't help but smile as they passed.

A small elevator took the group three floors up and opened into a foyer. They were already in the suite. To one side a full dining room, facing it a sunken seating area capable of entertaining twenty people, all fixtures and metal surfaces were in 18K gold plate. A large hot tub sat half-in and half-out of the living room through a set of double doors and out on a deck overlooking the pool. Bath bubbles burped over the edge.

Corpe pressed a button and a butler dressed in formal attire appeared from the foyer. "Thomas, my new friends and I want to have three bottles of Bollinger 1999 and a liter of Patron Gran Burdeos. Make some aperitivos, too. When you are finished you're done for the night. Don't interrupt us no matter what. Adios."

"All right, Corpe, let's party!" Daga and Cheyenne hit the water in the hot tub at about the same time, their warm-ups strewn along the way like bread crumbs for Corpe to follow.

He made it to the tub but his coordination in trying to enter slowed his full arrival until he fell headfirst over the edge. He came up for air between Daga's breasts, bubbles plastered across his face giving him the appearance of Moe in a Three Stooges skit.

Thomas finished up and exited discreetly, this party rather mild compared to rock stars and Asians. Better that he didn't have to deliver the drinks to the tub.

Daga and Cheyenne helpfully patted across the marble tile floor and gathered all the goodies. Corpe, screaming the entire time to hurry up, slapped the water like a toddler. The women clamored in false protest and jumped on Corpe as soon as they hit the water.

"Drink, drink, arriba, arriba!" The girls took turns pouring first champagne and then tequila down Corpe's mouth. At first, they had to defend themselves against clumsy advances and cheap feels but soon those occurred less often and eventually Corpe approached blackout stage. When he started floating on his back with his eyes closed and saliva ran down his chin, they knew the time had come.

Cheyenne and Daga pushed their target to the bottom of the tub and sat on him. Daga sat on his chest and Cheyenne his feet. Their heads bobbing above the water calmly like lily pads while the last breath of life seeped from El Corpulento.

Accidental drowning assisted by a blood alcohol level beyond .30 ranked third in the most common manner of death in Vegas behind gunshot and overdose of drugs. When one thought of it, .30 qualified as an overdose as well.

Sure, the cops would investigate. Thomas would tell them there were two beautiful girls with the deceased; everybody seemed to be having a good time, no readily seen animosity or domestic conflict. The coroner would find no bruising because Corpe hadn't resisted. The toxicology report would tell the sordid tale.

A guy comes to Vegas with all sorts of money, picks up a couple of chicks, they party, they leave when he passes out, he drowns in the hot tub. No sign of robbery or violence to say otherwise. Looks like another misadventure.

Cheyenne and Daga caught the shuttle back to Harrah's, walking the short distance across to the Venetian elevators. Using the shuttle and not a taxi meant no record of them leaving at a particular time. The two girls in blue sweat suits and ball caps, their hair pulled up beneath the hats, didn't look anything like the two women at the pool with oversized sun straws.

Cheyenne couldn't believe it. The first time it happened in the VIP room, Daga struck first and Cheyenne got caught up in the moment. But they had planned this in detail without even knowing at the time the exact target. Wolfe and Daga had a pair and a pair they were. Whose huevos won for biggest cojones could be the subject of argument endlessly. She'd put her money on the mambo momma.

XXV

DC TO VEGAS

Barnsworth Donovan Bailey chewed aggressively on the earpiece of his turtle shell glasses. He had a rogue agent on his hands, one with plenty of contract help, no other explanation would do. Yet some of the outcomes where the agent worked favored the political goals of POTUS if not entirely the citizens as a whole. Play dumb and allow whoever was running the ops to wipe out the vipers nest and he could fall back on plausible deniability if it got as far as Congress? A possible choice, but the venom coming out of the mayor's office through the President had a poisonous effect on his career aspirations. His turn to roll the shit downhill came when the ring on the other end of the phone stopped and a voice answered flat and without emotion.

"Yes?" Sam hated these calls from Bailey and for good cause.

"Guess what Sam. I got call from the President. He got a call from the mayor. Seems a strip club parking lot fills up with dead Mexican gangbangers covered in tattoos, a lower level cartel capo drowns in his hot tub, and an Asian Socal guy gets pinned to the strip with a crossbow bolt. What the hell is going on down there?"

"What happens in Vegas stays in Vegas, including dead bodies." Sam had answered flippantly but he knew nothing of the drowning.

"Look Sauria break this down for me so I can brief the President."

"The parking lot was our op but the cartel already had a hit on the guy. They opened fire, we returned it more accurately, and retrieved our objective. The guy that did the Asian kid won't be doing any more hits. We believe him to be one and the same. We gathered plenty of intel from him before he fell out of a plane on the Bravo side of the border. The mayor should like the body dump location. The drowning I don't know anything about. You know men with too much money to spend kill themselves accidentally everyday in Vegas?" As Sam finished the sentenced he silently said thanks that the dead capo didn't have a knife wound in his upper cervical vertebrae.

"All the dead men who kill themselves don't work for the cartels that happen to be your targets."

"I can't control the level of stupidity that the narco-terrorists choose to employ. He probably made them a bunch of money before he killed himself."

"Sam, when this is over, you and I are going to have an interesting talk back East."

"Can't wait." The phone on the DC side went dead and Sam picked up another phone to call Daga.

"Hey Sam, what do you need?" Daga had been waiting for this call since she and Chey had gotten back from the Rio.

"What did you do today?" Sam's question begged no specific answer instead he listened for hesitation or an over-detailed account of the day.

"We got bored and went over to the Rio, me and Chey."

"You guys run into anybody while you were there?"

'Yeh, a waitress and some tequila."

"Anything I should know about?"

"Nope. I got sunburned and so did Chey. There's a bunch of idiots over there with gang tats and deep pockets."

"Yeh, one of those idiots passed out and drowned in his hot tub."

"There's a news flash."

"Well, this one had been hanging with two chicas, one with café con leche skin and another with brown skin with a rose tint. Know anybody that fits that description?"

"Nope. They sound hot though. Anything else?"

"Yeh, don't leave the room without calling me. I'll send one of my guards to cover your door in case you get visitors." Keeping Daga under control always had an end point and he figured she had just reached it. Pulling Cheyenne along with her made for more distraction than he needed.

Wolfe couldn't stand being in lockdown. With most of the bad guys dead, he figured he could play a little more poker in the WSOP provided he wore a basic disguise. Sauria had a contact that did make-up for some of the shows on the strip and got him to come to the Venetian.

"While we are waiting for this guy, let's go over some ground rules. Los Zetas basically has contracts out on all of us. Every gangbanger wannabe trying to move up the ranks and make some cash on the side is itching to find us. You feel any kind of heat; you go to the restroom, drop your disguise and grab a cab. I don't care if you have the chip lead or not."

"No problem, Sam. The way my luck has been running I won't be there that long. Today's my last best chance. It is the senior tournament for a bracelet. You got to be fifty. Thanks for the fake ID."

"Don't try to pick up any grandmothers."

"Thanks for the reminder."

The door to the suite opened, one of the Varangian guards leading the way, and the make-up guy entered the room with a trunk on wheels large enough for a body. He had long blond hair with a chemical perm to give it the look of a poodle. Long, lean, and wearing jeans around his tiny hips with a motorcycle chain belt for accent; if this guy wasn't gay he did a great imitation. As he greeted Sam and Wolfe, any doubt concerning his sexual orientation got erased.

"Who's my plaything today?"

"The ugly one." Sam pointed at Wolfe and started laughing.

"Now, now don't be cruel. He looks a little like my high school boyfriend. Not handsome but rough and tumble, you know?" The ubiquitous flying wrist kept time with the cadence of his speech like a conductor's baton.

"Sam you just couldn't let me go play poker without making me pay a price, could you?"

"Dear me Wolfe, whatever could you be talking about?" Sauria settled into a chair to watch the show.

"I'm Randy by the way. Come along and sit on this chair. Let me have a look at you."

"Of course, your name is Randy." Wolfe sat down and shot Sam a look. "You know I'll get even for this."

Randy began assessing the material with which he had to work, running his hands through Wolfe's hair and then standing uncomfortably close in front of him "When was the last time you had your haircut?"

"In prison." Wolfe looked back at Sam and they both doubled over in spasms accompanied by poorly suppressed howling.

"You two will just have to have fun at my expense. Let's see now."

Two hours later, Randy presented the final product to Wolfe with a handheld mirror. Rebelle held his breath and looked. By then, Sauria had nearly bitten through his lower lip trying not to guffaw.

Gone to the floor were Wolfe's blond hairs and they were replaced with thick black curls just beyond his ears and collar. He looked like a 1980's guido from the Jersey shore. A porn star black moustache covered his upper lip.

"What do you think?" Randy seemed absolutely proud.

"Great. Thanks Randy." Sam slipped him a grand and Randy turned on his heels wheeling his trunk behind him like an owner walking his dog. He left feeling unappreciated for his efforts.

"I think you pissed him off, Wolfe."

"Oh, no." Rebelle put his hands to his cheeks Jack Benny style.

"OK. One more time. If you think you need to get out of there, lose the black weaves and moustache. Take this blond wig and hat. Wear two shirts. The outer of which is very bright and very distinctive. Underneath wear a common color and style. When you lose the hair and moustache lose the outer shirt as well, put on the wig and hat. Got any questions? Good. You just got a one month CIA course in disguise in three minutes. I hope you remember it."

"I'm fine Sam. Wish me luck." After a few more details, Wolfe let himself out of the suite and walked over to the shuttle for the Rio. Along the way Wolfe starting rehearsing his bad Rocky/Soprano accent and vocabulary. *You talkin' to me, goomba, gooma, gabagoo and stugat, t*he last four of which translated to a close associate, mistress, capicola, and this dick. Fuhgidaboutit. Go figure.

Wolfe entered the Rio without incident and began the half-mile walk to the buy-in cage next door to the Amazon room. As he walked, Wolfe tried to see if anyone looked at him strangely or did he blend with the usual crowd of nuts and eccentrics attending or playing at the WSOP. His dark glasses were more common than uncommon in this crowd of misfits. By the time he reached the convention space, he had nearly forgotten how he looked.

Wolfe wanted a bracelet badly but not so badly as to forfeit his life because of some gangbangers on coke. He would have to concentrate on both the game and his surroundings, one of which could be a full day's task, and in both instances a single mistake would be the end.

Rebelle walked up to the buy-in window and bought his entry. Picture identification, player's card from Harrah's, one thousand in cash or chips, all were necessary before the cashier finally printed his entry slip and handed it through the cage.

He stared down at it and read the information. He scanned to the portion most important. The table and seat number represented the first part of the tournament that required luck. Luck, skill and the weight of each in one winning a tournament were ongoing subjects of discussion among players. Some claimed it took only skill to win a tournament; that professionals could win with any two cards. Although true to a degree, professionals could also lose with any two cards as well.

An equally large number of people felt it took only well-timed luck and cojones. Wolfe fell somewhere between the two camps. Drawing a seat between Texas Dolly and Phil Hellmuth cannot be as conducive to winning as a seat between Billy Bob from Texas and a housewife from Canton, Ohio. On the other side, one's randomly selected chair may receive killer cards for the first day of the tournament giving one at least a temporary advantage. Wolfe felt the seat assignment qualified as a small piece of luck or not. Rebelle's own calculations were more like 70% skill, 20% luck, and 10% balls. The last ten percent often made the difference between getting paid or not, or winning the bracelet when it got to heads up.

Wolfe made his way over to the Amazon room and searched for his table number, 373. He had seat number one his least favorite. If the dealer were larger than average, seeing players ten, nine and eight became difficult and leaning to see them too obvious depending on what type of table presence one wanted to suggest.

Today's tournament had a projected field of over three thousand people, the final count unknown until the first card flew. Ten percent of the field would be paid, the house's cut another ten percent, and 2.7 million dollars split among three hundred players with the final table receiving two million of the kitty. Not too bad for two and half days work. The old timers were fond of saying *a hard way to make an easy living.*

The table began to fill and Wolfe started to assess his opponents. Three Asian males and an Asian female took seats 2-4-6-10. The female sat directly to Wolfe's left. Two leather-skinned cowboys, a SoCal surfer stuck in the 1960's, a barbecue magnate from Central Florida if the logo on his shirt could be believed, and an Italian from somewhere in the NE filled out the table. With Wolfe, that made two paisanos, if he remembered to stay in character.

SoCal started talking while the table waited for the tourney to begin. He looked Wolfe in the eye."Where you from?"

"Miami. Whad abou' you?"

"Cali. My whole life."

Wolfe shook his head in acknowledgement but didn't add anything to the conversation. Any truthful information given to another player about one's background, where one was born, what one did for a living, might be used to get a read. As Rebelle counted his stack, SoCal went around the table with similar questions.

He got practically nothing from the Asians, the cowboys were friendly and talkative, and the guido grunted but never responded otherwise. Only the barbecue man gave his life history before the game ever started. The tournament director gave last minute instructions and rules including the standard warning about f-bombs. From out of Wolfe's sight the familiar words 'shuffle up and deal' rang out and the entire room leaned forward in their chairs on cue.

Two hours and one break later, the cowboys were gone, Wolfe was card dead along with seat two, and the male Asians had the cowboys' money. The Italian had chipped away a little on their run when he hit pocket AA's in the small blind after seats four and six had raised and re-raised. The cowboys had been replaced by a couple of old Vegas-looking types.

Wolfe finally hit a starting hand on the button, A-K hearts. "Raise. Two thousand." Four times the big blind.

"Is this the first hand you've played?" Wolfe didn't respond. Seat four called, along with one other Asian and one of the Vegas types.

The dealer exposed the flop. 2-4-A rainbow. Seat four bet the pot, Vegas folded, and the other Asian called. Action to Wolfe. "Yo, what ya flop, a straight?' Nothing but silence stared back at Rebelle. No flap jaw players in this hand. Top pair, top kicker, Wolfe had to go with it. "All in."

Seat four called. The other two folded. His opponent held his cards face down although only the two of them were in the pot and no more bets could be made. Rebelle had decided it to be some sort of Western style they play in the Cali poker rooms, keeping one's cards facedown although all bets were made. A method intended to give less information to opponents for future hands. Rebelle didn't care. He showed his hand. Seat four couldn't help it and flopped his cards. He had the wheel straight, which meant that his whole cards were 3-5. What some describe as Gus Hanson hole cards. Only a full house could win for Rebelle.

Fourth street popped an 'A'. "Least I'm giving you a sweat."

"Not really. You're dead to ten cards. Three deuces, three fours, three kings, and an ace. Less than one in five chances." Professional players could calculate the odds of a hand like kids in a *Brainiac* classroom.

"Only one of those will do." The river came and Rebelle had the needed deuce. No jumping up and down on his part, no screaming, Wolfe silently and nonchalantly raked the chips to his chair and began to stack them.

"Lucky box." It came from the seat to his immediate left, the Asian female, with a smile.

"Yeh, by the time it got to the river it definitely qualified as a lucky card but the reason suited A-K is the third best starting hand is because, say for instance against a hand using a 3-5 to start, that if it does hit it wins. Where if he had hit a boat with 3's and 5's assuming the ace is still on the board his full house can be nullified by mine. I needed to play some hands."

Wolfe felt better about being back in the game. Rebelle glanced at the tournament screen and checked out the average chip count. Three hundred guys were gone and the average chips stood at twenty-five G. He didn't trail by much.

The first day had come and gone, no new players at the table because no one had gotten knocked out since the cowboys, the floor man not finding it necessary to move people off of full tables. Day two would start at noon the following day; Wolfe caught a cab at the Rio front entrance.

"Drop me at the IP."

"I don't know where that is."

"How long have you been doing this?"

"Two weeks."

"Oh. It's the Imperial Palace, next to Harrah's with an H."

"I don't know if I can do this."

"You can do this. Don't take me around back. This is the front driveway right off the strip."

Wolfe sat exhausted in the back seat and his patience for cabbies in Vegas trying to run the fare up didn't have much of a half-life. When one added the Eastern European or Middle Eastern accent, his self-control fell below zero on a scale of one to ten. A hack who pretended not to know the most direct route to one's destination likely would feel an uncomfortable feeling in his nether regions once Rebelle got done with the verbal emasculation.

The next day Wolfe woke fresh and ready to make a run for some money. Back at the same table but this day he had some cards. The thing about getting cards and getting called is pretty soon the table gets gun shy because they figure you for a hot streak. This unavoidable feeling by one's opponents then offers even more opportunities to steal pots. At the end of day two, Rebelle and twenty-nine others remained and he had a slightly above average chip stack. Sleep's embracing arms beckoned just a short ride away. His cell phone displayed 0145h. He headed for the front entrance.

On the long walk back to the main casino he passed at least ten Angelino gangstas working in pairs as they glanced in restaurants and auxiliary poker rooms, sometimes taking a stroll through and then exiting out a different door than the one through which they had entered. If they were looking for him, his disguise continued to hold up against unpracticed scrutiny.

He mentally went over Sam's instructions in case one of them actually knew how to see through a deception.

As Rebelle entered the main casino floor, he glanced to his left into the high roller salon. Rebelle instantly recognized him from one of Sam's photos in the CIA dossier. He sat at a five hundred minimum blackjack table playing heads up with the dealer. As is often the case, his stature didn't match his position of ruthless power.

José Jesús Dominguez. El Zarilla, the skunk, could have been anybody but how he carried his small frame even while sitting at the table made him noticeable to those who paid attention. Swarthy skin seemed to stretch thin as paper across a small featherweight build. Black on black clothing, short wavy black hair combed straight back, opaque dark dots for eyes, could be the perfect metaphors for his view of life.

Men who have spent a portion of their lives training to kill and then killing other people are almost incapable of hiding how we see them. They see the world through lenses much more clear than those of the general public.

Three beefaronis stood legs at parade rest against opposing walls, unmoving except the pairs of darting eyes sweeping the room constantly. Reflective lenses hid the motion but Rebelle knew and could feel his presence just outside the entrance draw the orbs in his direction. A target would not know if he had been seen. Wolfe knew he had been seen but not recognized. They would store his image in their memories and if the same image popped up again on their personal radar their interest in him would increase exponentially.

Yes, they had seen. Wolfe had seen as well.

XXVI

GRIM REAPER

Sam settled into the chair across from Major General James 'Hacksaw' Harrison. Sauria knew the Air Force general had fond memories of how he had earned the serrated moniker. When the US first occupied Iraq, boots were coming home without feet or with feet that didn't need shoes anymore. High casualties were being suffered at the hands of the Iranians who had taken the time between threats and actual action on the part of the US to prepare thousands of Iraqis in the building and operation of IED's. The US for some reason always finds it necessary to warn people before it invades.

Our people on the ground were riding around in Humvees that wouldn't stand up to a bad Detroit winter much less artillery shells masquerading as a bag of soccer balls. The Pentagon, especially Defense Secretary Rumsfeld, insisted our troops had what they needed to win and regardless you make do with what you have. The usual senseless rattle from someone watching from the sidelines, safety from afar always has a different perspective.

General Harrison, while assigned to the Pentagon's Systems Acquisition Office, took a hacksaw and manually cut a Humvee in half finishing the dissection in front of the Joint Chiefs of Staff. Shortly afterwards, the MRAP vehicle (Mine Resistant Ambush Protected) program got underway to the joy of anyone inclined to come home in one piece.

Following that success, Harrison had pushed for Predator drones to become platforms for Hellfire missiles. It was the result of that project that he found himself the commanding officer of the 11th Reconnaissance Wing at Nellis Air Force base. Reapers, the offensive version of the Predator, had become the US's preferred method of sneak attack and assassination in the wake of 9/11. The drivers for those drones were stationed at Nellis, lived in the suburbs of Las Vegas, wore civvies to and from the base, and might even be sitting next to you at a blackjack table after taking out some mujahedin for breakfast.

In was in this role as Al Queda's worst nightmare that he found Sam Sauria sitting in his office on a hot summer's day.

"How can I help you, Sam?" The general's husky voice sounded like that of a character from central casting. Chomping on a cigar would have completed the caricature. These outward features would be red herrings in an attempt to have possible adversaries underestimate him. Behind the façade, a formidable personal drive coupled with genius intellectual power made Harrison the kind of man one wanted on his side.

"I need to know about your Reaper program."

"Well, some of that is classified of course, but what I can tell you is......."

"My clearance goes as high as the DNI. Here is a letter stating as much and I'll wait for you to make a confirmation if you need to CYA."

"That won't be necessary. I did a little checking after you called for the appointment to see me, one of the prerogatives of my rank. I know you're the real thing it's just we're a little sensitive about our program here. What can I do for you?"

Sam chuckled to himself. Why is it always called a program when people are getting killed? The Nazis even called it a program.

"Well General, I need a quick briefing. I've got an operational plan but it depends on your tactical ability. What can those birds do?"

"Pretty much anything a piloted platform can do and better. It's designated a MALE, Medium Altitude, Long Endurance platform."

"Sounds like a sexual aid for men designed by a defense contractor and named by the Pentagon."

Hacksaw laughed till tears clouded his eyes. "That's a good one, hombre." His west Texas roots shining through all the salad on his chest. "Would you like some sipping whiskey?" Harrison pulled fifteen year old Dalmore single malt from his desk drawer. Soon two highball glasses shone golden three fingers deep. The one quip by Sam had lowered any existing barriers between the two men. Two old warriors planning more war and sipping whiskey, from their perspective, it didn't get any better.

"Sure. Don't mind if I do." Sam slipped into his best southern syntax. Adding ice cubes would have been like the Rape of the Sabines.

"Yeh, that bird can transit four hundred miles, loiter for fourteen hours, and return to base. Pilots can't do that even with a piss bag and extra fuel tanks. Being that it's medium altitude the cameras can read script on a piece of paper. Equipped with Hellfire missiles guided by on-board lasers, the noise signature of both the platform and the supersonic Hellfire give very little notice to the eventual target. We just circle around until they all get in a single dwelling and light'em up like the Fourth of July."

"How about air to air?"

"Well, like I said, we use Hellfire but we can load heat seeking Sidewinders if the mission calls for it. An Iraqi MIG26 shot down one of our early Predator models back in the day. That's one of the reasons we went to Reaper. Why?"

"The mission may call for it. Within a few hours general you will receive an Executive Order from POTUS. Carry out the mission as I know you will. Our United States will be safer because of your actions."

"I understand."

Sam raised his glass in a toast. "God bless America."

"God bless America." Both warriors, warriors of a different type, couldn't hide their emotions completely.

Sam rode back to the Venetian encapsulated with that warm fuzzy feeling one gets when one's plans start to come together. His mind ran through multiple scenarios while the Varangians drove. He couldn't wait to talk to Wolfe. While Sam headed south on Interstate15 from the 215 on ramp, Hacksaw Harrison received from his secretary the unscrambled fax from POTUS that Sam had indicated.

For the purposes of this Executive Order, Commander Sam Sauria, USN will direct your efforts without you having any question of his authority as it has come directly from this office. You are to follow his tactical plan. All available assets under your direct command are at his disposal. This remains in effect until otherwise notified. POTUS

Hacksaw read the order. He didn't know who this guy was but he carried a lot of weight. Harrison took another swig of Scotch and contemplated what lie ahead.

VENETIAN

Sam answered the door. China Doll stumbled through the door past the Varangian guards. She acted a little tipsy and irritated. "Sam, what do you need from me?"

"I don't need anything Anna Lee. You've done great. You helped us get to Cruz."

"I can't stay in the room any longer. I'm going batty. Where the hell is Wolfe? He leaves in the morning and stumbles in tired after midnight?"

"Since we took out quite a few of them, I let him play some poker if he wore a disguise."

"And I sit in a hotel room? I haven't heard from the other girls either."

"They're fine. Look Wolfe is on his way back from poker pretty soon, we'll talk. Okay?"

"Fine" Anna Lee slumped down in a chair.

Sam called Wolfe and told him to come by the suite. He poured China Doll a drink so that he could control the amount.

One and a half drinks later, Wolfe entered a little worse for the wear. If someone were to have told Wolfe as a young man that playing poker for fourteen hours could bring him to near total exhaustion, his response would have been disbelief. As a college student, he played cash games that lasted from Friday night after the other players had dropped their dates off till kickoff of the Browns game on Sunday afternoon, allowing for a few naps and snacks along the way. The glaring difference being that home games with unskilled players didn't require the concentration playing in the WSOP required.

"Need a drink?" Sam offered.

"One only. Tomorrow night at 1800h there's thirty of us left. First place is a bracelet and 425G."

"Good luck. Did you see anything while you were there?"

"Matter of fact I did. Zarilla playing heads up blackjack in the high roller room, he had three bodyguards with him."

"Well we know where he is. Did you see a bunch of Latinos?"

"On my way out I saw an eight man crew working in pairs checking out poker rooms, maybe looking for one of us. Not too many playing cards. I think their plan to wash money didn't work out for them as far as tournament poker. It's funny in that way. Sometimes people can't win even when they cheat. There's a guy back home like that. Runs a crooked game and loses. He doesn't have good support. Go figure. They'll probably stick to strip clubs and high stakes cash games away from the casinos for washing money. Their little gangstas didn't do so well."

"Okay. I've formulated a final solution. This operation terminates in three days, maybe less if Dominguez doesn't play along. I'm going to get Chey and Daga down here and brief it right now with all of us in the same room. Then we're all off to the races. Last one home buys the drinks."

Two hours later and relying on his copious speaking points, Sam had his team ready for the three pronged attack. Varangian guards escorted the foursome to their respective rooms, Daga glaring at China Doll the entire time while they waited for the elevator.

If Sam had anything to say about it, Los Zetas would be gutted like a whitetail deer after a field dressing. Unfortunately, cartels reminded him of bags of shit. You step on one end of the bag and shit squirts out the other.

Sam made his call to Major General Harrison and another to the administrator of the FAA sound asleep in his Georgetown townhouse. Emergency alert, there would only be approximately a sixty minute heads up. All crews to sleep on base and in uniform. Even old salt Sam Sauria, had sweaty cold palms.

VOODOO LOUNGE

"Would you prefer bottle service?" The diminutive cocktail waitress looked disproportionate to her newly purchased boobs. At least she pretended to be nice. That's all a server needs to remember in order to be successful. At least *pretend* to be nice, you don't have to like anyone just don't act like you're doing the customer a favor by waiting on him.

"Sure. Absolut Citron, please and a couple bottles of soda water with a plate of lemon slices."

"The soda water will be extra above the one hundred and fifty for the vodka."

"Of course it will. Thank you." Chey turned, facing Daga and China Doll. "You believe that bitch? Like women can't pay for their own drinks. This town can be as screwed up as Arkansas when it tries."

"Don't worry about it. Let's relax and see if we can help Sam."

The band wasn't a band. It consisted of some over-pumped twenty something trying his best to be on a Dr. Dre commercial with a turntable and poor taste in music. Daga missed the days when the music played live and consisted of blues, jazz, and Motown. Of course, the music is what brought them to the Voodoo deck high above Vegas.

"Oh, My God!" Anna Lee flapped her hands like an extra in *Clueless*. She began pointing speechless in the direction of the observation deck, her hand covering her mouth but not her bulging eyes.

"What? What?" Daga swiveled on her chair. She had seen a lot of things in Vegas but she had never been around a scene comparable to this performance.

A two-hundred pound man had another more slightly built male by the ankles and had him suspended over the railing, the last stop on the fall fifty-one floors direct to hell. The girls couldn't understand the ranting but the large man who apparently controlled the situation had a future as a temporary Hunter S. Thompson sidekick in a Johnny Depp sequel. The film production, likely to be based in Vegas during the 2010 midterm elections, would only add to the nonsense.

"Is he going to drop him?" Daga acted as interested as shocked.

"I don't know but falling bodies kill people who happen to be catching." As Chey spoke, the situation simmered down, the smaller man now hanging to the good side of the railing and the apparently insulted one bouncing off clientele on his way to negotiate the spiral staircase to the fiftieth floor.

"That got the adrenalin going. Let's get to our assignment, three gangstas before the end of the evening. First one to score, the others pick up the tab. Go." Daga showed full blown enthusiasm for what others would find distasteful.

Fifty-one floors below the girls Wolfe sat four hours into the final thirty with seventeen players remaining. Based on the numbers displayed on the tournament screen, Wolfe occupied last place and for the previous four hours, cold cards. His options were very limited. He could wait for his stack to hit eight times the big blind and push with any two cards under the gun, not the preferred choice. Secondly, he could go all in first chance he had the button and any kind of hand hoping for a call from whoever had the strongest but not dominating hand.

Against any random calling hand, two random cards were only 35-65 dogs. Two live cards were the key.

He pushed with 7-8 diamonds. The chip leader who had the button called. The flop came 4-4-7. Wolfe's cards were lying face up. He checked his opponent for a sign. Nothing, the button kept his cards down. Wolfe could be in the lead if the guy had anything but a four or a large pocket pair. The river and turn were blanks. No more help for Wolfe. The button flopped his cards. A pair of aces stared back at Wolfe. There goes the idea that luck is not a factor. The familiar words 'seat open table 323' rang out from the dealer. Rebelle walked with 22K.

The following morning, Barnsworth Donovan Bailey received another call from the mayor of Las Vegas about dead bodies ironically littering Sin City. Three specific bodies, all with gang tats and Cali driver licenses, found within Clark County, showing very little preliminary forensic evidence. The protest had become progressively muted from the Nevada end of the line over the days however the mayor still felt it necessary to call. He needed to at least pretend to care. The politico had become accustomed to the current conditions and the newspapers left it alone except for blurbs buried mid-paper. The coverage reminded one of beach towns where shark bites never occur in spite of the stitches. If the newspapers could be silenced or limited in their coverage, it meant at the minimum the mayor had not lost any supporters. He might as well make good out of bad. The LAPD sure as hell wouldn't care if LA had fewer gangbangers.

Sam's phone rang. His eyes at the Rio had Zarilla on the move. The watcher, dressed as a houseman, had been sweeping the same section of tile outside the entrance to the villas for four hours. Sauria hung up and called the task force commander. "He's moving, black stretch, leaving the convention center entrance, tail him. Let me know if he goes to the airport."

Twenty minutes later the commander called Sam. "He's at the private airport. He's boarding a GS-II Gulfstream, tail number T5632683D. The pilot filed a flight plan for Mexico City non-stop."

Sam had the commander repeat the tail number two more times as Sauria re-checked his notes. He hung up and called Nellis AFB. The next call went to the FAA.

Ground support personnel loaded the AIM-9X Sidewinders on to the unmarked Reaper painted black with radar absorption coatings. The Sidewinders, named for the desert snake that hunts prey by seeking body heat and then moving in for the kill in a fishtail S motion, perfectly matched nature's version in its distinctive movement and searching of heat. Sidewinder missiles could make all sorts of loops and dives before finding a heat source. More than one pilot had used evasive counter measures to avoid the sting of his own missile during a particularly dynamic air to air engagement. A common one, flying into the sun, didn't work at night.

The Sidewinder had been around in one version or another since engineers had discovered that Lead Sulfide affected electric conductivity when exposed to infrared radiation .i.e. heat. That basic physical reaction became the key component for what is known as heat seeking technology. This particular version being loaded was twenty-fourth generation now using Cadmium Sulfide for the reaction.

As the conductivity varied depending on the relative position of the heat source, the change could be tied to a gyro guidance system for target acquisition. Counter measures had been created over the years to confuse the targeting by muffling heat signatures and dispersing alternative heat sources like flares to hide a plane's position. Air Force One carried the most advanced counter measures for Sidewinders and other missiles using heat seeking technology.

The Reaper engine cranked up and the bird, looking like some fantastic toy for a spoiled rich kid or a man who never outgrew his boyhood, lifted into the desert sky. Major General 'Hacksaw' Harrison sat at the monitor, joystick in hand, driving the Reaper. He had dismissed the other personnel from the control module, a metal box resembling a shipping container on the far side of the base. The operational security so tight, he had chosen to do the driving himself.

The Reaper took up position over the Sonora Desert, lingering in a circle with thirty miles of radius. The flight path filed by Zarilla's pilot would take the Gulfstream over the NE corner of the some of the most remote territory in Northern Mexico. Flying due SE, Dominguez's plane would fly over Chihuahua State as it left Sonora and New Mexico. When it entered the Reaper's kill zone, justice would be done.

Meanwhile, the FAA had grounded or redirected all aircraft in the Phoenix-Tucson area with lame misinformation like excessive thunderstorms or failed radar. The media dutifully reported the reasons for the disruptions without any additional investigation. This makes glaringly clear the differences between reporters, journalists, and investigative reporters. Reporters repeat what they are told or see, journalists create controversy and discussion with opinion; investigative reporters do work to protect the citizens of the US. Reporters were being manipulated and therefore the people as well by the CIA as they had been many times before in the past.

Zarilla relaxed in the plush leather chairs of the Gulfstream. Yes, there had been trouble in Vegas, but the club was well on its way to coming back online with clean money and most of the actual casualties were hired guns except for his men who he suspected anyhow. Santa Muerte had worked her magic and now he headed home to the luxury and security of his fortress. Maybe with the recent aggressiveness of the US security and intelligence forces he should reconsider the offer by Dr. Basir Fasim concerning the PETN explosive.

As Dominguez pondered his choices, a USAF AWACS look down radar plane directed the Reaper to the one of the farthest reaches of its current radius. General Harrison moved the joy stick appropriately and armed the missiles on board. Lying in wait behind a ridge of the Sierra Madres, The Reaper squatted like a baseball catcher behind home plate as it waited for the AWACS to give the exact location and interception vector.

Hacksaw's headset squawked and the old F-14 pilot raised the Reaper into position as the Gulfstream came into view on his monitor bearing 270 degrees. Mumbling the old NATO code for live air to air missile launch, Fox 2, two Sidewinders left the Reaper at supersonic pace seeking the target's heat signature in the cold upper atmospheric temperature. The fact the missiles traveled at faster than the speed of sound meant of course they arrived before the target could hear their launch.

As a visual display, the fireball compared favorably with one of the desert sunsets that often framed the mountain peaks. A strange metal rain fell on the desolate sands in all manner of sizes for over five minutes. Oxymoronically, death represented the most human activity seen in the region for years.

Hacksaw notified Sauria that the mission had been completed successfully. Harrison had been involved during the first Iraqi war with some Iranian insertions and extractions which resulted in Iranian troops being eliminated. Those black ops paled greatly with operating an offensive weapon over US territory to dispose of a narco-terrorist. If Congress ever got a hold of this, he'd probably be dealing blackjack in downtown Vegas for his retirement.

A news report crawled across the bottom of the twenty-four hour news channel screen. '*Mexican authorities reported finding the wreckage of a private passenger jet in a remote area of the State of Chihuahua. The initial investigation suggests it is the wreckage of a plane belonging to a Mexican drug cartel. An onboard bomb is suspected as the cause of the downing. The shooting war along the US-Mexican border for control of the lucrative drug trade is the suspected motive. A highly placed unnamed source in the State Department stated.*'

Sam read the crawl. More excellent reporting from our friends in the media, he quietly mused. With any kind of luck, the story will be buried in the middle of Section A of *USA TODAY* on day one and gone by day two.

Sam wondered about these ops. His life and the lives of others risked ostensibly for the safety of the United States yet it would probably be days and not weeks before other narco-terrorists slipped into the space left by Zarilla.

The only end for this war would come when reward didn't compensate for risk to the cartels and American citizens either stopped using or legalized the drugs in a similar fashion to alcohol. When poor, unemployed people could become billionaires by cultivating and processing plants the event horizon looked more like infinity.

XXVII

HILTON HEAD ISLAND, SC

The sun shone brightly on Sam Sauria's crew. The weather played by the rules, an early cool fall breeze blowing in off the Atlantic to moderate the end of summer heat. The Tiki Hut had that 'it's over' feel to it, most of the college kids gone except for the usual few who had been seduced by Hilton Head and now had decided on a career in food and beverage with a minor in beach. They would worry about paying that 100K student loan some other time.

Rob Ingman, one of Hilton Head's premier minstrels and a fixture during season for as long as anyone could remember, serenaded the sunbathers fighting for their last few UV's before heading back to small towns in Ohio and other points North.

Sam set up shop at some tables in front of the band stand. Everyone had managed to arrive. Anna Lee, Cheyenne, Wolfe and Daga sat splayed across the deck soaking up rays with an assortment of drinks to go with the music.

Rob played one of his latest hits, *Real Man*, about a woman that comes to the Tiki Hut with false fingernails, dyed hair, breast implants, and a birthmark enhancement. Seems she just can't find a real man. It always made Wolfe's day when he heard it.

"Well boys, to use the vernacular, you done good."

"Do we look like boys?" China Doll piped up, waving her hand in the direction of Daga and Chey

"Think of team when I say boys. It's a friendly collective."

"Jesus, Sam. Don't get her going." Wolfe waved down Jamie the waitress and ordered another round.

"So how did everything go down?" Daga asked between sips of her favorite rum, aged Cruzan.

"I guess we'd say Okay. The problem is very much like North Korean infantry or dissatisfied young Muslim males. For everyone you eliminate, two more pop up. We slowed them down for awhile, but new faces will appear operating businesses with new names, laundering the same money.

They play hard. The other day cartel killers ambushed and killed two US embassy employees and family members working in Juarez, in the middle of the day. Our embassies and consulates in Mexico are on lockdown the same as they are in Pakistan. Families are being sent home.

Our national press is starting to give it all a little more play but the money is so good corruption is rampant on both sides of the border. Being in law enforcement is looking a lot like Colombia in the 1990's. Remember, *plata o plomo?* Tell them what it means Daga"

"Silver or lead. In other words, take the bribe or you and your family will be killed. No exceptions. They usually take the bribe."

"The other day Homeland Security estimated the entire cartel corridor from Matamoros to Tijuana had hired 10,000 new mercenary killers. They're armed to the maximum with weapons most of which are made here. Greed is a tough motive to beat. These are the people who threaten our security and who we must find a way to defeat."

"Another round please? I can't handle this" Cheyenne turned to make an order.

"Based on what Sam said, it sounds worse than Miami during the cocaine wars of the 1980's." Wolfe had experienced some of the overflow lawlessness from Florida during those days. "One could transport almost anything up the I-95 corridor and jump off to Hilton Head with very little difficulty and find oneself supplying a certain population with money literally to blow. Hell, one time the Feds found shrimp coolers full of money in a smuggler's back yard not fifty yards from the Intracoastal Waterway. The hardware stores sold a lot of shovels to locals the next day"

"Yeh, Wolfe you're right. It is worse. A lot worse."

"So why don't you retire?"

"That's just puts it in somebody else's lap. Besides, as long as I stay healthy, the boys in DC will call me whenever they feel they could use me. Why retire?"

"Well, don't stick that ugly mug out too far. One of those hombres might shoot it off." Daga gave Sam a big hug.

"I'm out of here. You guys take care. I'll call you if I need you."

"We know you will Sam, we know you will. Hey, wait a minute Sam. I could have done better at poker if I hadn't been working."

"Really? That's as close as you'll ever get. Besides with what we paid you guys you did Okay."

"Thanks for your support." Wolfe smiled. It's always worth a try to get a few more dollars from Sam.

Sam rambled off the deck escorted by a beautiful sky and parrot head music. Wolfe turned to the others.

"Come on. Let's go over to the Frosty Frog and grab some frozen daiquiris made with 190 grain alcohol."

"I'm in. If we have enough drinks we can all do the horizontal samba." Daga leapt off the deck and into the sand. The foursome walked arm in arm over to the nearby Frog.

Anna Lee leaned over to Wolfe. "Hey, while we're over there, tell me again about those two people missing at the marina and the suicide with multiple stab wounds, especially the suicide. That has a bad fish odor."

"Remember China Doll, when it doesn't make sense, follow the money. When the town takes on a project that doesn't appear logical, find out who is profiting. When owners on a board refuse to accept bids from prospective vendors with the same specs but reduced pricing, think motivation. When wealthy people go missing and a business associate stabs himself multiple times in order to commit suicide there's something hooey in the hot sauce. A first year pathology intern will tell you that multiple wounds are unusual in suicides. Besides, we don't investigate things. We help solve problems for Sam.

Anyways, forget about all that for awhile. We're going over to the World Headquarters of the Frosty Frog and have a few drinks with Pat. He might try to give you some Erie corn. I think he's addicted to it. He's considering going into rehab for it."

"What the hell is Erie corn?"

"I'm not sure. I think it's some kind of code. The bartender always looks at me funny when he's talking to Pat about it.

When we finish with the drinks we're going out to eat at Catch 22 and I'm getting the portobello app with lobster and shrimp followed by the day's fresh catch. Probably spent the day swimming before it got to my plate. When our bellies are full, we're going back to my place to crash. No more thinking. Relax and enjoy our little island paradise."

Daga glanced over to Wolfe. The look she gave Rebelle was Caribbean queen-speak for tonight would be one her voodoo loas would make unforgettable. "Remember the lyrics from your favorite song, _Little Red Riding Hood,_ mi Wolfie, '*even bad wolves can be good.*'"

Be sure to visit these local businesses that support old beach bums who write novels and play poker. See you at one of these places or the WSOP.

CATCH 22

FROSTY FROG

TIKI HUT

BEACH BREAK BAR

7935396R0

Made in the USA
Charleston, SC
23 April 2011